The Perfect Poison

Amanda Quick

piatkus

PIATKUS

First published in the US in 2009 by G.P. Putnam's Sons,
a member of Penguin Group (USA) Inc., New York
First published in Great Britain in 2009 by Piatkus
This paperback edition published in 2010 by Piatkus

A CIP catalogue record for this book
is available from the British Library.

ISBN 978-0-7499-0946-8

Typeset in Bembo by Phoenix Photosetting, Chatham, Kent
Printed and bound in the UK by CPI Mackays, Chatham ME5 8TD

Papers used by Piatkus are natural, renewable and recyclable
products sourced from well-managed forests and certified
in accordance with the rules of the Forest Stewardship Council.

Mixed Sources
Product group from well-managed
forests and other controlled sources
www.fsc.org Cert no. SGS-COC-004081
© 1996 Forest Stewardship Council

Piatkus
An imprint of
Little, Brown Book Group
100 Victoria Embankment
London EC4Y 0DY

An Hachette UK Company
www.hachette.co.uk

www.piatkus.co.uk

This one is for my fantastic sister-in-law, Wendy Born. With love and thanks for the Ameliopteris amazonensis.

And for Barbara Knapp, with my deepest appreciation and thanks for, among other things, introducing me to Mr. Marcus Jones.

I am very grateful to you both for opening a window on the wonderful world of nineteenth-century botany.

The Perfect Poison

One

Late in the reign of Queen Victoria . . .

Lucinda stopped a few feet away from the dead man, trying to ignore the fierce undercurrents of tension that raged through the elegant library.

The constable and the members of the grieving family were well aware of who she was. They watched her with a mixture of macabre fascination and barely concealed horror. She could hardly blame them. As the woman the press had once featured in a lurid scandal and a tale of shocking murder, she was not welcome in polite society.

"I do not believe this," the attractive, newly minted widow exclaimed. "Inspector Spellar, how dare you bring that woman into this household?"

"This will only take a moment," Spellar said. He inclined his head toward Lucinda. "If you would be so kind as to give me your opinion, Miss Bromley."

Lucinda was careful to keep her expression cool and composed. Later the family members would no doubt whisper to their friends and associates that she had appeared as cold as ice, just as the newspapers and the penny dreadfuls had portrayed her.

As it happened, the thought of what she was about to

1

do actually did chill her to the bone. She would far rather be home in her conservatory enveloped by the scents, colors and energy of her beloved plants. But for some reason that she could not explain, she found herself drawn to the work that she occasionally did for Spellar.

"Certainly, Inspector," she said. "That is why I'm here, is it not? I think we can safely say that I was not invited for tea."

There was a gasp from the widow's spinster sister, a severe-looking woman who had been introduced as Hannah Rathbone.

"Outrageous," Hannah snapped. "Have you no sense of the proprieties, Miss Bromley? A gentleman is dead. The least you can do is behave in a dignified manner and leave this household as quickly as possible."

Spellar gave Lucinda a veiled look, pleading silently with her to watch her tongue. She sighed and closed her mouth. The last thing she wanted to do was jeopardize his investigation or cause him to think twice about requesting her advice in the future.

At first glance one would be highly unlikely to guess Spellar's profession. He was a comfortably stout man with a benign, cheerful countenance, a voluminous mustache and a thin ring of graying hair, all of which served to distract others from the sharp, insightful intelligence in his blue-green eyes.

Few who were not well acquainted with him would guess that he possessed a true talent for noticing even the smallest clues at a murder scene. It was a psychical gift. But there were limits to his abilities. He could not detect any but the most obvious cases of poisoning.

Fairburn's body lay in the middle of the vast floral carpet. Spellar stepped forward and reached down to pull aside the sheet that someone had drawn over the dead man.

2

Lady Fairburn burst into a fresh cascade of sobs.

"Is this really necessary?" she cried brokenly.

Hannah Rathbone gathered her into her arms.

"There, there, Annie," she murmured. "You must calm yourself. You know your nerves are very delicate."

The third family member in the room, Hamilton Fairburn, set his well-modeled jaw in grim lines. A handsome man in his mid-twenties, he was Fairburn's son by a previous marriage. According to Spellar, it had been Hamilton who insisted on summoning a detective from Scotland Yard. When Fairburn had recognized Lucinda's name, however, he had been aghast. Nevertheless, although he could have refused to allow her into the mansion, he had not done so. He wanted the investigation to go forward, she thought, even at the cost of having such a notorious female in his house.

She walked toward the body, bracing herself for the disturbing sensations that always accompanied an encounter with the dead. No amount of preparation could entirely dampen the disorienting sense of utter emptiness that swept over her when she looked down at the figure on the floor. Whoever and whatever Fairburn had been while he was alive, that essence was gone.

She knew that traces of evidence that might provide clues to the manner of his death still clung to the scene, however. Spellar would certainly spot most of them. But if there was any indication of poison, it was her mission to detect it. The psychical residue of toxic substances remained not only on the body but on anything the individual had touched in those last moments.

There was often other, very unpleasant and much more obvious evidence, as well. In her experience most people who died after ingesting poison became violently ill before expiring. There were always exceptions, of

3

course. A long, slow, steady diet of arsenic did not usually produce such dramatic results at the end.

But there was no indication that Lord Fairburn had suffered from bouts of nausea before he died. His death could have been attributed to a stroke or a heart attack. Most families who moved in elevated circles, as the Fairburns did, would have preferred to accept such a diagnosis and thereby avoid the publicity that inevitably attended a murder investigation. She wondered what had made Hamilton Fairburn send a message to Scotland Yard. Clearly he had his suspicions.

She concentrated for a moment on visual cues but they told her little. The dead man's skin had turned a stark, ashen shade. His eyes were open, staring at nothing. His lips were parted in a last gasp. She noticed that he had been older than his wife by at least a couple of decades. That was not an unusual circumstance when a wealthy widower remarried.

Very deliberately, she stripped off her thin leather gloves. It was not always necessary to touch the body but direct physical contact made it easier to pick up nuances and faint traces of energy that she might not notice otherwise.

There was another round of shocked gasps from Lady Fairburn and Hannah Rathbone. Hamilton's mouth tightened. She knew that they had all seen the ring on her finger, the one the sensation press claimed she had used to conceal the poison that killed her fiancé.

She leaned down and lightly brushed her fingertips across the dead man's forehead. Simultaneously she opened her senses.

At once the atmosphere of the library altered in subtle ways. The scents that emanated from the large jar of potpourri swept over her in a heavy wave, a combination of dried geraniums, rose petals, cloves, orange peel, allspice and violets.

The colors of the roses in two tall, stately vases intensified dramatically, exhibiting strange hues for which there were no names. While the petals were still bright and velvety, the unmistakable reek of decay was clearly detectable. She had never understood why anyone would want to decorate a room with cut flowers. They might be beautiful for a short time but they were, by definition, in the process of dying. As far as she was concerned, the only suitable place for them was in a graveyard. If one wished to preserve the potency of a plant or bloom or herb, one dried it, she thought, annoyed.

The sad-looking filmy fern trapped behind the glass front of the Wardian case was dying. She doubted the exquisitely delicate little *Trichomanes speciosum* would last the month. She had to resist the urge to rescue it. There was scarcely a household in the country that did not boast a fern in the drawing room, she reminded herself. One could not save all of them. The fern craze had been going strong for several years now. There was even a name for it, *Pteridomania*.

With the ease of long practice, she suppressed the distracting energy and colors of the plant life in the room and concentrated on the body. A faint residue of unwholesome energy slithered across her senses. With her talent she could detect almost any type of poison because of the way the energy of toxic substances infused the atmosphere. But her true expertise was in the realm of those poisons that had their origins in the botanical kingdom.

She knew at once that Fairburn had, indeed, drunk poison, just as Spellar had suspected. What stunned her were the faint traces of a certain very rare species of fern. A cold chill of panic trickled through her.

She took a moment or two longer than necessary with the body, pretending to concentrate on her analysis.

In reality she used the time to catch her breath and steady her nerves. *Stay calm. Do not show any emotion.*

When she was certain that she had herself under control she straightened and looked at Spellar.

"You are right to be suspicious, sir," she said in what she hoped were professional tones. "He ate or drank something quite poisonous shortly before he died."

Lady Fairburn gave out a shrill cry of ladylike anguish. "It is just as I feared. My beloved husband took his own life. How could he do this to me?"

She collapsed into a graceful faint.

"Annie!" Hannah exclaimed.

She dropped to her knees beside her sister and removed a dainty vial from the decorative chatelaine at her waist. She pulled out the stopper and waved the vinaigrette under Lady Fairburn's nose. The smelling salts proved effective immediately. The widow's eyes fluttered.

Hamilton Fairburn's expression hardened into grim outrage. "Are you saying that my father committed suicide, Miss Bromley?"

She closed down her senses and looked at him across the vast expanse of the carpet. "I never said that he deliberately drank the poison, sir. Whether he took it by accident or design is for the police to determine."

Hannah fixed her with a seething glare. "Who are you to declare his lordship's death a case of poison? You are certainly not a doctor, Miss Bromley. Indeed, we all know exactly what you are. How dare you come into this household and hurl accusations about?"

Lucinda felt her temper stir. This was the annoying aspect of her consulting work. The public was consumed with a great fear of poison, thanks to the sensation press, which had developed a morbid infatuation with the subject in recent years.

"I did not come here to make accusations," Lucinda said, fighting to keep her voice even. "Inspector Spellar requested my opinion. I have given it. Now, if you will excuse me, I will take my leave."

Spellar stepped forward. "I will escort you outside to your carriage, Miss Bromley."

"Thank you, Inspector."

They left the library and went into the front hall, where they found the housekeeper and butler waiting. Both individuals were steeped in anxiety. The rest of what was no doubt a very large household staff remained discreetly out of sight. Lucinda did not blame them. When there was a question of poison, the servants were often the first to come under suspicion.

The butler hurried to open the door. Lucinda went out onto the steps. Spellar followed. They were met with a wall of gray. It was midafternoon but the fog was so thick that it masked the small park in the center of the square and veiled the fine town houses on the opposite side. Lucinda's private carriage waited in the street. Shute, her coachman, lounged nearby. He came away from the railing when he saw her and opened the door to the vehicle.

"I do not envy you this case, Inspector Spellar," she said quietly.

"So it was poison," Spellar said. "Thought as much."

"Unfortunately nothing so simple as arsenic, I'm afraid. You will not be able to apply Mr. Marsh's test to prove your case."

"I regret to say that arsenic has fallen somewhat out of favor of late now that the general public is aware that there is a test to detect it."

"Do not despair, sir, it is an old standby and will always be popular if for no other reason than it is widely

7

available and, if administered with patience over a long period of time, produces symptoms that can readily be attributed to any number of fatal diseases. There is a reason, after all, why the French call it inheritance powder."

"True enough." Spellar grimaced. "One can only wonder how many elderly parents and inconvenient spouses have been sped on their way to the Other World by that means. Well, if not arsenic, what then? I did not detect the smell of bitter almonds or notice any of the other symptoms of cyanide."

"I'm certain that the poison was botanical in origin. It was based on the castor bean, which, as I'm sure you know, is highly toxic."

Spellar's forehead creased. "I was under the impression that castor bean poisoning produced violent illness before it killed. Lord Fairburn showed no indication of that sort of sickness."

She chose her words with great caution, anxious to give Spellar as much of the truth as possible. "Whoever brewed the poison managed to refine the most lethal aspects of the plant in such a way as to produce a highly toxic substance that was extremely potent and very fast-acting. Lord Fairburn's heart stopped before his body even had a chance to try to expel the potion."

"You sound impressed, Miss Bromley." Spellar's bushy brows bunched together. "I take it that the skill required to prepare such a poison would be uncommon?"

For an instant his talent for keen observation sparked in his eyes. It disappeared almost immediately beneath the bland, slightly bumbling façade he affected. But she knew now that she had to be very careful.

"Extremely uncommon," she said briskly. "Only a scientist or chemist of some genius could have concocted that poison."

"Psychical genius?" Spellar asked quietly.

"Possibly." She sighed. "I will be honest, Inspector. I have never before encountered this particular blend of ingredients in any poison." And that, she thought, was no more or less than the absolute truth.

"I see." Spellar assumed a resigned air. "I suppose I shall have to start with the apothecary shops, for all the good it will do. There has always been a lively underground trade in poisons carried on in such establishments. A would-be widow can purchase a toxic substance quite easily. When the husband drops dead she can claim that it was an accident. She bought the stuff to kill the rats. It was just unfortunate that her spouse accidentally drank some of it."

"There are thousands of apothecary shops in London."

He snorted. "Not to mention the establishments that sell herbs and patent medicines. But I may be able to narrow the list of possibilities by concentrating on shops near this address."

She pulled on her gloves. "You are convinced this is murder, then? Not a suicide?"

The sharp gleam came and went again in Spellar's eyes. "This is murder, all right," he said softly. "I can feel it."

She shivered, not doubting his intuition for a second.

"One cannot help but observe that Lady Fairburn will look quite attractive in mourning," she said.

Spellar smiled slightly. "The same thought occurred to me, as well."

"Do you think she killed him?"

"It would not be the first time that an unhappy young wife who longed to be both free and wealthy fed poison to her much older husband." He rocked on his heels once or twice. "But there are other possibilities in that household. First, I must find the source of the poison."

Her insides tightened. She fought to keep the fear out of her expression. "Yes, of course. Good luck, Inspector."

"Thank you for coming here today." He lowered his voice. "I apologize for the rudeness that you were obliged to endure in the Fairburn household."

"That was in no way your fault." She smiled slightly. "We both know that I am accustomed to such behavior."

"That does not make it any more tolerable." Spellar's expression turned uncharacteristically somber. "The fact that you are willing to expose yourself to such behavior in order to assist me from time to time puts me all the more deeply into your debt."

"Nonsense. We share a common goal. Neither of us wishes to see killers walk free. But I fear you have your work cut out for you this time."

"So it would seem. Good day, Miss Bromley."

He assisted her up into the dainty little cab, closed the door and stepped back. She settled against the cushions, pulled the folds of her cloak snugly around her and gazed out at the sea of fog.

The traces of the fern that she had detected in the poison had unnerved her as nothing else had since the death of her father. There was only one specimen of *Ameliopteris amazonensis* in all of England. Until last month it had been growing in her private conservatory.

Two

The colorful posters in front of the theater heralded him as *The Amazing Mysterio, Master of Locks*. His real name was Edmund Fletcher and he was well aware that he was not particularly amazing onstage. Give him a locked house and he could slip inside, as undetectable as fog. Once on the premises, he could locate the home-owner's valuables, no matter how well concealed. Indeed, he had a talent for the craft of breaking and entering. The difficulty was that he had once again decided to try his hand at making an honest living. The attempt, like all previous efforts in that direction, was faltering badly.

He had opened to sparse audiences and the crowds were only getting thinner as the weeks went past. This evening nearly three-quarters of the seats in the tiny theater were empty. At this rate, he would be obliged to return to his other career very soon in order to come up with the rent on the first of the month.

They said that crime does not pay but it was certainly a good deal more profitable than the illusionist's profession.

"In order to satisfy all those present that there is no trickery involved, may I have a volunteer from the audience?" he said in a loud voice.

There was a bored silence. Finally, one hand shot up.

11

"I'll volunteer to make sure ye don't cheat," a man in the second row said.

"Thank you, sir." Edmund gestured toward the stage steps. "Kindly join me here in the spotlight."

The beefy man, dressed in an ill-fitting suit, made his way up the stage steps.

"Your name, sir?" Edmund asked.

"Spriggs. What do ye want me to do?"

"Please take this key, Mr. Spriggs." Edmund presented him with the heavy chunk of iron. "Once I am inside the cage, you will lock the door. Are the instructions clear?"

The man snorted. "Expect I can handle that. Go on with ye. Get inside."

It was probably not a good sign that the volunteer from the audience was giving directions to the magician, Edmund thought.

He moved into the cage and looked out at the silent crowd through the bars. He felt like an idiot.

"You may lock the door, Mr. Spriggs," he said.

"Right ye are, then." Spriggs slammed the door and turned the old-fashioned key in the big lock. "You're locked up good and tight. Let's see ye get out of there."

Chairs squeaked. The audience was getting restless. Edmund was not surprised. He had no idea how those watching him perceived the passage of time, although the number of people who had walked out was some indication, but from his perspective the performance seemed interminable.

Once again his gaze went to the solitary figure in the last row. In the low light of the wall sconce he could see only the dark silhouette in the aisle seat. The man's features remained veiled in shadows. There was something vaguely dangerous, even menacing, about him, however. He had not applauded any of Edmund's escapes but he had not booed or hissed, either. He simply lounged there, very still and very silent, taking in everything that happened on the stage.

Another little flicker of unease went through Edmund. Perhaps one of his creditors had become impatient and decided to send someone extremely uncouth around to collect. Another, even more alarming thought had also occurred to him. Perhaps some unusually insightful detective from Scotland Yard had finally stumbled over a clue at the scene of Jasper Vine's death that had led to him. Well, this was the reason even the lowliest of theaters provided convenient backstage doors that opened onto dark alleys.

"Ladies and gentlemen," he intoned. He made a show of adjusting his formal bow tie and palmed the sliver of metal concealed there. "Watch very carefully. I will now unlock this door with merely a touch of my fingers."

He elevated his senses and simultaneously brushed his hand against the lock. The door of the cage swung open.

There was a lackluster smattering of applause.

"I've seen fancier tricks from street magicians," a man in the second row shouted.

Edmund ignored him. He bowed deeply to Spriggs. "Thank you for your gracious assistance." He straightened, withdrew a pocket watch and dangled it in front of Spriggs. "I believe this belongs to you."

Spriggs started and then snatched the watch out of Edmund's hands. "Give me that."

He hurried back down the steps and stomped out of the theater.

"You're nothing but a well-dressed pickpocket," someone shouted.

The situation was deteriorating. Time to close the

show. Edmund moved to the center of the stage, making certain that he was in the middle of the spotlight.

"And now, my friends," he said, "it is time to bid you all adieu."

"Good riddance," someone called out.

Edmund bowed deeply.

"I want my money back," a man yelled.

Ignoring the jeering, Edmund gripped the edges of his cloak, raised them high and then drew the black satin folds closed, concealing himself from the audience. He heightened his senses again, generating more energy, and executed his final astonishment.

The cloak crumpled to the floor, revealing an empty stage.

There was, at long last, a gasp of amazement from the audience. The hissing and booing ceased abruptly. Edmund listened from the other side of the tattered red velvet curtain. He needed to devise more of such flashy, attention-grabbing tricks. There were two problems, however. The first was that elaborate and suitably dramatic stage props of the sort that would truly impress a crowd were expensive.

The second problem was that showmanship was not in his nature. He preferred to go unnoticed. He hated the spotlight and all that went with it. It made him decidedly uneasy to be the center of all eyes. *Face it, Fletcher, you were born for a life of crime, not the stage*.

"Come back out here and show us how you did that," someone shouted through the curtain.

The murmur of startled amazement that had rippled across the audience promptly metamorphosed into grumbling disgust.

"One halfway decent trick," a man complained. "That's all he's got."

Edmund started backstage toward his dressing room.

Murphy, the owner of the theater, loomed in the shadows. His plump little dog, Pom, was at his feet. With their broad heads and squashed-in noses, the two bore an uncanny resemblance. Pom bared his teeth and uttered a high-pitched growl.

"Difficult crowd," Edmund offered.

"Can't say as I blame 'em," Murphy said in a voice that sounded a lot like Pom's. His ruddy face tightened into a sour scowl. "Any magician worth his salt can escape from a locked cage or a pair of handcuffs. That last trick of yours isn't half bad but it's hardly unique, now, is it? Keller the Great and Lorenzo the Magnificent both make themselves disappear on a nightly basis. They make a lot of other things vanish, as well, including attractive young ladies."

"Hire an attractive young lady for me and I'll make her disappear for you," Edmund said. "We've discussed this before, Murphy. If you want fancier astonishments, you'll have to invest in more expensive props and pretty assistants. I certainly cannot afford them on what you pay me."

Pom snarled. So did Murphy.

"I'm already paying you far too much," Murphy snapped.

"I could make more driving a hansom. Get out of my way, Murphy. I need a drink."

He continued down the hall to the tiny closet he used as a dressing room. Murphy bustled after him. Edmund heard Pom's claws clicking on the wooden boards.

"Hold on, there," Murphy said. "We're going to have a talk."

Pom yipped.

Edmund did not slow his pace. "Later, if you don't mind."

"Now, damn it. I'm closing down your engagement.

Tonight was your last performance. You can pack your things and leave."

Edmund halted abruptly and turned on his heel. "You can't sack me. We have a contract."

Pom skidded to a stop and hastily retreated. Murphy drew himself up to his full height, which brought his large, bald head even with Edmund's shoulders. "There's a clause in the contract that says if the nightly receipts fall below a certain minimum for three performances in a row, I am free to terminate the agreement. For your information, the receipts have been below the minimum for over a fortnight."

"It's not my fault you don't know how to advertise and promote a magician's act."

"It's not my fault you're a mediocre illusionist," Murphy shot back. "It's all well and good to unlock safes and make a few items disappear and reappear, but that's very old-fashioned stuff. The public wants new and more mysterious astonishments. They want to see you levitate. At the very least they expect you to summon a few spirits from the Other World."

"I never claimed to be a medium. I'm a magician."

"One with only a couple of tricks up his sleeve. You're skilled with the art of sleight of hand, I'll give you that. But it's not enough for modern audiences."

"Give me another few nights, Murphy," Edmund said wearily. "I promise I'll come up with something suitably spectacular."

"Bah. That's what you said last week. I'm sorry for your lack of talent, Fletcher, but I can't afford to give you any more chances. I've got bills to pay and a wife and three children to feed. Our contract is finished as of now."

So it was back to a life of crime, after all. Well, at least it would be more profitable, if somewhat more dangerous. It was one thing to be let go because of a poor performance on the stage; quite another to be sent to prison because one had been caught robbing a house. But there was a certain thrill to the art of breaking and entering, a thrill he could not seem to come by in any legitimate fashion.

Deliberately he heightened his senses, charging the atmosphere with a whisper of energy. Murphy did not possess any noticeable degree of psychical talent but everyone, even the dullest and most irritating theater owners, possessed a little intuition.

"I'll be gone by morning," Edmund said. "Now go away and take your little dog with you or I'll make you both disappear. Permanently."

Pom squeaked in alarm and ducked behind Murphy.

Murphy's whiskers twitched and his eyes widened. He took a hasty step back, managing to step on Pom. The dog yelped. So did Murphy.

"Now, see here, you can't threaten me," Murphy stammered. "I'll summon the police."

"Never mind," Edmund said. "Making you vanish would require more effort than it's worth. By the way, before you remove yourself and the beast, I'll have my share of the receipts."

"Haven't you been listening? There was no profit tonight."

"I counted thirty people in the audience including the man who came in late and sat in the back row. Our contract specifies that you will give me half of the total you took in at the box office. If you propose to cheat me, I'll be the one summoning a constable." It was an empty threat but he could not think of anything else.

"In case you didn't notice, a good percentage of the crowd left before you finished," Murphy insisted. "I had to refund a great deal of money."

"I don't believe that you refunded so much as a penny. You are far too shrewd a businessman."

Murphy's face reddened with outrage but he reached into his pocket and removed some money. He counted it out very carefully and dutifully handed over half.

"Take it," he grumbled. "It's worth it to be rid of you. See to it that you clear out all your things. Anything left behind becomes my property."

Murphy picked up Pom, tucked the dog under one arm and stalked away toward his office at the front of the theater.

Edmund went into his dressing room, turned up the gas lamp and calculated quickly. There was enough to buy another bottle of claret and still have something left over for food tomorrow. There was no question, however, that his career as a member of the criminal class would have to resume immediately; tomorrow night at the latest. He would pack and go out of the theater via the alley just in case the unknown man in the last row was waiting for him in front.

He hauled his battered suitcase from under the dressing table and swiftly tossed his few possessions into it. The dramatic satin cape was still on the stage. He must not forget it. Not that he would be needing it any longer. Nevertheless, he might be able to sell it to some other struggling magician.

A knock on the door stopped him cold. *The man in the last row*. His intuition was strongly linked to his talent. It never failed him in situations like this.

"Damn it, Murphy, I told you I'd be gone by morning," he said loudly.

"Would you happen to be interested in another engagement?"

The man's voice was low and well educated. It resonated with cool control and raw power. Not your typical debt collector, Edmund thought, but for some reason he did not find that especially reassuring.

He elevated his senses, picked up his suitcase and cautiously opened the door. The man standing in the hall somehow managed to remain just beyond the reach of the gas lamp's weak glare. There was a lean, hard, predatory quality to the shadowy figure.

"Who the devil are you?" Edmund asked. He prepared to execute a little diversion.

"Your new employer, I trust."

Perhaps the return to a life of crime could be postponed for a time, after all.

"You wish to hire a magician?" Edmund asked. "As it happens, I'm open to an offer."

"I don't need a magician. Magicians use sleight of hand and props to achieve their astonishments. I want someone who truly does possess a preternatural talent for slipping in and out of locked rooms."

Alarm shafted through Edmund.

"I don't know what you're talking about," he said.

"You are not a stage magician, Mr. Fletcher. You do not depend upon fakery, do you?"

"I don't understand what you mean, sir."

"You possess a most unusual psychical ability, one that enables you to feel your way through the most complicated locks. It also allows you to create small illusions that distract the eye of those around you while you go about your work. You cannot actually walk through walls but one could easily believe that you are capable of such a feat."

"Who are you?" Edmund demanded, trying to conceal his astonishment.

"My name is Caleb Jones. I recently established a small investigation agency, Jones and Company, that handles inquiries of a most private and confidential manner. I am learning that upon occasion I require the assistance of consultants who possess particular talents."

"Consultants?"

"I am presently conducting an investigation that requires your unusual abilities, Mr. Fletcher. You will be well compensated, I assure you."

"You said your name was Jones. That rings a very loud bell. Any connection to the Arcane Society?"

"I can assure you that there are days when the connection is a good deal closer than I would like."

"What is it you wish me to do for you?"

"I want you to help me break into a securely locked and well-guarded building. Once inside, we will steal a certain artifact."

In spite of everything, Edmund felt his pulse quicken.

"I had rather hoped to avoid a life of crime," he said.

"Why would you want to do that?" Caleb Jones asked very seriously. "You have a talent for the profession, after all."

Three

$\mathcal{T}$he one insurmountable, damnably annoying difficulty that got in the way of trying to operate a
psychical investigation agency was that the business necessarily involved clients.

Caleb stepped down from the hansom and went up
the front steps of Number Twelve Landreth Square. He
raised the heavy brass knocker and let it fall a couple of
times.

Clients were the great drawback to what would otherwise have been an interesting and challenging profession. Discovering patterns and obtaining answers had
always fascinated him, some said to the point of obsession. He was still new at the investigation business but
already he could see that it promised a great deal of stimulation. It was also a welcome distraction from the other
matter that consumed him these days.

It was a great pity that there was no way to avoid
dealing with the individuals who brought their questions
to the Jones agency, however. Clients were always carrying on in a dramatic fashion. Clients got emotional.
After contracting for his services they pestered him with
messages demanding to know what progress he was
making. When he did provide answers, clients tended to
fall into one of two categories. Half flew into fits of rage.
The rest broke down weeping. Either way, they were

rarely satisfied. But, sadly, clients seemed to be a necessary part of the enterprise.

At least on this occasion he was about to interview a potential client who promised to be decidedly out of the ordinary. In spite of his customary antipathy toward those who approached the agency seeking investigative assistance, he could not suppress an odd sense of anticipation.

He had recognized her name, of course, the moment he opened her note. Lucinda Bromley, known in the sensation press as *Lucrezia* Bromley, was the daughter of the notorious Arthur Bromley. A brilliant botanist, Bromley had traversed the far corners of the world seeking out rare and exotic botanical specimens. His wife and daughter had often accompanied him. Amelia Bromley had died four years ago but Lucinda had continued to travel with her father.

The expeditions had come to an abrupt halt some eighteen months ago, when Bromley's longtime business partner, Gordon Woodhall, was discovered dead of cyanide poisoning. Immediately thereafter Arthur Bromley had committed suicide. Rumors that there had been a falling-out between the two men were splashed across the front pages of every newspaper in London.

The headlines following the murder-suicide were nothing, however, compared to those that had riveted the public less than a month later when Lucinda Bromley's fiancé, a young botanist named Ian Glasson, was found dead of poison.

The scandal was compounded by the sordid gossip that had swirled around the events immediately prior to Glasson's demise. Lucinda had been seen rushing away from a secluded corner of the gardens at the Carstairs Botanical Society, the bodice of her gown half undone. A short time later, Glasson had sauntered out of the same remote section of the grounds, still fastening his trousers. A few days later he was in his coffin.

According to the lurid stories in the newspapers, Lucinda had fed her fiancé a cup of poisoned tea. They said she had secreted the lethal dose in a hidden chamber of a ring she always wore.

It was in the wake of the Glasson poisoning that the press had bestowed the name Lucrezia on Lucinda. The reference was to the infamous Lucrezia Borgia, who was said to have poisoned any number of people. According to the legend, the lady had concealed the deadly substance in a ring.

The door opened. A formidable-looking housekeeper eyed him as though she suspected he had come to steal the silver.

"I'm here to see Miss Bromley," Caleb said. He gave the woman his card. "I believe I am expected."

The housekeeper studied the card with a disapproving frown then reluctantly stepped back.

"Yes, Mr. Jones. Follow me, please."

Caleb moved into a marble-tiled hall. A large mirror in a heavily gilded frame hung on the wall above an elaborately inlaid side table. The silver salver on top of the table designed to receive cards from visitors was empty.

He expected to be shown into the drawing room. Instead the housekeeper marched to the back of the house and through a library crammed with books, maps, globes and papers.

At the far end of the room the woman opened a set of French doors. Caleb found himself looking into a large conservatory. The fancifully designed glass-and-iron structure contained a verdant green jungle. Humid warmth flowed over him, carrying the scents of rich, fertile soil and thriving vegetation.

Other kinds of currents flowed from the conservatory, as well. He felt the unmistakable whispers of energy. It was a remarkably invigorating sensation. The atmosphere in the conservatory acted like a tonic on all his senses.

"Mr. Jones to see you, Miss Bromley," the housekeeper announced in a voice that was loud enough to carry to the far end of the conservatory.

The sea of greenery was so thick and so dense that Caleb did not notice the woman in the gardening apron and leather gloves until she appeared from behind a waterfall of purple orchids. A prowling excitement whipped through him, tightening muscle and sinew. An inexplicable sense of urgency unfurled. The word *invigorating* came to mind again.

He did not know what he had been expecting but whatever it was, Lucinda Bromley engineered an extremely rare feat. She caught him entirely by surprise.

He supposed that, given her reputation, he had been anticipating a sleek, sophisticated lady with a façade of charm and polish that might just possibly conceal a venomous heart. Lucrezia Borgia had a certain reputation, after all.

But Lucinda looked more like an absentminded, scholarly Titania, Queen of the Fairies. Her hair put him in mind of an exploded sunset. She had attempted to tame the frothy red curls with pins and a couple of ribbons but to little avail.

Intelligence lit her features, transforming a face that would otherwise have been described as passable into one for which the only suitable word was *riveting*. He realized that he did not want to look away. She peered at him from behind the sparkling lenses of a pair of gold-rimmed spectacles. Her eyes were a deep, fascinating shade of blue.

She wore a long, many-pocketed leather apron over a plain gray gown. In one hand she gripped a pair of pruning shears. The long, sharp blades of the tool had the appearance of some bizarre medieval weapon designed to be worn by an armored knight. A number of other equally dangerous-looking implements were festooned about her person.

"Thank you, Mrs. Shute," Lucinda said. "We'll take tea in the library, please."

Her voice was not at all fairy-like, Caleb decided, pleased. Instead of the irritatingly high tinkle of little elfin bells that so many women cultivated, her tone was warm, confident and determined. Energy radiated from her in an invisible aura. A woman of power, he thought.

He had met other women with strong talents. They were not that uncommon at the higher levels of the Arcane Society. But something inside him responded to Lucinda's energy in a way that was new and oddly unsettling. He had to fight the urge to move closer to her.

"I'll fetch the tea, ma'am," Mrs. Shute said. She turned and went back through the doorway.

Lucinda gave Caleb a cool, polite smile. He could feel the wariness in her. She was not certain that she had done the right thing by sending for him, he realized. Many clients developed reservations after making the appointment.

"Thank you for coming here today," she said. "I know you must be very busy, Mr. Jones."

"It was no imposition at all," he said, mentally dismissing the long list of pressing projects and responsibilities that would otherwise have occupied his attention. "Happy to be of service." It was certainly the first time he had ever said that to a client. He suspected it would be the only time.

"Shall we go into the library?"

"As you wish."

She untied her dirt-stained apron and slipped it off over her head. The ungainly assortment of tools and implements in the pockets clanked. He watched her strip off the thick leather gardening gloves. There was, indeed, a ring, he noticed, just as the press had reported. It was fashioned of heavy, intricately worked gold and decorated with dark blue lapis and an amber gemstone. The ring looked old and vaguely Renaissance in style. It was certainly large enough to conceal a small compartment, he thought, intrigued.

She stopped in front of him and gave him an inquiring look.

He realized that he was standing there, directly in her path, staring. He pulled himself together with a monumental effort of will and stepped aside to let her enter the library. When she went past him he deliberately heightened his senses, enjoying the little rush of energy that stirred the atmosphere. Oh, yes, definitely a woman of power.

Lucinda seated herself behind a cluttered mahogany desk and indicated the chair across from her.

"Please sit down, Mr. Jones."

She was defining their relationship quite clearly, he realized, amused; making it obvious that she perceived herself to be the one in command and that she intended to retain the upper hand in their association. He found the subtle, unspoken challenge as stimulating as her aura.

He lowered himself into the chair she indicated. "In your note you mentioned that the matter was urgent."

"It is." She clasped her hands very tightly together on top of the blotter and fixed him with a very steady look.

"Have you, by any chance, heard of the recent death of Lord Fairburn?"

"Saw something about it in the morning papers. Suicide, I believe."

"It may have been. That is still to be determined. The family, or at least one member of the family, Fairburn's son, has asked Scotland Yard to investigate."

"I had not heard that," he said.

"For obvious reasons, the family would like the inquiry to remain quiet."

"How did you come to learn of it?"

"The detective who is conducting the investigation asked me to give my opinion. I have consulted for Mr. Spellar on a number of occasions."

"I know Spellar. He is a member of the Arcane Society."

"Indeed." She gave him a defiant little smile. "As am I, Mr. Jones."

"I am aware of that. No one outside the Society would likely be aware that the Jones agency even exists, let alone know how to contact me."

She flushed. "Yes, of course. Forgive me. I fear that I am occasionally inclined to be somewhat defensive." She cleared her throat. "My family has something of a reputation. I'm sure you're aware of the gossip."

"I have heard a few rumors," he said neutrally.

"I do not doubt that." Her fingers tightened visibly until her hands appeared clenched, not merely clasped together. "Will those rumors affect your decision concerning whether or not to accept my case?"

"If they did, I wouldn't be here. I should think that much would be obvious, Miss Bromley. As I'm sure you're aware, the Arcane Society does not always conform to the same rules that govern the social world." He paused a beat. "And neither do I."

"I see."

"I suspect you have heard gossip about me, as well."

"Yes, I have, Mr. Jones," she agreed quietly. "It is one of the reasons I asked you to come here today. Among other things, it is said that you are greatly intrigued by mysteries."

"To a fault, I'm told. But in my own defense I will say that I am only intrigued by very interesting mysteries."

"Yes, well, I'm not sure my situation will qualify as interesting to you but I assure you I find it extremely worrisome."

"Why don't you tell me a little more about your mystery?"

"Yes, of course." She straightened and squared her elegant shoulders. "As you may know, I possess a certain amount of botanical talent. Among other things, I can detect poison. If that poison is based on herbs or plants, I can usually determine the precise nature of the ingredients in the toxic substance."

"You deduced that Lord Fairburn was poisoned?"

She gave him a wry smile. "You do indeed jump straight to the appropriate conclusion, I see. Yes, he most certainly drank some very lethal concoction. The only question now is whether it was a case of suicide or murder. To be honest, I think it highly unlikely that Inspector Spellar will be able to prove the latter."

"It is notoriously difficult to prove a case of murder by poison even when there is strong evidence, as in the case of arsenic or cyanide. It is too easy to convince a jury that it was an accident or that the victim took his own life."

"Yes, I know. But if there are extenuating circumstances—" She stopped abruptly.

"Why are you so concerned with the outcome of this

case, Miss Bromley? Surely it is Spellar's responsibility to decide if it was murder, not yours."

Lucinda drew a deep breath and visibly braced herself. She was trying to conceal her tension but he could detect the undercurrents as clearly as if he could see her aura. She was not just anxious about the outcome of the Fairburn case; she was frightened.

"When Inspector Spellar summoned me to view the body at the Fairburn town house yesterday," she said slowly, "I confirmed that—"

"You viewed the body?"

She gave him a quizzical frown. "Well, yes, of course. How else could I assess the possibility of poison?"

He was stunned. "Good Lord. I had no idea."

"No idea of what?"

"I understood that Spellar occasionally asked you to consult but I did not realize that you were obliged to physically examine the bodies of the victims in order to give an opinion."

She raised her brows. "How did you think that I went about providing my consultations?"

"I suppose I didn't," he admitted. "Think, that is. I just assumed that Spellar brought you some of the evidence. The poisoned cup, perhaps, or the victim's clothing."

"I can see that you do not consider what I do for Inspector Spellar to be suitable work for a lady."

"I didn't say that."

"No need." She waved one hand, dismissing his attempt to vindicate himself. "I assure you that you are not alone in your view. No one, with the exception of Inspector Spellar, approves of what I do. Actually, I don't think that Spellar entirely approves, either, but he is dedicated to his profession and, therefore, more than willing to take advantage of whatever assistance I can provide."

"Miss Bromley—"

"Given my somewhat unusual family history, I am quite accustomed to disapproval."

"Damn it, Miss Bromley, you will not put words in my mouth." He was on his feet before he realized what he was doing, flattening his palms on the desktop. "I am not passing judgment on you. Yes, I was astonished to discover that your consulting work requires you to view the bodies of the victims. You will concede that sort of thing is, generally speaking, a somewhat uncommon occupation for a lady."

"Is it?" She unclasped her hands and sat back quickly. "And just who do you think is usually responsible for attending to those who become gravely ill and die in the vast majority of households? Most people do not go to hospitals to die, sir. Most people die at home and it is women who are at the bedside when the end comes."

"We are talking about people who are murdered, not those who expire from natural causes."

"Do you think one sort of death more violent than the other? If that is so, then you have not been called upon to witness many passings. I assure you, a so-called natural death can be far more dreadful, more painful, more lingering than one brought on by a quick case of poison or a bullet to the head."

"Devil take it, I cannot believe I am engaged in this ridiculous argument. I did not come here to discuss your consulting work, Miss Bromley. I am here because you sent for me. I suggest we get on with our business."

She gave him a steely glare. "You're the one who started the quarrel."

"The hell I did."

She blinked and angled her chin. "Do you always use that sort of language when you are in the company of a lady, sir? Or is it that you feel free to employ such colorful vocabulary because of the particular lady you happen to be with at the moment?"

He smiled grimly. "My apologies, Miss Bromley. But I must admit that I'm surprised to learn that a lady who consults at murder scenes is shocked by a little rough language."

She matched his smile with a very chilly one of her own. "Are you implying that I am not a proper sort of lady?"

He straightened abruptly, turned and stalked to the window. "This is the most bizarre conversation I have had in ages. Also the most pointless. If you will be so good as to tell me why you summoned me here today, perhaps we could get on with this meeting."

A sharp knock on the door interrupted him. He turned to see the housekeeper enter the room with a tray of tea things. Mrs. Shute glowered at him, letting him know in silent but no uncertain terms that she had overheard the heated discussion.

"Thank you, Mrs. Shute," Lucinda said smoothly, just as though she were not thoroughly annoyed with her visitor. "You may leave the tray on the table. I'll pour."

"Yes, ma'am."

With another disapproving look at Caleb, the housekeeper departed, closing the door quietly.

His language really had been quite appalling. It was true that he had never been known for his drawing room manners. He had little patience with social niceties. But he was generally not so lost to propriety that he cursed in the presence of females of any station or background.

Lucinda rose and went to sit on the sofa. She picked up the teapot.

"Milk and sugar, sir?" she asked, poised and composed,

just as if there had been no argument. Her cheeks were somewhat flushed, however, and there was a militant sparkle in her eyes.

When all else fails, pour a cup of tea, he thought.

"Neither, thank you," he said, his voice still a little gruff.

He tried to analyze the new, bright intensity that emanated from Lucinda. She was not precisely glowing, but she seemed a little more energized.

"You may as well sit down again," she said. "We still have a great deal to talk about."

"I'm amazed that you wish to engage my services given my language."

"It is not as though I am in a position to ask you to leave, sir." She poured tea with a graceful hand. "Your services are unique and I find myself in need of them." She set the pot down. "So it appears that I am stuck with you."

He felt the edge of his mouth start to curve in spite of his mood. He took the cup and saucer and sat down in an armchair.

"And I, Miss Bromley, appear to be stuck with you," he said.

"Hardly, sir. You are quite free to decline my request for your investigative services. We both know that you do not need the exorbitant fees that I'm certain you intend to charge me."

"I could certainly walk away from the money," he agreed. "But not from this case."

Her cup paused halfway to her lips. Her eyes widened. "But I have not yet told you what it is that I wish you to investigate."

"It does not matter. The case is not what interests me, Miss Bromley." He swallowed some of the tea and lowered the cup. "You do."

She did not move. "What on earth are you talking about?"

"You are a most unusual female, as I'm sure you're well aware. I have never met anyone quite like you. I find you—" He broke off, searching for the right word. "Interesting." *Fascinating* would have been closer to the truth. "Therefore, I expect that your mystery will prove equally stimulating."

"I see." She did not appear pleased, nor did she seem insulted. If anything she looked resigned; perhaps a little disappointed although she hid the reaction well. "Given your odd choice of a career, I suppose it makes sense."

He did not like the sound of that. "In what way?"

"You are a gentleman who is attracted to puzzles." She set her cup down very carefully on the saucer. "At the moment, I am something of a mystery to you because I do not conform to the model of female behavior that is generally held to be acceptable by society. Therefore you are curious about me."

"It is not that," he said, irritated. He paused, aware that she was correct, in a manner of speaking. She *was* a mystery to him; one he felt compelled to explore. "Not exactly."

"Yes, it is exactly that," she countered. "But you are drinking the tea that I just poured for you, so I will not hold it against you."

"What the devil are you talking about?"

She gave him another cool smile. "Very few gentlemen have the courage to drink tea with me, Mr. Jones."

"I cannot imagine why any man would hesitate." He smiled faintly. "It is excellent tea."

"It is said that the poison that killed my fiancé was fed to him in a cup of tea that I poured."

"What's life without a little risk?" He took another

33

healthy swallow and put the cup down. "Now then, about the matter you wish me to investigate. Would you care to give me the details? Or would you prefer to spar awhile longer? Mind you, I have no objection to the latter. I find the sport quite stimulating."

She stared at him for a heartbeat or two, her eyes unreadable behind the lenses of her eyeglasses. Then she burst into laughter. Not the light titter of ballroom giggles or the low, seductive laugh of a woman of the world. Just genuine, feminine laughter. She had to set down her cup and dab at her eyes with her napkin.

"Very good, Mr. Jones," she managed finally. "You are as unusual as I had been led to believe." She crumpled the napkin and pulled herself together. "You're right. It is time for the business at hand. As I said, Inspector Spellar called me in to view Lord Fairburn's body."

"And you concluded Fairburn had been poisoned."

"Yes. I told Spellar as much. I also gave him to understand that the basis of the poison was the castor bean plant. But there were some unusual aspects to the case. The first is that whoever concocted the lethal brew must have been very learned in botanical and chemical matters."

"Why do you say that?"

"Because he knew how to make an extremely refined, powerful and quick-acting version of the poison. Lord Fairburn was dead before he had time to become ill. That is extremely uncommon in the case of botanical poisons. The victim is usually stricken first with a number of obvious physical symptoms. I'm sure I need not go into detail."

"Convulsions. Vomiting. Diarrhea." He shrugged. "I believe we have already established that I prefer not to mince words."

She blinked again in a way that he was coming to recognize as an indication that she had been caught off guard. It was a small sign, but a telling one.

"Indeed," she said.

"You say that the speed with which the poison acted led you to believe that it was concocted by a scientist or chemist?" he said.

"Yes, I think so. As I'm sure you're aware, there are any number of potentially poisonous substances available in the apothecary shops. One can buy arsenic and cyanide without any difficulty whatsoever. And who knows what is in some of those appalling patent medicines that are so popular? But the poison that was employed to kill Lord Fairburn was not one that could be purchased so easily. Nor would it have been simple to prepare."

His talent quickened. "You are saying that it was produced in a laboratory, not in an apothecary's back room."

"I am saying more than that, Mr. Jones. I believe I know who concocted the poison that killed Lord Fairburn."

He did not move, did not take his eyes off her. Interesting was not the half of it, he thought. Even fascinating failed to describe Lucinda Bromley.

"How do you know this, Miss Bromley?" he asked.

She took a deep breath. "In addition to the traces of the castor bean plant, I recognized another ingredient in the poison that killed Fairburn. It was derived from an extremely rare fern that once grew in my conservatory. I believe the poisoner called upon me last month in order to steal it."

With that he suddenly comprehended the true nature of the case.

"Damnation," he said very softly. "You did not inform Spellar about your visitor or the theft, did you?"

"No. I dared not tell him about the traces of the *Ameliopteris amazonensis* that I detected in the poison that Lord Fairburn drank. He would have been forced to come to the obvious conclusion."

"That you were the one who brewed the poison," Caleb said.

Four

There was a disturbing tension in his aura. she had sensed it the moment he walked into the conservatory. In a weaker man such an imbalance of energies would have resulted in serious illness of a psychical nature. She suspected that Caleb Jones was unconsciously controlling the disharmony through the sheer power of his will. She doubted that he was even aware of the strange, unwholesome currents that pulsed around him.

The state of his psychical health was not her problem, she reminded herself, not unless it prevented him from conducting a thorough investigation. Her intuition told her that would not be the case. Determination and resolve emanated far more strongly in his aura than did the unnatural currents. Caleb Jones was a man who would finish whatever he set out to do, no matter the cost.

This meeting was the very last thing she had wanted but she had not been able to come up with any alternative. Her circumstances were dire and the problem was of a psychical nature. That meant she required an investigation firm that could deal with the paranormal. The only one she was aware of was the recently established Jones agency.

Unfortunately, becoming involved with the firm

meant having to deal with a member of the Jones family, by all accounts an eccentric and dangerous lot. The Arcane Society was a notoriously secretive organization and the powerful members of the Jones clan—descendants of the founder—were always at its heart. Rumor had it they were very good at the business of protecting the Society's—and their own—dark secrets.

She had guessed that Caleb Jones would be frighteningly adept at the business of getting at the truth. It was said that everyone in the family possessed a strong talent of one kind or another, and she had expected Caleb to demonstrate an expertise for his unusual profession.

What had stunned her was the frisson of intense curiosity, indeed outright fascination, that she had experienced when she first sensed his presence in the conservatory. The thrilling little shivers of awareness that were sparkling through her now could only be described as alarmingly sensual in nature. The sensations were disturbing and disorienting; the sort of emotions that might have been forgiven in an innocent young lady of eighteen but which were quite inappropriate in a woman of twenty-seven years; a woman of the world.

For heaven's sake, I'm officially on the shelf; a spinster. And he's a Jones. What on earth is happening to me?

There was a compelling strength in Caleb Jones but also a dour, melancholic air. It was as if he had examined life with the full powers of his intelligence and talents and concluded that it had little in the way of joy to offer him but he would nevertheless persevere. Even if she had not known that he was a direct descendant of Sylvester Jones, the founder of the Society, she would have recognized Caleb as a powerful talent.

Something else burned hot in him, as well, an all-consuming intensity, a single-mindedness of purpose, which she knew would be a two-edged sword. In her experience there was often only a very fine line between the ability to concentrate intelligently on an objective and an unhealthy obsession. She suspected that Caleb had crossed that line more than once. That knowledge taken together with the disharmony in his aura was alarming but she had little choice now. Jones might very well be all that stood between her and a charge of murder.

She fastened the invisible corset of her composure snugly around herself and prepared to move forward with her plan.

"Now you understand why I asked you to come here today, Mr. Jones," she said. "I wish you to investigate the theft of my fern. I am convinced that when you discover the thief, you will also discover that he is the one who concocted the poison that killed Lord Fairburn. You will find him and hand him over to Inspector Spellar, along with the appropriate proof of his guilt."

Caleb's brows rose. "All without dragging your name into the matter, I assume?"

She frowned. "Well, yes, of course. That is the whole point of hiring someone like you to make private inquiries, is it not? One expects a guarantee of confidentiality in this sort of thing."

"So they tell me."

"*Mr. Jones.*"

"I'm still somewhat new at this business of making private inquiries but I have discovered that clients seem to think that there are a number of rules that I must follow. I find that assumption to be tedious and irritating."

She was appalled. "Mr. Jones, if you came here today under false pretenses, be assured that I will go straight to the new Master of the Society and register a complaint about your services in the strongest possible terms."

"Probably best not to bother Gabe at the moment. He's got his hands full trying to reorganize the Governing Council. Seems to believe he can actually get rid of some of those doddering old fools who are still playing at alchemy. I've warned him that a few of them might become dangerous if they find out that they are to be replaced but he insists that an element of democracy is what is needed to put the Society on the path for the new century."

"Mr. Jones," she said sternly. "I am trying to discuss my case with you."

"Right. Where were we? Ah, yes, confidentiality."

"Well, then? Are you prepared to guarantee that you will keep everything pertaining to this matter confidential?"

"Miss Bromley, this may come as a surprise to you, but I keep most things confidential. I am not a sociable man. Just ask anyone who knows me. I despise drawing room conversation and, while I always listen to gossip because I find it is often a source of useful information, I never engage in it."

She had no trouble believing that. "I see."

"You have my promise that I will keep your secrets."

Relief washed through her. "Thank you."

"With one exception."

She froze. "What is that?"

"While the services of my firm are available to all members of the Arcane Society, it is understood that my first responsibility is to protect the secrets of the organization."

She brushed that aside impatiently. "Yes, yes, that was made clear by Gabriel Jones when he announced the establishment of your firm. I assure you, my problem has nothing to do with Arcane Society secrets. This is a

40

simple matter of plant theft and murder. My only goal is to stay out of prison."

Icy amusement flickered in his eyes. "A sensible ambition." He removed a small notebook and a pencil from an inside pocket of his elegantly cut coat. "Tell me about the theft."

She put aside her cup and saucer. "A month ago a man named Dr. Knox called upon me. He claimed to have been referred by an old friend of my father's. Like you, Mr. Jones, I do not go out into society. Nevertheless, I occasionally enjoy the company of others who are as interested in botany as I am."

"Knox was, I take it, very keen on rare plants?"

"Yes. He requested a tour of my conservatory. Said he'd read all of my father's books and papers. He v very enthusiastic and knowledgeable. I saw no reason to refuse."

Caleb looked up from his notes. "Do you frequently provide such tours?"

"No, of course not. This isn't Kew Gardens or the Carstairs Botanical Society."

The old anger shafted through her. She managed, just barely, not to allow it to show in her expression but she could feel her jaw clenching slightly. She suspected that the very observant Mr. Jones noticed the small movement.

"I understand," he said.

"In any event, following my father's death and the death of my fiancé, there have been very few requests for tours, I assure you."

She thought she glimpsed something that might have been sympathy in his expression but it vanished in a heartbeat. She must have been mistaken, she decided. It was unlikely that Caleb Jones would recognize such a delicate sensibility if he fell over it.

"Please continue with your account, Miss Bromley," he said.

"Dr. Knox and I spent nearly two hours in the conservatory. Before long it became obvious that he was particularly interested in my medicinal plants and herbs."

Caleb stopped writing again and gave her a sharp, searching look. "You grow medicinal plants?"

"They are my specialty, Mr. Jones."

"I didn't know that."

"Both of my parents were talented botanists but my mother's chief area of interest was the study of the medicinal properties of plants and herbs. I inherited her fascination with the subject. After she died, I continued to accompany my father on his plant-hunting expeditions. The specimen that captured Dr. Knox's attention was a very unique fern that I discovered in the course of our last journey to the Amazon. I called it *Ameliopteris amazonensis* after my mother. Her name was Amelia."

"You discovered this fern?"

"Not exactly. The people of a small tribe who live in that part of the world deserve that credit. But after I returned from the expedition I could find no reference to it in any books or papers. This library, I assure you, is very extensive."

Caleb examined the crammed shelves with a considering expression. "I can see that."

"A healer in the tribe showed the fern to me and explained its properties. She called it by the name her people had given it, which translates roughly as Secret Eye."

"How is the fern used?"

"Well, the tribe employs it in certain religious ceremonies. But I doubt very much that Dr. Knox is a religious man, let alone that he observes sacred rites that are practiced by only a small group of people who live in a very remote village in South America. No, Mr. Jones, he used my fern to somehow make the poison act more quickly and to mask the taste and smell."

"Do you know what effect the fern has when it is used in the villagers' ceremonies?" Caleb asked.

The question surprised her. Most people would have dismissed out of hand the beliefs of a people who lived in a far-off land.

"The tribe's healer claimed that a tisane made from the fern could open what her people refer to as an individual's secret eye. I'm certain the villagers believe that is what happens when one drinks the brew but that is the thing with religion, is it not? Belief is everything."

"Do you have any notion of what the healer meant by opening the secret eye?"

His intense, unexpected interest in the properties of the fern itself, rather than the theft, was starting to concern her. Some of the rumors she had heard about Caleb Jones implied that he might be something other than merely eccentric.

It was too late to show him the door, she thought. She had already told him her secret. In any event it was not as if she could replace him. There were a great many people in London who claimed to possess psychical talents. Indeed, the paranormal was all the rage. But as every sensible person within the Arcane Society knew, the vast majority of such practitioners were frauds and charlatans. She desperately needed Caleb Jones's talents.

"I do not pretend to be an expert on the healer's religious beliefs," she said carefully. "But according to her, *secret eye* was the term the villagers employed to refer to what you and I would call an individual's dream state."

A great and alarming stillness came over Caleb Jones.

"Son of a bitch," he said, his voice chillingly soft. "Basil Hulsey."

She gave him a disapproving glare. "More ungentlemanly language, Mr. Jones? Really, do you find it so astonishing that there are those outside England who have an understanding of the paranormal? It is not as though we are the only ones who possess a psychical side to our natures."

She broke off abruptly because Caleb had come up out of his chair with the force of a volcano erupting. He crossed to the sofa, hauled her to her feet and into his arms.

"Miss Bromley, you cannot know how helpful you have been. I vow, I could kiss you in gratitude."

She was so stunned that she could not even utter a ladylike protest. Something resembling a startled little squeak came from between her lips and the next thing she knew, his mouth was covering hers and hot energy began to flare in the atmosphere.

Five

She understood intuitively that the kiss was meant to be a fast, meaningless gesture brought on by the wholly inexplicable excitement that appeared to have overcome the obviously well-controlled Mr. Jones. Nevertheless, she knew she ought to have been shocked to her very core by such a breach of etiquette.

Stolen kisses were the province of cads who took advantage of innocent young ladies and daring lovers who managed to slip away from overheated ballrooms into the shadows of night-darkened gardens. Among the respectably married set, such kisses were the signature of illicit liaisons.

There was a word for a woman who allowed a gentleman to take such outrageous liberties: *loose.*

Ah, but she had been called so much worse, she thought.

In any event, this was no clandestine moment of passion such as might be enjoyed by two people in love. It was merely a flash of uncharacteristic exuberance from a man who, she suspected, rarely allowed himself to indulge in strong passions.

The kiss should have ended as suddenly as it had begun, leaving little more than a momentary awkwardness between them. Instead, like lead transmuted into gold in an alchemist's crucible, the embrace went from startling to searing in a disorienting instant.

Caleb's hands tightened abruptly on her arms. He pulled her closer and deepened the kiss. His mouth was now warm and heavy on hers, intoxicating. It was as though he offered her an irresistible elixir laced with dark and dangerous promises.

A frisson of startling clarity shivered through her. A door opened somewhere, providing a glimpse into a fabulous garden filled with exotic, impossibly vibrant plants, flowers and herbs that, until now, had existed only in her dreams. It was a world of thriving energy and life, a place of mystery and enchantment.

Her initial astonishment evaporated, replaced by a wave of deliciously disturbing heat. The thrilling warmth sweeping through her was not the only new sensation in the atmosphere. All her senses, the psychical as well as the physical, suddenly blazed across the spectrum. She experienced an electrifying awareness that was focused entirely on Caleb Jones.

He muttered something she could not understand; words that surely belonged to the night; words that were far too arousing ever to be spoken in daylight. His breathing roughened. Another rush of heady excitement snapped through her when he urged her lips apart with his own. Then his hands were moving, sliding around her so that he could pin her against the length of his hard frame.

She was trembling now, not with fear but with anticipation. The magical garden beckoned, filled with wild green life that gave off a marvelously seductive energy. She wrapped her arms around Caleb's neck and allowed herself to sink deeper into the embrace and into the dangerous currents that whirled around them.

So this is passion, she thought. *Oh, my goodness. I had no idea.*

Caleb released her with such jolting force that she reeled back a step.

"Damnation." He looked at her in stark disbelief. If he had been in the grip of desire a moment ago, one would never know it now. His iron control closed around him like the bars of a prison cell. "Forgive me, Miss Bromley. I do not know what came over me."

It took her a few seconds to find her tongue.

"Think nothing of it," she finally managed in what she hoped was an airy, woman-of-the-world manner. "I realize that you intended no insult. You were clearly stricken with professional enthusiasm."

There was a short pause. He did not take his eyes off her.

"Professional enthusiasm?" he repeated in an oddly neutral tone of voice.

It dawned on her that her eyeglasses were askew. She concentrated hard on adjusting them. "I quite understand, of course."

"You do?" He did not sound pleased.

"Yes, indeed. That sort of thing has happened to me on more than one occasion."

"It that so?" He looked fascinated now.

"It affects the nerves, you know."

"What affects the nerves?"

She cleared her throat. "A sudden onslaught of professional enthusiasm. Why, it can even overcome a man of your obvious powers of self-mastery." She went behind her desk and more or less collapsed into her chair, still trying to catch her breath and slow her pulse. "Obviously the, er, excess stimulation you experienced a short time ago was inspired by some clue I must have unwittingly provided you. I trust that bodes well for the investigation."

For a few unsettling seconds he did not move. He stood there gazing down at her as though she were some heretofore unknown specimen that he had encountered in Mr. Darwin's study.

Just when she thought she could not endure the scrutiny any longer, he turned toward the French doors and contemplated the massed greenery on the other side.

"A very insightful observation, Miss Bromley," he said. "You did, indeed, provide me with a clue. I have been searching for a connection like this for damn near two months."

She clasped her hands again on top of the desk and tried to bring some order to her scattered senses. It seemed to her that she could still feel sensual energy swirling in the room. Clearly the kiss had overstimulated her imagination.

"This has something to do with a person named Basil Hulsey?" she asked.

"I am certain of it. But just to be sure, would you describe the man you knew as Knox?"

"He was smallish. Quite bald. Rather unkempt and disheveled. I remember that his shirt was stained with chemicals. He wore glasses." She hesitated. "There was something spindly about him."

"Spindly?"

"He reminded me of a very large insect."

"That certainly matches the description I was given." Satisfaction underscored the words.

"I would appreciate an explanation, Mr. Jones," she said.

Caleb turned to face her. Every aspect of his countenance and posture was once again coldly composed and resolute. But she sensed the anticipation of the hunter just beneath the surface.

"It's a long story," he said. "I do not have time to go into all the details. Suffice it to say that approximately two months ago an infernally brilliant and psychically gifted scientist named Dr. Basil Hulsey caused the Society a great deal of trouble. Murder was involved. Perhaps you read the reports of the Midnight Monster in the press?"

"Yes, of course. Everyone in London followed that dreadful case in the papers. It was such a relief when news came of the Monster's death." She paused, searching her memory. "But I do not recall any mention of a Dr. Hulsey."

"The situation was decidedly more complicated than either the press or Scotland Yard realized. You must trust me when I tell you that Hulsey was involved. Unfortunately he fled before he could be apprehended. I have been searching for him but the trail had gone cold. Until now."

"Surely finding Hulsey is a job for the police."

"There is no point turning the case over to the authorities until I find the bastard and some evidence of his crimes," Caleb said. "But even when I do track him down, it may not be possible to secure the sort of proof that will stand up in a court of law."

"In that case, what on earth will you do?" she asked, bewildered.

Caleb looked at her with no trace of emotion. "I'm sure I'll think of something."

Another shiver went through her. This time the sensation had nothing whatsoever to do with passion. She decided it would be best not to press Caleb on the subject of his plans for dealing with Hulsey. That was Arcane Society business. She had her own problems. Probably best to change the subject.

"Why would this Dr. Hulsey steal my fern?" she asked.

"It is just the sort of specimen that would interest him. Hulsey's expertise is dream research. Some time ago he concocted a potion that induced lethal nightmares. Most of his victims died."

She shuddered. "How dreadful."

"After Hulsey vanished, I discovered some of his notebooks. It is clear that he has been fascinated with dreams for some time. He is convinced that in the dream state the veil between the normal and the paranormal is very thin, almost transparent. His goal is to learn how to manipulate that state. Dr. Hulsey's chief problems appear to be of a financial nature, however."

"What do you mean?"

Caleb began to pace the room, his fiercely etched features set in hard lines of intense concentration. "Every indication points to the fact that Hulsey came from a poor background. I don't think that he has any social connections and certainly no fortune of his own. Setting up a well-equipped laboratory is expensive."

"In other words, he requires a patron to finance his research."

Caleb glanced back over his shoulder, looking pleased with her conclusion. *It is as if I were a bright child or an intelligent pet dog that had just passed some test,* she thought. *How very annoying.*

"Precisely." Caleb continued to prowl the room. "His last patrons were not primarily interested in dream research, however. They had a different goal in mind. They employed him to re-create the founder's formula."

He stopped and watched her very intently, obviously awaiting a reaction of some sort. She did not know what he expected so she merely nodded.

"Go on," she said politely.

He frowned. "You do not appear surprised, Miss Bromley."

"Should I be?"

"Most of those within the Society believe that the formula is nothing more than a legend associated with Sylvester the Alchemist."

50

"I recall my parents speculating on the possible composition of such a formula on a few occasions. Is that so odd? The founder's drug, if it ever existed, would have been botanical in nature and my parents were very talented botanists. It was perfectly natural that they would have had some interest in it."

"Damnation." Caleb's voice roughened with frustration. "So much for the deepest, darkest secrets of the Society."

She waited but there was no apology for the rude language this time. She supposed she had better become accustomed to Caleb's lack of drawing room manners.

"If it is any consolation, my parents eventually concluded that any formula that could enhance one's psychical talents would be extremely dangerous and inherently unpredictable," she said. "We simply do not know enough about the psychical senses to risk tinkering with that aspect of our natures."

"Your parents were very wise," Caleb said. There was great depth of feeling in every word.

"They were also convinced that it was highly unlikely that Sylvester ever achieved his goal of creating such an elixir. After all, he lived in the late sixteen hundreds. People still believed in alchemy in those days. He would not have had the advantages of modern science."

"Unfortunately, your parents were wrong," Caleb said grimly. "Sylvester did, indeed, concoct a recipe for such a formula. The damn stuff works but there are, as Mr. and Mrs. Bromley suspected, some vicious side effects."

Astonished, she could only stare at him for a moment. "Are you certain?"

"Yes."

"What are these side effects you mentioned?" she

asked, suddenly intrigued, in spite of herself. She was a botanist, after all.

He stopped at the far end of the room and looked at her.

"Among other things, the drug is highly addictive," he said. "What little we know of its effects comes from Sylvester's old journals and the notes of those who have tried to re-create it."

"Hulsey is not the first to attempt to concoct the drug?"

"Unfortunately, no. Some time ago a man named John Stilwell also conducted experiments on the formula. He died in the process. His journals and papers were confiscated by the new Master of the Society."

"Gabriel Jones, your cousin."

He inclined his head to acknowledge that fact and continued. "Those records are now secure in the Great Vault at Arcane House. I've studied them. A couple of things were readily apparent. According to Stilwell, once a person starts taking the drug, he cannot stop. If he does, he will likely go insane."

"A most dangerous poison, indeed." She pondered the information. "But you say it works?"

He hesitated, looking very much as if he wanted to deny the truth.

"Evidently," he said finally. "Although to what extent and for what period of time are open questions. No one who has taken the drug has ever lived long enough to supply us with much in the way of helpful information."

She drummed her fingers on the arm of the chair. "No one you know personally, you mean."

He shot her a sharp, searching look. "No offense, Miss Bromley, but under the circumstances, I find that a rather odd statement."

"What of the founder himself, Sylvester Jones?"

Caleb appeared first startled and then, to her astonishment, he actually smiled a little. It was, she decided, a very charming smile. What a pity he did not indulge in the expression more often. Then again, they were discussing murder and other assorted subjects that did not generally elicit amusement.

Caleb walked across the room and came to a halt directly in front of her desk. "I will tell you a Jones family secret, Miss Bromley. We are all convinced that it was probably the drug that killed our ancestor. But as he was already an old man at the time, there is no way to prove that he died of anything but natural causes."

"Hmm."

"We do know that the old alchemist was drinking the formula at the time of his death and that he expected it to add several decades to his life span. It is safe to say that the stuff did not achieve that objective but whether or not it actually killed him has never been determined."

"Hmm."

"Your interest in the subject is starting to concern me," Caleb said dryly. "Perhaps I should remind you that we are discussing a matter that is considered by the Master and the Council to be the Society's most closely guarded secret."

"Are you threatening me, Mr. Jones? If so, you will have to take your turn. At the moment I am far more concerned with the possibility of going to prison than I am with the consequences of offending the Master and the Council."

His mouth kicked up again at the corners and amusement glinted in his eyes. "Yes, I can see that."

"About Hulsey," she prompted.

"Right. Hulsey. As I said, he is obsessed with his research. We destroyed his old laboratory, and, as it happens, those who funded his experiments are no longer in a position to continue financing him. But I suspected that he would not remain inactive for long. It is not his nature."

She wondered what, exactly, had happened to Hulsey's former financial backers but decided it would not be prudent to inquire.

"Do you think that he has found another patron?" she asked instead.

"Or someone involved in trying to concoct the drug has found him."

She understood. "Hulsey will not have hesitated to make a Faustian bargain with his new backer."

"Hulsey may be a modern man of science but after reading his notebooks, I can assure you that at his core he thinks like an alchemist. Some men would bargain with the devil in order to gain gold. Hulsey would sell his soul in exchange for a fully equipped laboratory."

"You said you were tracking Hulsey but you lost the trail?"

He rubbed the back of his neck in a gesture that underlined his frustration. "Hulsey's notebooks listed many of the rare drugs, spices and herbs that he uses in his experiments. I have tried to keep watch on London's apothecaries and herbalists, thinking that sooner or later he would start acquiring the items he requires. But the task has proved far beyond the scope of my small agency. Do you have any notion of how many establishments there are in this town that sell medicinal potions, herbs and spices? There are literally hundreds, if not thousands."

She smiled ruefully. "I recently had a similar discussion with Inspector Spellar. The number is in the thousands, sir. And you must not forget the patent medicine dealers. Some of them sell some very rare and exotic tinctures and elixirs. To say nothing of the herbalists."

His jaw hardened. "As you no doubt suspect, thus far I have had no luck spotting a pattern of purchases that would point to Hulsey."

"Why are you so sure that this Dr. Hulsey is the one who stole my fern?"

"It is possible that I am grasping at straws. But there is a very satisfactory logic about this entire affair. Whoever stole your fern had to be aware of its unusual psychical properties. He also must possess a great deal of scientific knowledge. In terms of probabilities, there cannot be a great many men of that description running around London at the moment. And the timing is right. It has been a little more than eight weeks since Hulsey disappeared. He has had ample opportunity to sell his services to another patron."

"I suppose that is true."

Caleb pulled out his pocket watch and frowned at the time. "Damn."

"What now, Mr. Jones?"

"I have a great many more questions for you, Miss Bromley, but they must wait until tomorrow. There is another extremely urgent investigation which requires my attention tonight. Preparations must be made." He dropped the watch back into his pocket. "When that affair is concluded, I will be free to concentrate on Hulsey."

He started toward the door without any pretense of a polite farewell.

Alarmed, she leaped to her feet. "One moment, if you please, Mr. Jones."

He turned, his powerful hand on the doorknob, and elevated an impatient brow. "Yes, Miss Bromley?"

"Let us be clear on one very important point, sir," she

said firmly. "I am hiring you to investigate the theft of my fern. If it so happens that your mad scientist, Hulsey, is the one who stole it and prepared the poison that was given to Lord Fairburn, well and good. But I am most certainly *not* employing you to apprehend some crazed alchemist who is trying to perfect the formula. Your task is to keep me out of prison. Do we have an understanding?"

He gave her the first full smile he had bestowed upon her.

"We do, indeed, Miss Bromley," he said.

He opened the door.

"Furthermore, I insist that you make frequent and regular reports on your progress to me," she called after him.

"Never fear, Miss Bromley, you will hear from me again. And soon."

He went out the door into the hall.

Her heart sank. *I'm doomed.*

There was no doubt in her mind but that, as far as Caleb Jones was concerned, the Arcane Society's interests would always come first. She could only pray that her desperate attempt to avoid a murder charge would coincide with Caleb's plans to capture Hulsey. If he was forced to choose between the two objectives, she knew she would come second.

Six

The stench of unwholesome excitement rising from the ranks of cowl-draped men was so thick that it seemed to darken the very atmosphere inside the ancient stone chamber. The shifting shadows cast by the lanterns appeared to Caleb's heightened senses as living, breathing entities that pulsed and throbbed in terrible rhythms, strange beasts of prey waiting to gorge on the blood that had been promised.

With an effort of will, he suppressed the imagined monsters. It was not easy. The ability to perceive dangerous patterns and dark connections where others saw only random chance was his gift. It was also his curse. While his ability to make huge intuitive leaps on the basis of only a few vague hints or clues was certainly useful, it had some unfortunate side effects. Lately he had begun to worry that the dazzling, multidimensional mazes he constructed in his mind when he was working on a problem were not merely the product of his strong talent but rather full-blown hallucinations created by a fevered brain.

From his position in the second row he had a clear view of the altar and the arched, curtained doorway on the far side. A boy of about twelve or thirteen lay stretched out on the surface of the stone slab, wrists and ankles bound with rope. He was awake but dazed, either from fear or a stiff dose of opium. Probably the latter, Caleb thought. He gave thanks for that small blessing. The boy was not alert enough to comprehend the danger.

This was not the way he had wanted to handle the case but by the time he had received the message from his informant, it had been too late to come up with any other plan. As it was, there had been barely enough time to attempt a rescue.

The first rumors of the existence of the cult had reached him only a few days ago. When he had realized that the man who had established it was powerfully talented and quite possibly dangerously unhinged, he had consulted immediately with Gabe. Neither of them had seen any way to build a case that could be handed over to the police, at least not before grave violence had been done. They had concluded that the Jones agency had no choice but to act.

The low chanting started in the front tier of hooded figures and spread swiftly to the second and third rows. It was a mix of mangled Latin with the occasional Greek word thrown in for effect. Caleb doubted that any of those standing with him actually understood what was being said. The acolytes were all young males in their teens and, judging by their accents, they had come from the streets.

He had done a quick head count when he and the others filed into the chamber. There were fifteen figures arrayed in ranks of five in front of the altar. Two more acolytes stood at either end of the stone slab. One was somewhat taller than the other and more solidly built. A man, not a youth. The leader and his closest associates had not yet appeared.

The harsh rumble of the chant grew stronger and louder. Caleb absently translated while he watched the curtained doorway.

. . . Great Charun, oh Demonic Spirit, we seek the power you promise to those of us who follow the true path . . .

. . . Praise to our master, the Servant of Charun, who commands the forces of darkness . . .

The black velvet curtains that covered the arched doorway were abruptly swept aside. A youth in flowing gray robes that were far too big for him strode solemnly into the room. He gripped the hilt of a jeweled blade in both hands. The lantern light seemed to flare a little higher. It glinted on the malevolent weapon. Power hissed and slithered across Caleb's senses.

No doubt about it, he thought, the group had found the dagger that had been used by the ancient Etruscan cult. A nasty paranormal artifact if ever there was one.

A hush fell over the crowd. The sick energy of unholy lust intensified in the chamber. Caleb slid his hands into the folds of his robes and gripped the handle of his revolver. The gun would be of only limited use against the large gang of tough young males. He would be able to get off a shot or two but the acolytes would soon overwhelm him. Mindlessly enthralled by their leader, they would sacrifice themselves for him, he had no doubt. That aside, the last thing he wanted to do tonight was shoot some poor boy who'd had the misfortune to come under the mesmerizing influence of the master of the cult.

"Behold the Servant of Charun and show him all honor," the boy holding the dagger intoned in a voice that cracked a little. "Tonight he will reach through the Veil to summon great powers."

Another figure appeared in the doorway, his tall, thin frame shrouded in black robes. Large rings glinted on his fingers. The cowl concealed his features.

Even from where he stood in the second row, Caleb sensed the dark, sick energy around the Servant.

The acolytes fell to their knees. Caleb reluctantly did the same.

The Servant of Charun looked at the boy holding the dagger.

"Is the sacrifice ready?"

"Yes, my lord," the boy said.

The intended victim surfaced from his drug-induced stupor.

"What's this?" he mumbled, the words slurred. "Where the bloody hell am I?"

"Silence," the boy holding the dagger ordered.

The sacrifice blinked a few times, still disoriented. "Is that you, Arnie? What are ye doin' in that silly-looking robe?"

"Silence," Arnie shrieked. He sounded very young and very scared.

"Enough," the leader decreed. "He should have been gagged and blindfolded. It is not fitting that the sacrifice look upon the face of the Servant of Charun."

Always hard to get good staff, Caleb thought. He could almost sympathize. He had lost track of how many housekeepers he'd gone through in the past few years.

"Yes, my lord," Arnie said hastily. "I'll take care of the business."

He hesitated, uncertain what to do with the dagger. Then he set it down on the altar.

"Give me the dagger," the Servant of Charun commanded.

The taller of the two hooded acolytes standing at the altar moved slightly as though to pick up the blade and hand it to the leader. His hand brushed against the weapon. The atmosphere around the blade blurred ever so slightly, as though it had been enveloped in fog. In the next instant the artifact disappeared altogether.

For a few seconds no one moved. Everyone, including

the Servant of Charun, just stood there, staring at the place where the blade had been a heartbeat earlier. Caleb took advantage of the collective confusion to get to his feet. He went swiftly toward the altar.

The Servant of Charun looked up, still bewildered, and saw Caleb coming toward him. He finally appeared to grasp the fact that the situation had become complicated.

"Who are you?" he shouted. He moved back, one hand raised as though to ward off a demon.

Caleb showed him the gun. "There's been a small change in tonight's performance."

The Servant stared at the gun. "No. Impossible. Charun will not allow you to harm me."

The boy on the altar sat up with a groggy air. The ropes that had bound his wrists and ankles had been severed.

"What's going on?" he said.

The dagger reappeared in the hand of the tall acolyte.

"We're leaving," the acolyte said.

He scooped up the boy, tossed him over his shoulder and disappeared through the curtained doorway.

"Stop him," the Servant of Charun shouted.

There was a mad scramble as several hooded figures tried to get through the opening at once.

Glass shattered on stone. Caleb realized one of the lanterns had been knocked to the floor. There was an ominous whoosh. Flames leaped high, snapping eagerly at nearby robes.

"Fire," a boy yelled.

Hoarse, terrified shouts reverberated through the chamber, echoing off the stone walls. There was a great thunder of shoes and boots as the frightened acolytes rushed to jam the only two exits.

A panicked youth intent on escape caromed into Caleb. The impact sent him sprawling. The gun flew from his hand and skidded out of reach across the floor.

"Son of a bitch," Caleb muttered. This was not going well.

He rolled to his feet in time to see the Servant dashing toward the curtained doorway. He leaped forward and managed to seize the back of the other man's cowl. He yanked hard.

The Servant of Charun did not go down but he reeled back against the altar. His cowl fell away, revealing the aquiline face of a man in his early thirties. His hand plunged into the folds of his robes and emerged with a pistol.

"Damn you," he roared. "I'll teach you to interfere with Charun's Servant."

He pulled the trigger but he was off balance and quite frantic. Not surprisingly, he missed by a wide margin. Before he could make a second try, Caleb was on him.

They hit the unforgiving stone floor with a bone-rattling thud. The muffling, entangling robes proved a great hindrance to landing solid blows. In the rising tide of firelight Caleb saw his opponent's pistol on the floor.

The cult leader fought back like a man who was, indeed, in the grip of a demonic possession. But there was no science in his efforts, just a great deal of wild thrashing, punching and screaming. There was also a great deal of odd cursing.

"You will burn in Charun's dungeon of fire, unbeliever."

"By the power of Charun, I command you to die."

The man was truly mad, Caleb thought. He was not just another dangerous criminal talent who had set himself up as the head of a cult. The Servant actually believed in the demon lord that he had created in his own demented mind.

"We have to get out of here," Caleb said, trying to reach some remnant of sanity in the man's disordered brain.

"It is Charun." The leader struggled to his knees, suddenly fascinated by the flames. "He is here." In the flaring light there was awe and euphoric wonder on his face. "He has come to deliver me from you. Now you will pay with your soul for daring to assault one who serves the demon."

The flames had reached a cloth-draped table. The black fabric quickly caught fire. Heavy smoke roiled through the room. The leader appeared utterly trans-fixed by the growing inferno.

Caleb picked up his gun and brought the butt of the weapon down quite forcefully against the back of the other man's skull.

The leader slumped forward.

Caleb dropped the gun into his pocket. Staying low in an effort to avoid the worst of the smoky atmosphere, he pulled out a large handkerchief and clapped it across his nose and mouth. A quick glance around told him that they were the only two people left in the chamber.

Once again he seized the cowl of the Servant's robe and used it to drag the unconscious man across the stone floor.

He hauled his burden past the black velvet curtain. The air on the other side of the doorway was much sweeter but the passageway was unlit. Darkness loomed.

He dropped the handkerchief and flattened one hand on the wall of the stone tunnel. Behind him there was another violent whoosh as the velvet curtain fell to the flames. He did not look back. Using the old stones and the scent of fresh air as a guide, he made his way toward the far end of the tunnel, dragging the leader behind him.

Lantern light splashed ahead, pushing aside the darkness. A moment later a figure loomed. The glary yellow light illuminated a familiar face.

"Imagine meeting you here, cousin," Caleb said.

"What the devil kept you?" Gabriel Jones reached down to assist with the unconscious leader. "The plan was for you to come out with Fletcher and the boy."

"Didn't want to risk losing this bastard." Caleb sucked in the clean air. "Then there was a small problem with a fire."

"Yes, I can see that. Who is he?"

"Don't know his name yet. Calls himself the Servant of Charun. Whoever he is, he's mad as a hatter. Fletcher and the boy are safe?"

"Yes. They're waiting for us outside. So are Spellar and some constables. They've rounded up several of the cult members."

"No point arresting them. They were all young, gullible street boys. I'm quite sure that whatever belief they had in the powers of their demon lord just got extinguished."

They emerged from the tunnel to find several frightened acolytes and a considerable number of constables milling around the yard of the old, abandoned inn that had served as the cult's temple. Lanterns lit the chaotic scene.

Edmund Fletcher hurried toward him. The boy he had rescued was at his heels.

"Are you all right, sir?" Edmund asked.

He radiated an exultant excitement. Caleb recognized the aftereffects that often accompany a close brush with danger combined with the powerful thrill that comes from pushing one's talent to the maximum degree. He was starting to feel a similar rush of sensation, himself.

It was not the first time he had experienced this sort of edgy intoxication. What he did not comprehend was why he was suddenly thinking of Lucinda Bromley.

"I'm all right," Caleb said. He started to cough but he managed to clap Edmund's shoulder. "You did excellent work back there. You got us inside without drawing any attention, through all those locked doors, and you got the boy out safely. A fine performance."

Edmund grinned. "Will you have other assignments for me, do you think?"

"Don't worry. I'm certain that the Jones agency will have occasional use for a man of your talents."

The boy looked up at him. "Beggin' yer pardon, sir, but Mr. Fletcher and I have been talking about your detective agency. It sounds like very interesting work. Would you have any need for an agent with my skills?"

Caleb looked down at him. "What is your name?"

"Kit, sir. Kit Hubbard."

"What sort of skills do you possess, Kit Hubbard?"

"Well, I can't make items disappear like Mr. Fletcher here does," Kit said seriously, "but I'm very good at finding things."

"What do you mean?"

"It's a skill that just sort of came to me in the past year or so. I never used to be able to do it, not the way I do now."

Strong psychical talents usually appeared at puberty.

Caleb exchanged a look with Gabe. Until recently, membership in the Arcane Society had been largely limited to those who had been born into it or who had married into it. Secrecy had been critical to the survival of the organization for centuries. In previous eras those who claimed to possess psychical powers had been accused of witchcraft. That dangerous history had kept the group from actively recruiting outsiders with talent, regardless of their social class.

But the world was changing. This was the modern age, and the new Master of the Society was a very modern-thinking man.

Gabe studied the boy. "That sounds like a very interesting talent, Kit."

Kit gestured at the jeweled dagger Edmund Fletcher still held. "I'm the one who found that blade for Mr. Hatcher, there."

They all looked at the cowled leader, who was just beginning to stir.

"That's his name?" Caleb asked. "Hatcher?"

"That's what Arnie called him," Kit said. "Arnie works for him, you see. He told me that if I brought that dagger to Mr. Hatcher, I'd get more money than I'd ever seen in my life. Well, I found it for him, all right. It was in an old house on Skidmore Street. The owner died a long time ago and no one ever cleaned out the basement. The next thing I knew, I woke up on that slab of rock with Arnie holding the damn blade over my head."

"I'd like to hear more about your talent, Kit," Caleb said. "I'm almost certain my agency could use a young man of your abilities."

Kit grinned. "Do you pay well, sir?"

"Very well. Just ask Mr. Fletcher, here."

Edmund laughed and ruffled Kit's hair. "One job for the Jones agency will take care of the rent for a few months and leave some money left over to buy your mother a pretty new bonnet."

"Ma will like that," Kit declared, gleeful.

"More likely she'll think you've taken up a life of crime," Caleb said. "Which might not be all that far from the truth."

Spellar loomed out of the shadows. He nodded toward Gabe.

"Thought I'd better warn you that the rumors are already on the streets, sir," he said. "The gentlemen of the press will be arriving at any moment. This tale is going to be a sensation in the papers in a day or so. I know you don't want the Society or the Jones name involved if it can be avoided."

This was the modern age, Caleb thought, but there were still sound reasons for cautious dealings with the press.

"Thank you, Inspector," Gabe said. "It is obviously past time for the agents of the Jones agency to take their leave." He looked at Kit and Edmund. "You two will come with us. We'll convey you to your lodgings. I expect Kit's mother is more than a little concerned about him."

Kit looked at Hatcher. "What will happen to him? Will he go to prison?"

Hatcher chose that moment to start babbling to Spellar.

"Charun came to save me," he said. "He produced a great storm of fire. But a ghost from the Other Side dared to stop him." He stared at Caleb, eyes wide and feverishly bright with rage. "Tremble in terror, phantom. You will soon feel the wrath of the Demon."

Spellar looked at Kit. "I think it's far more likely that this gentleman will soon find himself in an asylum."

Some of the heady energy that had been resonating through Caleb faded. An icy chill took its place.

"A fate worse than death," he said quietly.

Seven

Caleb let himself into the front hall of the darkened house and went upstairs. When he reached the landing he walked down the hall and unlocked the door to his library-laboratory. Inside, he turned up the gas lamps and surveyed the vast room that was either his refuge or his private hell, depending on circumstances and his mood. Lately the resemblance to the netherworld had been growing stronger.

The majority of the Society's collection of paranormal relics and artifacts were kept in Arcane House, a remote mansion in the country. But many of the ancient records of the organization, some dating back to the late 1600s when the Society was founded, were housed here. His branch of the family had been responsible for them for generations.

The most valuable items in his collection, including several of the private journals of Sylvester Jones, were secured in the large vault built into the stone wall of the old house.

The laboratory that adjoined the library featured the very latest apparatus. He was not a psychically gifted scientist; his true talents lay in another direction, but he was fully capable of carrying out a large number of experiments. He knew his way around the various instruments and devices arrayed on the workbench.

He had always been drawn to the mysteries of the paranormal. Lately, however, what had once been a keen intellectual interest had become what he knew his closest relatives and friends considered an unhealthy obsession.

They whispered that it was in the blood; that in this generation of Joneses, he was the true heir to the brilliant but darkly eccentric Sylvester. They worried that the founder's lust for forbidden knowledge had passed down through Caleb's branch of the family tree, a dark seed waiting to take root in fertile ground.

The dangerous plant did not flower in every generation, they said. According to family legend, it had appeared only once after Sylvester, in Caleb's great-grandfather Erasmus Jones. Erasmus had been born with a talent like the one Caleb possessed. Less than two years after marrying and fathering a son, however, he suddenly started to exhibit increasingly odd eccentricities. He sank swiftly into madness and finally took his own life.

Caleb knew that everyone in the Jones clan believed that the changes they were witnessing in him had begun with the discovery of Sylvester's tomb and the journals of alchemical secrets it had contained. Only he and his father knew the truth, however. Even within the extensive and psychically powerful Jones family, it was still possible to keep a secret if one grasped it tightly enough.

He walked through the maze of shelving that held the old leather-bound volumes and came to a halt in front of the cold fireplace. There was a cot and two chairs near the hearth. He usually slept here and took his meals here. This was where he received the occasional visitor. He rarely used the other rooms. Most of the furniture in the household was shrouded in dust covers.

A small table held a decanter and two glasses. He

poured himself a measure of brandy and went to stand at the window, looking out at the darkest hour of the night.

His thoughts took him back to another very dark night and what everyone had believed was his father's deathbed. Fergus Jones had dismissed those keeping the vigil around him—the nurse, an assortment of relatives, the servants—all except Caleb.

"Come closer, son," Fergus said, his voice weak and hoarse.

Caleb moved from the foot of the bed to stand at his father's side. He was still stunned by the suddenness of the crisis. Until three days ago his father had been a fit and healthy man of sixty-six years, showing no signs of anything more debilitating than some mild discomfort in his joints, which he treated with salicin. A hunter, like so many males in the Jones line, he had always enjoyed a hearty constitution and seemed destined to live to a ripe old age as had his father before him.

Caleb had been assisting Gabe in an inquiry into the theft of the founder's formula when he received the urgent summons informing him that his parent had succumbed to a sudden infection of the lungs. He left his cousin to pursue the investigation on his own and hurried to the family estate.

Although he had been anxious, in truth he had expected that his father would recover. It was not until he walked into the solemn, heavily draped household and listened to the doctor's grim prognosis that he understood just how dire the situation had become.

His relationship with his father had always been close; even more so following the untimely death of his mother, Alice, who had died in a horseback riding accident when he was twenty-one. Fergus had never remarried. Caleb was the sole offspring of the union.

A fire blazed on the hearth, heating the sickroom to an uncomfortable temperature because, although his entire body was hot to the touch, Fergus had complained of the chill. The unnatural sensation of cold, the nurse had explained with an air of morbid satisfaction, was one of the sure indications of the approach of death.

Fergus looked up at him from the stack of pillows. Although he had been sliding in and out of a delirium for most of the day, his eyes now held a feverish clarity. He grasped Caleb's hand.

"There is something I must tell you," he whispered.

"What is it?" Caleb said. He tightened his grip on his father's hot hand.

"I am dying, Caleb."

"No."

"I confess that I had planned to leave this world a coward. I did not think that I could bring myself to tell you the truth. But I find that I cannot, after all, leave you in ignorance, especially when there may be some small chance—"

He broke off on a racking cough. When the fit was over he lay quietly, gasping for air.

"Please, sir, do not exert yourself," Caleb pleaded. "You must conserve your strength."

"Damn it to hell. This is *my* deathbed and I will spend what energy I have left as I wish."

Caleb smiled slightly in spite of his devastated spirits. It was oddly reassuring to hear the familiar, gruff determination in his father's voice. The men and women of the Jones family were all fighters.

"Yes, sir," he said.

Fergus narrowed his eyes. "You and Alice were the two great blessings bestowed on me over the course of my life. I want you to know that I have always been grateful that the good Lord saw fit to let me have time with both of you."

"I am the most fortunate of sons to have you for a father, sir."

"I regret to say that you will not thank me for siring you after I tell you the truth about yourself." Fergus closed his eyes in pain. "I never did tell your mother, you know. It was my gift to her. Alice died without ever realizing the danger you will confront."

"What are you talking about, sir?" Perhaps Fergus was hallucinating again.

"I still hesitate to tell you of the truth," Fergus whispered. "But you are my son and I know you well. You would curse me to your own dying day if I held back knowledge of such a vital nature. Given what I am about to say, you will doubtless abominate me anyway."

"Whatever it is you feel you must confide, sir, I assure you, it could never drive me to hate you."

"Wait until you hear what I am about to tell you before you judge." Another violent cough interrupted Fergus. He gasped a few times and finally recovered his breath. "It concerns your great-grandfather, Erasmus Jones."

"What about him?" But a cold trickle of knowing slithered down Caleb's spine.

"You possess a talent very similar to his."

"I am aware of that."

"You also know that he went mad, set fire to his library and laboratory and jumped to his death."

"You think I face the same fate, sir," he said quietly. "Is that what you are trying to tell me?"

"Your great-grandfather was convinced that it was his talent that drove him mad. He wrote about it in his last journal."

"I have never heard that Erasmus Jones kept any journals."

"That is because he destroyed all but one of them in the fire. He was convinced that the vast amount of research he had done with the aid of his talent was meaningless. But he held back one journal because, in the end, he was still Erasmus Jones. He could not bear to destroy his own secrets."

"Where is this journal?"

Fergus turned his head to look across the room. "You will find it in the hidden compartment of my safe along with another little volume, a notebook that he preserved with the journal. His son, your grandfather, gave them to me on his deathbed, and now I bequeath them to you."

"Have you read them?"

"No. Neither did your grandfather. We couldn't."

"Why not?"

Fergus managed a snort. "Erasmus was Sylvester's heir to the core. Like the old bastard, he invented his own private code for use in his journals. The notebook is also written in code. Neither your grandfather nor I dared show either book to anyone else in the family who might have been able to decipher it because we feared the secrets it might contain."

"Why did you and Grandfather keep the journal and the notebook?"

Fergus looked up at him, his feverish eyes remarkably steady. "Because the first page of the journal is written in plain English. Erasmus addressed a message to his son and his future descendants. The note instructed them to preserve both volumes until such time in the future when another male with Sylvester's talent appeared."

"Someone like me."

"Yes, I'm afraid so. Erasmus believed that the notebook

contained the secret to recovering his sanity. He failed to discover that secret in time to save himself. He was convinced that sometime in the future one of his line would face the same crisis. He hoped that his descendant would be able to alter his own fate by solving the mysteries in that damned volume."

"What is the second volume?" Caleb asked.

"According to Erasmus, it is Sylvester's last notebook."

He remained by his father's bedside until dawn. Fergus opened his eyes just as the first light of day appeared.

"Why the devil is it so damned hot in here?" he growled. He glared at the blaze on the hearth. "What are you trying to do? Burn down the house?"

Stunned, Caleb pushed himself up out of the uncomfortable chair in which he had spent the night. He looked down into his father's eyes and saw at once that they were no longer bright with fever. The crisis had passed. His father lived. A relief unlike anything he had ever experienced in his life cascaded through him.

"Good morning, sir," he said. "You gave us a bit of a scare during the past few days. How are you feeling?"

"Tired." Fergus rubbed the gray stubble on his chin with one hand. "But I do believe I'm going to live after all."

Caleb smiled. "So it appears, sir. Are you hungry? I'll send downstairs for some tea and toast."

"And perhaps some eggs and bacon, as well," Fergus said.

"Yes, sir." Caleb reached for the velvet bellpull hanging beside the bed. "Although you may have to do some persuasive talking to convince the nurse that you are ready for a proper breakfast. Between you and me, she looks a bit tyrannical."

Fergus grimaced. "She'll be disappointed that I failed to meet her expectations. She was sure I'd cock up my toes by dawn. Pay the woman and send her off to the next poor, dying bastard."

"I'll do that," Caleb said.

Eight

Caleb found the sleek little black-and-maroon carriage precisely where Mrs. Shute had told him it would be in Guppy Lane. In the morning light the neighborhood displayed an air of proud, hardworking respectability. It was only a short distance from Landreth Square but it was many leagues away in terms of social status. What in blazes was Lucinda doing here?

A thin man dressed in a coachman's hat and multi-caped coat lounged against the iron railing that guarded the front area of a small house. Caleb got out of the hansom, wincing a little when his bruised ribs protested the small jolt. He paid the driver and then walked toward the man on the railing.

"Mr. Shute?"

"Aye, sir." Shute watched him with slightly squinted eyes. "I'm Shute."

"Mrs. Shute gave me this address," Caleb said. "I am looking for Miss Bromley."

Shute angled his head toward the doorway to the house. "She's inside." He took out his pocket watch and examined the time. "Been there for an hour. Might be a while longer."

Caleb studied the door. "A social call?" he asked neutrally.

"Not exactly. She's got business inside that house."

"Is that so?"

"You came here this morning because you were curious about what would bring a lady like Miss Bromley to this part of town."

"You are a very astute man, Mr. Shute."

"Thought she might be in some danger, did ye?"

"Crossed my mind." The other possibility, of course, was that she was having an affair. For some obscure reason that had bothered him just as much.

"Mrs. Shute and I were raised in this neighborhood." Shute looked at the row of narrow houses across the street. "Mrs. Shute's aunts live in number five over there. Retired after nearly forty years of service in a wealthy household. When their employer died, the heirs let them go without a pension. Miss Bromley pays their rent."

"I see," Caleb said.

"I've got a couple of cousins at the end of the lane. Miss Bromley employs the girls as maids in her household. Mrs. Shute and I have a son. He and his wife and their two little ones live in the next street. My son works for a printer. Miss Bromley's father got him the job a few years ago."

"I think I'm beginning to understand, Mr. Shute."

"My grandchildren attend school. Miss Bromley helps out with the fees. She says an education is the only sure way to get ahead in the modern age."

"Obviously a lady of advanced notions."

"Aye." Shute aimed a thumb over his wide shoulder, pointing toward the door to the house behind him. "My sister's daughter and her family live here."

"You've made your point, Mr. Shute. My concerns for Miss Bromley's safety were groundless. She is in no danger here."

"There's folks in this neighborhood and the nearby

streets who would slice the liver out of anyone who tried to hurt a hair on Miss Bromley's head with nary a moment's hesitation and then toss the body into the river." Shute's eyes tightened a little more. "Been in a fight, have ye?"

"I was involved in a small altercation last night," Caleb said. He had done his best to conceal his bruised eye by pulling up the high collar of his long coat and angling the brim of his hat but there were limits to such a disguise.

Shute nodded, unperturbed. "You got the better of your opponent, I take it."

"I would say so. He is headed for an insane asylum."

"Not the usual ending for a fistfight."

"It was not the usual sort of fistfight."

Shute gave him a speculative look. "I reckon not."

The door to the little house opened. Lucinda appeared in the doorway. She carried a large black leather satchel in her ungloved hand. She had her back turned toward Caleb as she spoke to a woman in a worn dress and apron.

"Do not worry about trying to get food into him," Lucinda said. "The important thing is to make sure that he takes a few sips of the tisane several times an hour."

"I'll see to it," the woman vowed.

"The little ones lose all of their fluids so quickly when they are struck by this sort of stomach ailment. But I'm sure Tommy will recover in a day or two, provided he continues to take the tisane."

"I do not know how to thank you, Miss Bromley." The woman's face registered both exhaustion and relief. "I didn't know what else to do except call you. The doctor would likely have refused to come to this neighborhood." Her mouth twisted. "You know how it is.

78

He would have assumed we could not afford his fees. In any event, it wasn't as if Tommy had broken a bone. I suspected that it was something he ate that made him ill. Everyone around here knows that when it comes to that kind of thing, you are far more knowledgeable than any doctor."

"Tommy will be fine. I'm sure of it. Just keep giving him the tisane."

"I will, Miss Bromley. Never fear." The woman leaned out of the doorway and waved at Shute. "Good morning, Uncle Jed. Tell Aunt Bess I said hello."

Shute straightened away from the railing. "I'll do that, Sally."

Lucinda turned in the doorway and saw Caleb for the first time.

"What on earth are you doing here, Mr. Jones?"

"I arrived at your address at eight o'clock to deliver my report on the progress of my investigation and to ask you some questions," he said. "You weren't at home."

"Good heavens." She stared at him, quite stunned. "You called at *eight o'clock* in the morning? No one does business at that hour."

"Evidently you do." He nodded toward the house from which she had just emerged.

"My business here is of an entirely different nature."

He took the satchel from her. It was surprisingly heavy. "When I discovered that you were not at home I decided to track you down. You will recall that you insisted upon a daily report?"

"I don't recall using the word *daily*," she said. "I believe the words I employed were *frequent* and *regular*."

"I took *frequent* and *regular* to mean *daily*."

She looked up at him from under the brim of her small, ribbon-trimmed hat. "Never say that you mean to call upon me every day at eight o'clock in the morning. That is outrageous." She broke off suddenly, eyes widening behind the lenses of her spectacles. "What happened to you, Mr. Jones? Did you suffer an accident?"

"Something along those lines."

He handed her into the dainty carriage and followed her with some caution. Nevertheless, the movement sent another jolt through his bruised ribs. He knew Lucinda noticed.

"When we get back to my house I will give you something for the pain," she said.

"Thank you." He set the satchel on the floor of the vehicle. "That would be greatly appreciated. Took some salicin but it hasn't done much good."

The miniature leather seats had never been intended to transport a man of his size. Gingerly, he sat down across from Lucinda. There was no way to prevent his trousers from brushing up against the draped folds of her gown. One severe bounce and she would be across his thighs. Or he would find himself on top of her. The images heated his blood and made him forget about his ribs.

"In addition to something for the pain, I have another tisane for you," Lucinda said.

He frowned. "What is it for?"

"There is some tension in your aura."

"I didn't get much sleep last night."

"The imbalance I sense will not be alleviated by sleep. It is caused by some problem of a psychical nature. I believe my tonic will ease it. I prepared it after you left yesterday."

He shrugged and looked out the window. "You appear to enjoy something of a reputation in this neighborhood, Miss Bromley."

"A reputation that is quite different from the one I

80

hold in the polite world, do you mean?" She smiled at a woman who was waving from a doorway. When she turned back to face him the smile was gone. "It's true that the people in Guppy Lane trust me not to poison them."

"As do I," he said, too weary and sore to allow himself to be provoked.

"Evidently," she said, relaxing a little. "Well, sir, what do you have to report?"

He discovered that he had to work hard in order to concentrate on any subject other than Lucinda's faint, tantalizing scent and the gentle currents of enticing energy that threatened to drug his senses. Sitting this close to her had a disturbing effect on his usually well-ordered thoughts. It was the lack of sleep, he thought.

Or perhaps there was a simpler explanation. He'd been too long without the therapeutic release of a sexual encounter. It had been several months now since the tepid liaison with a certain attractive widow had ended, as all such connections did, with the usual sense of relief.

Nevertheless, it struck him as strange that he had not been aware of missing the occasional bout of that particular type of physical exercise until yesterday when he had been inexplicably overcome by the urge to kiss Lucinda. And, just as inexplicably, the same nearly irresistible urge was riding him hard once again. He really needed to get more sleep.

"Sir?" Lucinda said somewhat sharply.

He forced himself to apply his powers of self-mastery. "I told you yesterday that before I could give my full attention to your investigation I had to deal with another matter. That business was concluded last night."

Curiosity sparkled in her eyes. "Satisfactorily, I assume?"

"Yes."

She studied his face. "Can I assume that the other urgent matter accounts for your bruises, sir?"

"Things became somewhat complicated," he admitted.

"There was a brawl?"

"Of a sort."

"For heaven's sake, what happened?"

"As I said, the business is concluded. Now then, this morning I took some time to compose a plan for the investigation into the theft of your fern."

"What time did you get to bed last night?" she asked.

"What?"

"How much sleep did you get?"

"A couple of hours, I think. I wasn't watching the clock. About my plan—"

"How much sleep did you get the night before?"

"Why the devil do you wish to know that?"

"When I spoke with you yesterday, it was clear that you'd had very little sleep the previous night, as well. I could sense it in your aura."

He was starting to get irritated. "I thought you sensed tension in my aura."

"I did. Presumably that is what is causing your inability to get a good night's rest."

"I told you, I was working on another case. The situation had come to a crisis point. There has been little time for sleep lately. If you don't mind, I have some questions, Miss Bromley."

"Breakfast?"

"What of it?"

"Did you have any?"

"Coffee." He narrowed his eyes. "My new housekeeper gave me a muffin on the way out the door this morning. I did not have time for a full meal."

"A hearty breakfast is very important for a man of your constitution, sir."

"My constitution?"

She cleared her throat. "You are a strong, hearty man, Mr. Jones, not just physically but psychically, as well. You require a great deal of energy. Sleep and a sound breakfast are critical to your well-being."

"Damnation, Miss Bromley, I did not track you down at eight o'clock in the morning to listen to a lecture on my sleeping and eating habits. If you don't mind, we will return to the subject of your missing fern."

She sat very straight in the tiny seat and folded her hands in her lap.

"Yes, of course," she said. "Very well, then, what brings you out at eight o'clock in the morning?"

He was overcome with the ridiculous urge to defend himself. "Miss Bromley, when I am involved in an investigation I cannot be bound by the social world's arbitrary dictates on matters such as the proper time of day for calls and visits." Aware that he sounded surly, he nevertheless plowed on. "I make no apologies for my methods. It is how I work, regardless of whatever project I happen to have undertaken. But this particular investigation is, as I informed you yesterday, of great importance to me and to the Society. I will conduct it my way."

"Yes, you did make it quite clear that you are keenly interested in Dr. Knox," she said coolly. "Very well, what is it you wish to know?"

"Yesterday you told me that Hulsey—"

"Knox."

"For the sake of clarity we are going to refer to Knox as Hulsey," he said. "At least until I turn up some proof indicating that the two names do not refer to the same individual."

She studied him with an expression of grave curiosity. "You're very sure that Knox is this Dr. Hulsey you've been looking for, aren't you?"

"Yes."

"It is your talent that has convinced you of that conclusion?"

"My talent combined with facts," he said, impatient as he always was when someone asked him to explain how his psychical abilities functioned. Damned if he knew, he thought. "That is what my talent does, Miss Bromley. It allows me to make connections between odd facts."

"I see. Are you occasionally wrong in your conclusions?"

"Rarely, Miss Bromley. My talent is what it is."

She inclined her head. "Very well, sir. Please continue."

"You said that Hulsey was referred to you by one of your father's old acquaintances."

"Lord Roebuck, an elderly gentleman who has a long-standing interest in botany. Unfortunately, he has become quite senile in the past few years."

"Did Roebuck know of the psychical properties of the fern and that the specimen was in your conservatory?"

"I do not see how he could have any knowledge of it. As I told you, my father and Mr. Woodhall and I brought the fern and a great many other interesting specimens back with us from our last expedition. That was some eighteen months ago. Poor Lord Roebuck had already become senile by then. He never left his house. He certainly never toured my conservatory. No, I really don't think he could have known much about my fern."

"Yet a month ago Hulsey somehow not only learned

of the existence of the fern but also that it possessed paranormal properties. It would have taken an expert to recognize the unique aspects of that plant, correct?"

"Not just any expert," she said, "one with talent."

"Then someone else *with talent* must have viewed that fern. That person told Hulsey about it."

"Well, I have shown a handful of people around the conservatory in recent months."

He frowned. "Only a handful?"

"As I told you yesterday, I have not had many visitors since my father's death. I can certainly give you the names of those who have called upon me recently."

"Let us concentrate on those who toured the collection shortly before Hulsey showed up."

"That will be a very short list."

"Excellent." He took out his notebook and pencil. "There is something I do not understand about this situation, Miss Bromley."

She smiled faintly. "I'm astonished to hear you admit that there is anything you do not comprehend, Mr. Jones."

He ignored that, frowning a little. "Your conservatory contains an astonishing collection of exotic and unusual plants. Why don't you receive more visitors?"

"You would be amazed how a few rumors of poison can affect one's social life."

"A decline in social calls is understandable. But one would think that any botanist worth his salt would be unable to resist the prospect of a tour of your conservatory."

She gave him a considering look. "Does it ever occur to you, sir, that not everyone is endowed with your ability to separate logic from emotion?"

"Frequently, Miss Bromley," he said. "I admit that it is one of the things that complicates my work as an investigator. I can find connections and intuit conclusions but I have discovered that I cannot always explain *why* individuals act as they do. Hell, I can't even predict how the clients will respond when I give them the answers they pay me to obtain. You would be floored by how many of them become furious, for example. I certainly am."

Her mouth twitched a little at one corner. "Yes, I can see how you might find emotions a complicating factor."

"Well, we must come back to the matter of your reputation some other time. For the moment, we will stay focused on Hulsey."

"What did you say, Mr. Jones?"

"I said that, for the moment, we must stick to the problem of Hulsey."

"Yes, I heard you, but why on earth would you want to concern yourself with the matter of my reputation?"

"Because it is an interesting problem," he said patiently.

Nine

Lucinda finished supplying Caleb with the very short list of people who had toured the conservatory in the weeks before Knox had requested a tour, just as Shute halted the carriage in Landreth Square.

Caleb looked out the window. "It appears that you may have a more active social life than you believe."

She followed his gaze and saw a lovely young blond-haired woman in a severe, russet brown traveling gown. The lady had just alighted from a hired carriage. The coachman was wrestling with a large trunk.

"My cousin Patricia," Lucinda exclaimed. "She will be staying with me for a month. I was not expecting her until this afternoon. She must have caught an earlier train."

"Miss Patricia," Shute called from the top of the box. "Welcome back to London. It is a pleasure to see you again."

"It is wonderful to see you, also, Shute," Patricia said. "It has been ages. My parents asked me to convey their greetings and best wishes to you and your family."

"Thank you, miss."

The door of number twelve opened. Mrs. Shute appeared.

"Miss Patricia," she exclaimed. "It is so good to have you back with us again."

"Thank you, Mrs. Shute," Patricia said. "I apologize for catching you by surprise like this. I know I was not expected until later today."

Mrs. Shute beamed. "Nonsense, I've had your room ready for days."

Caleb opened the carriage door and kicked down the steps. He squeezed out of the small vehicle with great care and then turned to offer his hand to Lucinda.

"Lucy." Patricia rushed forward.

Lucinda opened her arms to hug her. "Patricia, I am so happy to see you again. It has been much too long." She stepped back. "I would like you to meet Mr. Jones. Mr. Jones, my cousin Miss Patricia McDaniel. If you know anything about the study of paranormal artifacts, you will have heard of her father, I'm sure."

Caleb bowed over Patricia's hand with a grace that startled Lucinda. The man might eschew polished manners most of the time but clearly he was capable of employing them when it suited him.

"A pleasure, Miss McDaniel," Caleb said, releasing Patricia's gloved fingers. "I presume that your father is Herbert McDaniel?"

Patricia dimpled up at him. "I see you do know your archaeologists, sir."

"Certainly those who are members of the Arcane Society and who are as brilliant as McDaniel," Caleb agreed. "I was intrigued by his paper on that Egyptian funerary text that recently came into the Society's collection. Fascinating insights into the psychical aspects of ancient Egyptian religion."

Lucinda smiled proudly. "Perhaps you have heard that the Council has appointed Patricia's parents to catalog the Egyptian antiquities in the Society's museum at Arcane House?"

"I recall Gabe mentioning that McDaniel and his wife

would soon be starting work on the project. It is about time that collection was cataloged."

"Patricia will also be working on the collection," Lucinda said. "She has a talent for deciphering dead languages."

"There is a great need for that ability at Arcane House," Caleb said. "How long will you be staying here in London?"

Patricia smiled. "Just until I find a husband."

Lucinda opened her mouth but it took a few seconds before she could form a single word.

"What?" she squeaked.

"Mama and Papa feel that I ought to get married," Patricia said. "I agree. There is no time to waste."

For the first time in her life, Lucinda felt in need of a dose of smelling salts. She forgot about Caleb, the Shutes and the driver of the hired carriage. She stared at Patricia in mounting alarm.

"You're *pregnant*?" she gasped.

Ten

"*I* am so sorry for giving you such a fright, Lucy." Patricia helped herself to more eggs from the silver serving dish on the sideboard. "I do apologize."

"Your apology would be more acceptable if you could manage to stop laughing," Lucinda grumbled. "You nearly shattered my nerves."

"Nonsense," Patricia said. "You are made of sterner stuff. I suspect that if I had turned up on your doorstep, pregnant and desperate for a husband, you would have lost no time finding one for me. Don't you agree, Mr. Jones?"

"I'm certain Miss Bromley is more than capable of accomplishing any task she undertakes," Caleb said, buttering a slice of toast.

Lucinda glowered at him down the length of the table. It had no doubt been a mistake to invite him in for breakfast but she had found herself unable to resist. He was clearly relying entirely on his formidable will to overcome exhaustion, the bruises from the previous night's adventure and the strange disharmony in his aura. The man needed food and then he needed sleep. She could offer the former. The healer in her would not allow her to do otherwise.

Nevertheless, she had expected him to turn down her invitation to breakfast. To her astonishment, he had accepted with alacrity, just as though he dined with her on a regular basis. Now he sat at the head of the table, filling the sunny morning room with the aura of his masculine vitality, and ate scrambled eggs and toast with the air of a man who had been hungry for a long time.

The neighbors must surely be talking, she thought. But given the notoriety that already swirled around the household, a mysterious gentleman caller was a mere bagatelle.

"I think we have had quite enough conversation on such a delicate subject," she said sternly. "I suggest we discuss something else. Anything else. You have had your little jest, Patricia."

"The thing is, I was not joking, Lucy."

"What do you mean?" Lucinda demanded.

Patricia carried her heavily laden plate to the table and sat down. "I will not tease you any more about the misunderstanding concerning my not-so-delicate condition. But I was quite serious when I told you that I am here to find a husband. I think one month should be sufficient for the task, don't you?"

Lucinda nearly dropped her coffee cup. At the end of the table Caleb swallowed another forkful of eggs and regarded Patricia with an interested expression.

"How do you propose to go about the business?" he asked, genuinely curious.

"Why, the same way Cousin Lucy did, of course." Patricia poured some coffee for herself. "It was a very efficient and very logical approach."

Caleb looked at Lucinda.

"It was a disaster," Lucinda snapped, suddenly quite cross. "Surely it will not have escaped your attention, Patricia, that not only am I not happily married, my fiancé died of poison and everyone thinks I'm responsible."

"Yes, well, I do understand that matters did not work out precisely as planned," Patricia said soothingly. "But that does not mean that the underlying method was at fault."

Caleb appeared fascinated now. "Describe this method to me, Miss Patricia."

"It was really quite straightforward," Patricia said, warming to her topic. "Lucy made a list of attributes that she required in a husband. She gave the list to her father, who then assessed the gentlemen of his acquaintance and their sons to see which among them came closest to meeting her requirements."

"The candidate Papa and I selected was Ian Glasson," Lucinda said coldly. "He proved somewhat less than satisfactory."

"I understand." Patricia was undaunted. "But I believe that the problem was that you left one thing off your list."

"What was that?"

"Psychical compatibility," Patricia declared with an air of modest triumph. "It was the missing ingredient."

"And just how was I supposed to assess that require-ment?" Lucinda demanded.

"That's the thing, you see," Patricia said. "You couldn't. You were, in effect, working blind in that department. But Mama told me that there is now a matchmaker in the Society who can assess that very quality."

Caleb nodded. "Lady Milden."

Lucinda and Patricia both turned to him.

"You know her?" Patricia asked excitedly.

"Certainly. She's the great-aunt of my cousin Thaddeus Ware." Caleb frowned. "Which makes her a relation of mine, I think, although I'm not quite sure how."

"Would you be so kind as to arrange an introduction?" Patricia asked.

Caleb ate some of the kippered salmon. "I'll send her a note today informing her that you wish to employ her services."

Patricia glowed with excitement. "That is very kind of you, sir."

Lucinda stirred uneasily. "Patricia, I'm not sure this is a good idea."

"Sounds perfectly sound to me," Caleb said. He looked at Patricia. "What are the requirements on this list of yours?"

"Actually, I merely adopted Lucinda's list," Patricia explained. "And then added the psychical compatibility factor."

"What was on Miss Bromley's original list?" Caleb asked.

"Well, among other things, the candidates must first and foremost hold modern views concerning the equality of women," Patricia said.

Caleb nodded, evidently in full accord with that requirement.

"Go on," he said.

"Suitable candidates will also demonstrate intellectual interests that are compatible with my own," Patricia continued. "After all, we will be spending a great deal of time in each other's company. I expect my husband to be able to discuss not only archaeology but the paranormal aspects of the subject."

"Makes sense," Caleb agreed.

"He will need to be in good health, of course, both physically and psychically."

"A legitimate requirement when one is talking about producing offspring," Lucinda put in quickly when she noticed that Caleb was frowning a little.

"He must also be broad-minded about my talent," Patricia said. "Not every man is prepared to tolerate a wife who possesses strong psychical abilities, I'm sorry to say."

"Probably best to seek a mate within the Society, in that case," Caleb said.

"That is my thought, as well," Patricia agreed. "And last but not least, the candidate must possess a positive and cheerful disposition."

"Well, of course," Lucinda said. "That goes without saying."

Caleb stopped looking intrigued. His expression hardened. "I understand the concern with the other requirements, but why the devil is a positive, cheerful disposition important?"

"Really, sir," Lucinda said briskly, "I would have thought it obvious. An agreeable temperament is an essential quality in a husband. The mere thought of putting up with a man who is inclined to melancholia and dark moods is enough to make any intelligent woman elect to remain a spinster for life."

Caleb's jaw tensed. "A man has a right to the occasional dark mood."

"Indeed," Lucinda said. "But the operative word is *occasional*. No woman should be forced to tolerate such behavior on a regular basis."

"Best to avoid the problem at the start by selecting the right husband," Patricia said. "A cheerful, positive temperament is definitely a critical requirement."

"Huh." Caleb went back to his eggs with a disgruntled air.

It struck Lucinda that he appeared to have plunged into a decidedly dark mood. She looked at Patricia. "The added requirement of psychical compatibility is an excellent notion. And I agree that employing a professional matchmaker is very wise. The great hurdle you face, I'm afraid, is me."

Patricia stared at her. "What do you mean?"

Lucinda sighed. "You and your parents have spent a goodly part of the last year and a half in Italy and Egypt. You do not comprehend how things have changed for me since my father and his partner and my fiancé died. The gossip about the poisonings, you know."

"What of it?" Patricia demanded. "Never say your friends and neighbors actually believed that nonsense."

"I'm afraid most did believe it," Lucinda said simply. "What is more, I think it is safe to say that, as long as you are closely associated with me, Lady Milden will decline to take you on as a client. The challenge of trying to overcome the notoriety that surrounds this household would be too much for any matchmaker."

Caleb looked up from his scrambled eggs. "You don't know Lady Milden."

Eleven

"*I* must say, Lucy, I quite like Mr. Jones." Patricia paused in front of a stand of foxglove. "But he is decidedly out of the ordinary, isn't he?"

"That is putting it mildly," Lucinda said. They were in the wing of the conservatory devoted to traditional medicinal herbs and plants. Her mother had called it the Physick Garden. "But I suspect that is part and parcel of his unusual psychical nature."

"Very likely." Patricia leaned down to examine some feverfew.

"He is, I think, quite powerful," Lucinda said. She paused by the aloe that she used to treat minor burns and wounds. "Such strength requires a great deal of self-mastery. And self-mastery of that degree can produce some quirks and a dash of eccentricity."

Caleb had left an hour ago, taking his tisanes with him. Patricia had disappeared upstairs for a time to supervise the unpacking of her trunk. When she had come back down, she had insisted on a stroll through the conservatory.

"One can certainly understand a touch of eccentricity." Patricia wandered over to look at the pale pink flowers of the tall valerian plants. "Papa says that very strong talents who do not control their paranormal senses are in danger of being overwhelmed by them."

"It is a popular theory in the Society and I think there is, indeed, some risk of that occurring." Lucinda fingered the large, broadly oval leaves of a Solomon's seal. "In my work, I have sometimes encountered individuals who were mentally unstable due to illness of a psychical nature. It has not escaped my notice that such people are usually rather strong talents."

Patricia cleared her throat delicately. "One hears certain rumors concerning the Jones family. Evidently there is more than a dash of eccentricity in the blood. They are descended from the founder, after all."

"Yes, I know, Patricia. But if you are implying that Caleb Jones might be a bit unhinged, you are wrong." She did not know why she felt obliged to defend Caleb but she could not seem to help herself. "He is a complex man who controls an unusual and very strong talent. That accounts for any odd behavior you may have noted."

"Does it explain the bruises on his face that I saw this morning?" Patricia asked smoothly.

"Mr. Jones suffered an accident of some sort last night. One of the tisanes I gave him is designed to alleviate the bruising." She would not mention the reason she had given him the other medicinal tonic, she thought. Something told her that Caleb Jones would not appreciate having the odd tension in his aura discussed by all and sundry.

"I see." Patricia moved on to survey the yellow flowers of the Saint-John's-wort. "One would have thought that he would have been married by now. Don't you find it strange that he is still single?" She looked up with an expression of polite inquiry. "He *is* still single, isn't he?"

"Oh, yes." Lucinda frowned, considering the issue more closely. "As to why, I have no notion."

"Whatever his eccentricities, he is a Jones," Patricia pointed out, straightening. "The heir to a fortune and a bloodline that goes all the way back to Sylvester the Alchemist. Most men of his years and background would have wed long ago."

"Mr. Jones is not *that* old," Lucinda said sharply. But she knew that Patricia was right. Caleb could not put off marriage much longer. A gentleman of his station had a certain responsibility to his family.

Now why was that such a depressing thought? she wondered.

"He must be nearly forty," Patricia said.

"Nonsense. Mid-thirties, I should think."

"Late thirties."

"Are you saying that he is too old for marriage? Rubbish. It is obvious that Mr. Jones is in his prime."

"I suppose that depends on your point of view," Patricia said very seriously.

"You are nineteen, Patricia. Wait until you are my age. A gentleman in his thirties will appear entirely different to you."

"I never meant to imply that you were old." Patricia whirled around, red-faced. "Please forgive me, Lucy. You know I did not intend any such thing."

"Of course you didn't." Lucinda laughed. "Do not concern yourself. You did no grave injury to my feelings." She paused and raised her brows. "Can I assume from this conversation that Mr. Jones is too advanced in years to be added to your list of candidates?"

Patricia wrinkled her nose. "Definitely."

"I'm sure you're aware that in the polite world young ladies of your age are frequently married off to men old enough to be their fathers and sometimes old enough to be their grandfathers."

Patricia shuddered. "Luckily for me, Mama and Papa

hold modern views. They would never try to coerce me into marrying a man I did not love." She clasped her hands behind her back and studied a clump of shrublike wormwood. "How long have you known Mr. Jones?"

It occurred to Lucinda that, what with one thing and another, there had been no opportunity to explain Caleb's presence in her life. She pondered whether to break the news that she was in danger of becoming a suspect in a murder case.

It would probably be best to keep quiet about her predicament, at least for the time being, she thought. The truth would only alarm Patricia and distract her from the project of finding a husband.

"Mr. Jones and I met quite recently," she said.

"A few weeks ago, perhaps? You never mentioned him in any of your recent letters."

"This is the second day of our association. Why do you ask?"

"What?" Patricia spun around, genuinely shocked. "You've only known him two days and he takes break-fast with you?"

"Well, he didn't get any sleep last night and he didn't eat this morning. I suppose I felt sorry for him."

Patricia's eyes widened a little more. Then she burst into a spate of giggles. "Really, cousin, you astonish me."

"What's so amusing?"

"Kept him occupied all night, did you?" Patricia winked. "You are more modern in your thinking than even I had believed. Does Mama know? I suspect not."

"You misunderstand," Lucinda said, baffled by the reaction. "I wasn't the one who kept Mr. Jones busy last night. He was involved with another project until dawn."

Patricia stopped giggling. "Mr. Jones is involved with someone else? How could you possibly bring yourself to share him?"

"Well, he is a professional," Lucinda pointed out. "I'm sure he has a number of affairs going on at the moment. I am in no position to demand his services full-time."

"His services?" Patricia's voice rose. "You *pay* him?"

Lucinda frowned. "Well, of course."

"Isn't that a little, umm, unusual?"

"In what way?"

Patricia widened her hands. "Well, I suppose I have always assumed that if there was a financial consideration involved in that sort of liaison, it was the man who paid the woman, not the other way around. But now that I consider the matter closely, I can see where, given modern notions of equality—"

"Liaison?" Horrified, Lucinda considered fainting for the second time that day. "Mr. Jones and I are not involved in anything of the sort. Good heavens, Patricia, whatever gave you that idea?"

"Let me think," Patricia said dryly. "There is the little matter of your returning home with him in a carriage very early in the morning. I had every reason to assume that the two of you spent the night in a secluded location."

"You are quite mistaken."

"And then you invited him in for breakfast. What else was I to think?"

Lucinda drew herself up and gave her a frosty glare. "Your assumptions could not be more wrong. Mr. Jones tracked me down in Guppy Lane this morning because of a business matter. We conferred in the carriage on the way back here, and when I discovered that he had not

100

slept or eaten I felt compelled to offer him a meal. That is all there is to it."

"Why?" Patricia said.

"Why what?"

"Why did you feel compelled to feed him? He's a Jones. He probably has a kitchen full of servants just waiting to prepare meals for him."

The logic of the question bothered Lucinda more than it should have. Why had she invited Caleb in for breakfast?

"He obviously does not look after himself," she said. "It is in my own best interests to keep him fit and healthy."

"Why?" Patricia asked again.

Lucinda threw up her hands. So much for trying to keep her association with Caleb unexplained. "Because he is the only person standing between me and prison, possibly the only one between me and a hangman's noose."

Twelve

The door to the laboratory opened just as Basil Hulsey was about to put the latest version of the formula into the water dish. Jolted by the interruption, his hand jerked, spilling several drops of the drug onto the floor. The six rats watched him through the bars of the cage, malevolent eyes glittering in the glow of the gas lamp.

"What in blazes?" Hulsey yelped, furious.

He whirled around, intending to chastise the hapless person who had dared to enter his domain uninvited. He was forced to swallow his anger when he saw who had stormed into the room.

"Oh, it's you, Mr. Norcross," he muttered. He adjusted his spectacles on his nose. "Thought it was one of the street boys the apothecary uses to deliver the herbs."

His new financial backers were just as arrogant and just as obsessed with the founder's formula as his previous patrons. They were all the same, he thought, men of wealth and rank whose only interest in the drug lay in the power they believed it would give them. They had no appreciation for the wonders and mysteries of the chemistry involved; no comprehension of the difficulties that had to be overcome.

Unfortunately, rich gentlemen who were willing to finance scientific experiments of the sort that interested him were hard to come by. Two months ago, following the collapse of the Third Circle, he had found himself between patrons. All of his equipment and several valuable notebooks had been destroyed or confiscated by the Society. The last thing he had wanted to do was become involved with the Order of the Emerald Tablet again. But its members seemed to be the only people around who were willing to pay for his unique talent.

"We have just learned that Caleb Jones was seen calling on Lucinda Bromley this morning," Allister Norcross said.

Unnerving energy shivered through the space between them. Hulsey was instantly thrown into a state of anxiety. Allister Norcross had probably never been what anyone would call normal. Now, his talent heightened by the drug, he was quite terrifying.

In looks, he was unremarkable. He possessed the sort of features that appealed to the ladies but he was not so pretty that men found him effeminate. His brown hair was cut in a fashionable style and his elegantly tailored coat and trousers emphasized his lithe, athletic frame. It was not until one got close to him that one realized he was unhinged.

Heart pounding, Hulsey took an instinctive step back. He came up hard against the cage. It shuddered under the impact. He heard the scurrying of little clawed feet behind him and quickly moved away.

Yanking off his spectacles, he fished a stained handkerchief out of his pocket. He often found that polishing his glasses calmed his nerves.

Norcross scowled at the cage and then looked away. He did not like the rats. Probably because they did not frighten easily, Hulsey thought. Or perhaps it was because he sensed that he might have more than a little in common with them when it came to savage impulses.

Hulsey positioned the glasses back on his nose and attempted to compose himself.

"I don't understand, sir," he said. He had a nasty suspicion that he was missing something of great importance here. He did not like the feeling. "Is there a problem?"

"You fool. Caleb Jones has become involved in this affair and it is your fault."

Alarm shot through Hulsey. So did outrage.

"I have no notion what you are t-talking about," he stuttered. "You cannot blame me if your Circle has come to Jones's attention. I c-can assure you I had no hand in whatever has occurred."

"We are reasonably certain that Jones is, as yet, unaware of the existence of the Seventh Circle. We intend to see to it that remains the case. Steps will be taken."

"Uh, what sort of steps?" Hulsey asked, more nervous than ever. His talent was of great use to the Seventh Circle but the one thing that had been impressed upon him during his short association with the Third Circle was that the Order of the Emerald Tablet did not tolerate failure or serious mistakes.

"That is none of your affair," Norcross said. "But bear in mind that you are responsible for the problem of Caleb Jones. I have been sent here today to inform you that the leader of the Circle is extremely displeased by your careless actions. Do you understand me, Hulsey?"

"H-how can you blame me for the fact that Jones has paid a call on Miss Bromley?" Hulsey asked, bewildered.

"You're the one who stole that damned fern from her conservatory."

"What in blazes does that have to do with Jones? I took that fern a *month* ago. I doubt that Miss Bromley even noticed it was missing. She certainly didn't call in Mr. Jones to investigate at that time."

"We do not yet know precisely why Jones has become associated with Bromley now, but the leader suspects that it has something to do with that bloody fern. It is the only connection."

Hulsey glanced uneasily at the fern. It sat in a pot on a workbench, its delicate fronds spilling forth in a fountain of vibrant green. It was a magnificent and most unusual specimen with a number of intriguing psychical properties. His experiments thus far had convinced him that it held the potential to take him to the next level of his dream research. To have left it in Bromley's conservatory would have been an intolerable waste.

"I really don't see how my removing the fern could have anything to do with this," he said soothingly. "Perhaps Jones's interest in Bromley is of a personal nature."

"He's a *Jones*. A man of his rank and status would have no reason to pay a personal call upon the daughter of a notorious poisoner, a woman who is rumored to have followed in her father's footsteps. As far as we have been able to discern, no one of note in the social world calls upon Miss Bromley. The only people she sees are her relations and a few brave botanists."

"Per-perhaps Jones wanted to tour her conservatory," Hulsey said hopefully. "Everyone in the Society is aware that he is a man of wide-ranging intellectual and scientific interests."

"If it transpires that Caleb Jones decided to call upon Lucinda Bromley for reasons of scientific curiosity, it would be the most astonishing of coincidences. You know how those of us with talent feel about coincidences."

"That conservatory is crammed with specimens. In

the unlikely event that Miss Bromley did discover that the fern was gone, it is ridiculous on the face of it to think that she would go so far as to employ a private inquiry agent to look for it. And even more ludicrous to think that Jones would actually take such a silly case. It is just a plant, after all, not a diamond necklace."

Norcross moved forward through the alternating shadow-and-glare cast by the gas lamps. "For your sake, you had better be right. Because that fern is a direct link to you, and you are linked to us."

Hulsey shivered. "I assure you, there is no way Jones could ever make the connection. I used a different name when I called upon Miss Bromley. She has no way of knowing who I am."

Norcross's mouth twisted in disgust. "You are an idiot, Hulsey. Go back to your experiments and your rats. I will take care of the problem you have caused."

Anger surfaced in Hulsey, momentarily suppressing his fear. He drew himself up to his full height. "I resent your remarks, sir. There is no other man alive in England today who can even begin to compare to me when it comes to the study of the chemistry of the paranormal. *No one*. Why, it would require another Newton to compete with me."

"Yes, I know, Hulsey. And that is all that is saving you at this moment. Trust me when I tell you that if there was another Newton available, hell, if there was anyone else who possessed your skills and talents, the leader would have ordered your execution in a heartbeat."

Hulsey stared at him, appalled.

Norcross withdrew a gold snuffbox from his pocket, flipped open the hinged lid with a graceful motion and took a pinch of the contents. He inhaled the powder with a sharp, practiced snort. Then he smiled his slow, terrifying smile.

"Do you understand me, Hulsey?" he asked very softly.

The strong currents of energy struck Hulsey with the force of a blow, shattering his already shaky nerves. He was no longer merely frightened, he was paralyzed with terror. Under the onslaught of Norcross's talent, his pulse began to beat so quickly and so erratically that he thought he might faint. He gasped for breath but all the oxygen seemed to have been pumped out of the room.

It was as if he confronted some dread monster of the night, a creature out of a nightmare. The logical side of his nature assured him that this was no vampire or supernatural phantom standing in front of him. It was just Norcross employing his bizarre talent to induce a sense of mindless panic. But that knowledge did nothing to assuage the sensation.

Unable to support himself any longer, Hulsey collapsed to his knees and began to rock back and forth. He heard a high, keening shriek and realized it was coming from his own throat.

"I asked you a question, Hulsey."

Hulsey knew he must answer but he could not. When he opened his mouth the only noise that emerged was an incomprehensible stutter.

"Y-y-yessss," he managed.

Evidently satisfied with the reaction, Norcross gave him another razor-sharp smile. Hulsey was vaguely amazed that fangs did not appear. He realized the mind-numbing fear was receding. He discovered that he could breathe again.

"Excellent," Norcross said. He pocketed the snuff-box. "I do believe that you comprehend me very well, indeed. Get up, fool."

Hulsey grabbed the edge of the workbench and hauled himself erect. It was not easy. He had to maintain his grip in order to keep himself from collapsing a second time.

Norcross went out the door, closing it in a calm, controlled manner that was, in its own way, just as unnerving as the wild, predatory excitement that had burned in his eyes a moment ago.

Hulsey waited until his pulse had slowed somewhat. Then he sank down onto the stool.

"It is all right," he said aloud. "You can come out now. He is gone."

A door cracked open. Bertram came cautiously into the room. He was clearly shaken.

"Norcross is mad," Bertram whispered.

"Yes, I know." Hulsey massaged his aching head.

"What do you think he meant when he said steps would be taken to make sure Jones does not connect the fern to you?"

Hulsey looked at his son. Bertram was a mirror image of himself at twenty-three and a brilliant talent in his own right. His psychical abilities and, hence, his interests were a little different—no two talents were ever identical—but they complemented each other very well in the laboratory. Bertram made the ideal research assistant. Someday, Hulsey thought with a touch of paternal pride, his son would make bold inroads into the mysteries of the paranormal.

"I don't know what he meant," Hulsey said. "The important thing is that whatever the steps are, they don't affect us."

"How do you know that?"

"Because if they did, we'd both be dead by now."

Wearily, Hulsey got up from the stool and went back to the cage. The rats watched him intently. They were new, replacements for the six that had died last week. He picked up the flask and emptied the rest of the contents into the water dish. The thirsty rats rushed forward to drink.

"Are all patrons so unreasonable?" Bertram asked.

"In my experience, the answer is yes. They're all cracked."

Thirteen

Victoria, Lady Milden, managed to appear at once austere and very fashionable. Her silver-gray hair was dressed in an elegant chignon. She wore an expensive, beautifully draped gown of dove gray.

It was evident from the outset that she approached her role as a matchmaker not only with enthusiasm, but with a brisk determination that would have been appropriate for a field marshal. She received Lucinda and Patricia in the cozy study of her new town house.

"I am impressed with your list of requirements," she said to Patricia. "In my experience, few young people approach marriage with such a degree of logic."

"Thank you," Patricia said. "Lucy was my inspiration for the list."

"Indeed?" Victoria gave Lucinda a thoughtful look and then returned to the list. "Well, I must say you've been very thorough. I'm especially pleased to see that you are aware of the importance of psychical compatibility."

"Mama said that she thinks it is critical."

"Your mother is very wise." Victoria put down the list and removed her glasses. "If only more couples would pay attention to that aspect. It is the key to marital happiness, especially among those with above-average talent."

"There is something I would like to clarify here," Lucinda said. "What, precisely, is meant by psychical compatibility?"

Victoria assumed a professorial air. "You are familiar with the notion that everyone produces unique currents of energy across a spectrum."

"Yes, of course," Lucinda said. "Do you read auras?"

"In a limited fashion," Victoria said. "I perceive certain wavelengths on the spectrum. It so happens that those are the very wavelengths that are critical to the success of intimate relationships."

Patricia leaned forward a little, fascinated. "In what way?"

"It is really very simple," Victoria said. "If the wavelengths of the two people involved do not resonate harmoniously, it is a certainty that the couple will not know any degree of true emotional intimacy or happiness. My talent allows me to determine whether the resonating patterns are, indeed, compatible."

"How very gratifying to know that you employ such a scientific approach to your work, Lady Milden," Patricia said.

"The problem for me," Victoria continued, "is that, while I can use my questionnaires and personal interviews to estimate the probability that two people will be well matched, I nevertheless must see the potential bride and groom together before I can be sure that they will resonate properly."

"How do you proceed?" Lucinda asked, intrigued.

"The first step is for me to prepare a list of candidates for Patricia." Victoria tapped the sheet of paper in front of her with one finger. "I shall, of course, keep her requirements in mind. But I warn you that it may be impossible to satisfy all of them."

For the first time, Patricia appeared uneasy. "I really do not know if I can compromise on any of those specifications. Each requirement on my list is very important to me."

"Never fear," Victoria said. "If the wavelengths resonate with a sufficient degree of harmony, you will discover that you can make a few compromises."

Patricia did not look entirely reassured. "How will you compile your list of gentlemen?"

Victoria waved one hand to indicate a long row of file drawers. "As it happens, I have been literally swamped with applications from members of the Society ever since I let it be known that I was available for this sort of consultation. I shall go through my records, pull out those of the young men I believe would be the most suitable and arrange for you to meet them."

"It sounds a rather lengthy process," Patricia said. "I was hoping to be engaged within the month."

"Oh, I don't think there will be any problem." Victoria smiled. "In my experience, once two people of talent who resonate well together actually meet, the attraction is almost instantaneous." She gave a ladylike sniff. "Not that the individuals involved are always willing to admit to that attraction, even to themselves, let alone to each other."

"I'm sure I won't have any problem recognizing the right candidate immediately," Patricia said.

"In addition, parents sometimes raise barriers to the marriage because they disapprove of the prospective bride or groom for one reason or another," Victoria said. "There is often considerable work for me to do in order to pull off a successful match."

"My parents hold very modern notions on marriage," Patricia assured her. "As I told you, it was my mother's idea that I come to London to consult with you."

"That is good to know," Victoria said. "It bodes well."

A thought struck Lucinda. "What happens if two individuals who resonate well together are already married to other people?"

Victoria tut-tutted. "That is a very sad situation and one which I am obviously unable to resolve. I regret to say that, given the inclination of so many people to marry for financial and social reasons rather than psychical compatibility, the problem arises all too often. The result is that illicit liaisons are quite common."

"Oh," Lucinda said quietly. "Yes, I suppose that does explain why there are so many people engaged in affairs."

"How will you arrange for me to meet the eligible gentlemen in your files?" Patricia asked.

"Several extremely efficient mechanisms for introducing clients to a great many candidates already exist," Victoria assured her.

"What are they?" Lucinda asked.

"The traditional methods, of course. Balls, parties, the theater, lectures, gallery receptions, teas and so on. People have used such techniques for generations to make introductions. The difference, of course, is that I accompany my clients to such events and assess the patterns of all those they meet."

Lucinda froze. "I'm afraid balls and parties are out of the question."

Victoria looked at her. "I don't see why."

"Lady Milden, I will be quite honest with you. I can afford to put on a ball or a party of some sort for Patricia but I'm sure you are aware of the notoriety that surrounds my family. I doubt very much that anyone on your list of candidates would accept an invitation from me. I cannot offer anything useful in the way of social connections."

"Yes, Miss Bromley, I am well aware of the gossip. But I do not think we need let a few unfortunate rumors get in the way of a successful match for your cousin."

"Unfortunate rumors?" Lucinda could not believe her ears. "Madam, we are talking about murder by poison and my father's so-called suicide. All of the talk is baseless, I assure you. Nonetheless, the taint of scandal cannot be easily washed away. You know how it is in the social world."

"I know how it is within the Arcane Society's social world," Victoria said calmly. "Rest assured, in that realm, an invitation from a member of the Jones family cannot be ignored."

"I don't understand," Lucinda said, utterly bewildered now.

"As it happens, there is a very important Society affair coming up later this week," Victoria said. "My son and daughter-in-law are giving a large reception to celebrate the engagement of my nephew, Thaddeus Ware, and his lovely fiancée, Leona Hewitt. A great many high-ranking members of the Society will be present, including the new Master and his wife. I will see to it that you, Miss Patricia, and the eligible gentlemen I have selected will all be on the guest list."

"Good heavens," Lucinda whispered, awed by Victoria's daring.

For her part, Patricia was suddenly hesitant. "The lectures and gallery receptions sound fine, Lady Milden, but I'm afraid I've had very little experience of the social world."

"There is no cause for alarm," Victoria assured her. "I will be there to guide you every step of the way. All part of the service that I provide."

"But if you accompany me, everyone will know that

I am in the market for a husband," Patricia pointed out. "Won't that make things a trifle awkward?"

"Not in the least," Victoria said. "Discretion is also part of the service. Trust me, I receive invitations to every important Society affair." She winked. "You will not be my only client at the ball."

"I think it would be best if I did not attend," Lucinda said, feeling more than a little desperate. "My presence will only generate comment and speculation. Patricia's last name is McDaniel. If I am not there it is quite possible that none of the other guests will realize that she is related to me."

"Nonsense, Miss Bromley." Victoria put her reading glasses back on and reached for a pen. "I can assure you that when it comes to dealing with the social world, timidity never pays. The weak get trampled. Only the strong, the bold and the very clever survive."

In spite of her unease, Lucinda almost laughed. "You sound as though you subscribe to Mr. Darwin's theories."

"I cannot speak for every species on earth," Victoria said, dipping her pen into the inkwell, "but there is no doubt but that Mr. Darwin's notions most certainly apply to the polite world."

Lucinda studied her for a moment. "Something tells me that the real reason we might be able to carry off your breathtaking scheme is because we will have the support of the Jones family."

Victoria looked at her over the rims of her eyeglasses. "Within the Arcane Society, the Jones family sets down the rules, Miss Bromley."

"And outside the Society?" Lucinda asked.

"Outside the Society, the Joneses follow their own rules."

Fourteen

The knock on the door the following morning came just as Lucinda and Patricia were sitting down to breakfast. Mrs. Shute set the coffeepot on the table and cast a disapproving look in the direction of the front hall.

"Can't imagine who that could be at this hour," she said, wiping her hands on her apron.

"Perhaps someone is ill and needs Lucy's advice," Patricia said, reaching for a slice of toast.

Mrs. Shute shook her head in an ominous manner. "Those from the neighborhood who send for Miss Bromley always come around to the kitchen door. I'll go and see who it is."

She left the morning room, grim-faced.

Patricia smiled. "I pity whoever has the misfortune to be standing on the front steps."

"So do I, but it serves him right for knocking on front doors at eight-thirty in the morning," Lucinda said. She reached for the newspaper. The headline of the *Flying Intelligencer* made her gasp. "Good heavens, Patricia, listen to this—"

She broke off in midsentence when she heard the low rumble of a familiar masculine voice.

"That sounds like Mr. Jones," Patricia said, sparkling with excitement. "He must have some news. Perhaps he has solved the case and discovered the identity of the person who poisoned Lord Fairburn."

"I doubt that." Lucinda put down the paper, trying to suppress the little rush of anticipation that soared through her. "Surely he hasn't had enough time to interview all the people on that list of visitors that I gave him."

Caleb loomed in the doorway. "You're right, Miss Bromley. I am only partway through your list. Good morning, ladies. You're both looking very fine today." He surveyed the platter of fried eggs and broiled haddock with an expression of riveted interest. "Am I interrupting your breakfast?"

Well, of course he was interrupting breakfast, Lucinda thought. He was a detective. Surely he could detect the obvious. She studied him closely and was relieved to see that he appeared a good deal more rested than he had the day before. The bruises on his face were still quite colorful but they looked less painful. She was also gratified to sense that the tension in his aura had lessened somewhat. The tisanes were working.

"Please do not concern yourself, sir," she said quickly. "I assume you are here because you have some news at least?"

"Unfortunately I have made very little progress in the investigation." Caleb gazed at the gleaming silver coffeepot as though it were a rare work of art. "But some new questions have arisen. I was hoping you could answer them for me."

"Certainly," she said. It dawned on her that he looked famished. She frowned. "Have you eaten yet?"

"Didn't have a chance," Caleb said a little too glibly. "New housekeeper hasn't got the hang of my schedule yet. They never do."

Patricia looked quite blank. "Who never does what, sir?"

117

"Housekeepers," he said, gliding toward the array of food with what Lucinda considered a decidedly surreptitious manner. "They never get the hang of my schedule. Breakfast is never ready when I require it. Expect Mrs. Perkins will be giving notice soon, just like the others." He studied the haddock with a reverent expression. "That looks quite tasty."

There was nothing for it but to invite him to sit down, Lucinda thought.

"Please join us," she said brusquely.

Caleb gave her an unexpected smile. It transformed his features. She caught her breath. He had fascinated her from the start but now she suddenly realized that he was quite capable of charming her, as well. That was unsettling. She had believed herself immune to masculine wiles since the discovery that Ian Glasson had deceived her.

"Thank you, Miss Bromley, I believe I will," he said.

He picked up a plate and began to serve himself with an alacrity that aroused even more suspicion. When he had left yesterday morning he had inquired about her customary breakfast hour. She had told him eight-thirty, thinking he wished to time his next visit so as not to interfere with the morning meal. She glanced at the tall clock. It was eight-thirty-two. That was not a coincidence, she concluded. Caleb Jones was not a man who made mistakes of that sort.

Patricia was doing her best to stifle a giggle. Lucinda gave her a repressive glare and then looked at Caleb.

"I take it there is a high turnover in staff in your household, Mr. Jones?" she said coolly.

"It's not as though I require a large staff." He piled eggs on his plate. "I'm the only one who lives in the house. Most of the rooms are closed off. All I require is

118

a housekeeper and someone to take care of the gardens. I don't like a lot of people running around when I'm trying to work. It's distracting."

"I see," Lucinda said neutrally. Now she, too, was struggling to swallow laughter.

"I don't understand it." Caleb walked to the table and sat down. "Housekeepers come and go like trains. They last a month, two at most, and then they give notice. I am forever having to send a note around to the agency that supplies staff, requesting a new housekeeper. It is extremely annoying, I don't mind telling you."

"What seems to be the chief complaint?" Lucinda asked.

"The chief complaint is that they all give notice."

"I was referring to the housekeepers, sir. Why do they leave your employ with such regularity?"

"Any number of reasons," he said vaguely. He took a large bite of the eggs, chewed with enthusiasm and swallowed. "Several have told me that it alarms them to hear me walking around in my library and laboratory late at night. They say it sounds as though the house is haunted. Superstitious nonsense, of course."

"Quite," Lucinda murmured.

"Others claim to have been frightened by certain experiments that I occasionally conduct. As if a little flash powder ever hurt anyone."

"Actually, it has been known to do just that, sir," Lucinda said. "There have been any number of serious accidents among photographers who employ various dangerous chemicals to concoct flash powder."

Caleb shot her an irritated look. "I have yet to burn down the house, Miss Bromley."

"How nice for you, sir."

He went back to his food. "In general, the complaint I've heard most often from housekeepers is my schedule."

"Have you got one?" Lucinda asked politely.

"Of course I've got a schedule. The fact that it changes daily depending upon whatever projects I happen to be working on is not my fault."

"Hmm."

Patricia, evidently concluding that it was time to move on to a new subject, stepped in quickly.

"Lucy was just about to read the headlines in the paper," she said.

"What have you got there?" Caleb asked. He glanced at the newspaper in Lucinda's hand. When he saw the masthead, he shook his head in disgust. "Right. The *Flying Intelligencer*. Don't believe even a fraction of what you read in that rag. It thrives on sensation."

"Perhaps." Lucinda contemplated the headline. "But you must admit this is a very thrilling account of a most bizarre crime. Just listen."

She began to read aloud.

BLOODY HUMAN SACRIFICE
THWARTED BY SPIRITS
by
Gilbert Otford

Invisible hands from the Other World are credited with halting a gruesome occult rite, thereby saving the life of an innocent young boy. Those at the scene recounted a horrifying experience to this correspondent.

Impossible though it may be for readers of this newspaper to believe, police confirmed that a strange cult devoted to demonic forces has been practicing dreadful rituals in the very heart of London for some weeks.

On Tuesday night of this week the group intended to sacrifice a boy who had been kidnapped off the streets for the purpose. Astonishingly, witnesses tell of invisible paranormal forces from beyond the Veil intervening at the last moment to save the life of the intended victim.

The cult leader called himself the Servant of Charun. Police identified him as Mr. Wilson Hatcher of Rhone Street. The boy who was intended as the sacrifice fled the scene in stark terror and was unavailable for comment.

The police arrested a number of people, including Mr. Hatcher, whom authorities believe to be insane.

This correspondent spoke with an informant who confided that there were rumors to the effect that the intended victim of the ritual was rescued not by spirits but by members of a secret society dedicated to psychical research. . . .

"Huh." Caleb spoke around a bite of toast. "Gabe won't like that. But I suppose a few rumors can't be helped."

Lucinda lowered the paper.

"Yesterday was Wednesday morning," she observed.

"Yes, it was." Caleb smiled at Mrs. Shute, who had just set a cup and some silverware in front of him. "Thank you, Mrs. Shute. The haddock is excellent this morning, by the way."

"I'm glad you are enjoying it, sir." Beaming, Mrs. Shute went back through the door that connected to the kitchen.

Patricia looked at Caleb. "Why does it concern you

that the newspaper correspondent may have heard some gossip about the Arcane Society, Mr. Jones?"

"There is a conviction among the members of the Council that it is best that the Society does not become fodder for the sensation press." Caleb scooped jam out of a pot. "I agree. But I doubt very much that a little gossip about the existence of yet another secret society of psychical researchers will do any great harm. There are, after all, a host of groups and organizations devoted to the study of the paranormal in London. What is one more?"

"This was why you got no sleep on Tuesday night, isn't it?" Lucinda tapped the newspaper with her forefinger. "You were the unseen hands from beyond the Veil who rescued that young boy. That explains your bruised ribs and black eye."

"I was present, but I wasn't alone." Caleb spread the jam on a slice of toast. "A young gentleman named Fletcher, who possesses a most unusual talent, was the one who got me in and whisked Kit off that altar and out of the sacrificial chamber. I was there only to make certain that the leader did not escape when the police moved in. Would you kindly pass the coffee, Miss Bromley?"

"How did this gentleman accomplish such an amazing feat?" Patricia asked.

"His talent is the ability to manipulate energy in such a way as to distract the eye. In a sense he can make things, and even himself, disappear, at least for a short period of time. He is also very, very good at getting through locks. In essence, he is the ultimate magician." Caleb paused, considering. "Although, for some reason, he was never very good onstage. I suspect that something about being in the spotlight made him uneasy."

"He can actually make things disappear?" Patricia asked. "Why, that is astonishing."

"Probably carries some fern seed in his pocket," Lucinda said dryly.

Patricia frowned. "But there is no such thing as fern seed. Ferns reproduce by spores."

"Ah, but the ancients were convinced that all plants had to spring from seeds," Lucinda said. "They couldn't find any seeds in ferns so they concluded that they were invisible. By extension, people believed that carrying fern seeds on one's person would make one invisible, too. Remember the line from Shakespeare's *Henry the Fourth*?"

"We have the receipt of fern-seed," Caleb quoted around another mouthful of eggs. *"We walk invisible."*

Patricia was enthralled. "This Mr. Fletcher sounds like a most interesting gentleman. I take it he works for your agency now, Mr. Jones?"

"Only on an occasional basis." Caleb poured coffee for himself. "I prefer not to inquire into his other sources of income."

Lucinda studied his still-colorful eye. "How often does your career as an investigator place you in jeopardy, sir?"

"I assure you, I do not spend every night engaging in fisticuffs with crackbrains who operate cults."

She shuddered. "I should hope not."

"I usually have better things to do with my time," Caleb added.

"Why did you become involved in the case, sir?" Patricia asked.

Caleb shrugged. "Gabe has persuaded the Council that the Society has an obligation to deal with particularly dangerous criminals who happen to possess psychical powers. He fears that the police cannot always cope effectively with such villains."

123

"He's probably right," Lucinda said, helping herself to more coffee. "Furthermore, given the public's fascination with the paranormal these days, it would not be at all helpful if reports of villains with psychical powers began appearing in the press. It would take very little to turn curiosity and interest into fear and panic."

Caleb paused in mid-chew and gave her an odd look.

She raised her brows. "What is it?"

He swallowed. "That is exactly what Gabe says. The two of you evidently take a similar view of such matters."

"What was the cult leader's talent?" Patricia asked.

"Hatcher had a gift for attracting, deceiving and manipulating others in a way that can only be described as mesmeric, although his talent was not, strictly speaking, that of a hypnotist," Caleb said. "Probably should have gone into the patent medicine line. He came to my attention when he began recruiting boys off the streets for his cult."

"Why do you speak of Mr. Hatcher's talent in the past tense?" Lucinda asked.

Caleb's expression grew abruptly somber. "Because it appears that he can no longer employ it on anyone other than himself."

Patricia's eyes widened. "What do you mean?"

"He has become a victim of the very deception he practiced on the members of the cult," Caleb explained. "There is no question but that Hatcher was unbalanced to begin with but the events of Tuesday night pushed him deeper into the imaginary world he created as the basis of his cult. Now he actually believes that he succeeded in piercing the Veil between this world and the Other Side but that instead of summoning a demon he could command, dark forces came through to destroy him."

"What a chilling sort of justice," Patricia whispered.

"Yes," Caleb said, his voice suddenly devoid of all inflection. "I suppose you could say that."

He drank coffee and looked into the mirror that hung on the wall at the opposite end of the table as though he could see into another dimension. Whatever he saw there did not elevate his spirits, Lucinda thought. A sense of deep knowing whispered through her. *He fears the same fate that overtook Hatcher.* But that was nonsense. As she had told Patricia, Caleb had complete mastery of his talent.

Then again, did anyone have complete control of all of their senses?

She put the paper down on the table. "About your questions, Mr. Jones," she said firmly.

Caleb jerked his attention away from the mirror and whatever dark thoughts had drawn him inward for a moment. He focused on her, his expression sharpening once more.

"I spoke with the three botanists on your list yesterday, Weeks and Brickstone and Morgan. All claimed to be unacquainted with anyone of Hulsey's description, and I'm inclined to believe them."

"I agree," Lucinda said. "That leaves the apothecary, Mrs. Daykin, who requested a tour a week or so before Hulsey called on me."

"Yes, it does." He fished a notebook out of his pocket and flipped it open. "Today I intend to speak with her. Something about her interests me."

"What is it that caught your attention?"

"Just a hunch."

She smiled. "Your talent is at work, you mean."

He ate half the toast in a single bite. "That, too. I've already checked the records. She is not a registered member of the Society. But do you think there is any possibility that she has a talent akin to your own?"

"Definitely," Lucinda said. "She is not nearly as strong as I am, though. I did hint at the possibility that she possesses some psychical ability while she was here but she acted as if she did not comprehend my meaning."

"She might not realize it," Caleb said. "A lot of people with moderate amounts of talent take their abilities for granted and consider them normal. It is only when such powers are particularly strong or of an unusual or disturbing nature that one questions them."

"Yes, I suppose that's true."

Caleb reached into his coat and brought out his pencil. "Very well, I will assume that Mrs. Daykin has a measure of talent. What else can you tell me?"

"Very little, I'm afraid. I met her only the one time when she sent around a note requesting a tour. She appeared to be in her late forties. She called herself Mrs. Daykin but I got the impression from something she said that she lives alone above her shop."

Caleb looked up at that. "Are you saying you don't think she is married?"

Lucinda hesitated, thinking about the question. "I'm not sure. As I said, it was just an impression. Perhaps her husband is dead. She wore no sign of mourning, though. She did mention once during her visit that she has a son, however. A woman with a child out of wedlock would very likely use the married title."

"Does she do well in her business?"

"I cannot say for certain. I have never visited her shop. But she was certainly well dressed, and she wore a rather expensive-looking cameo necklace. My guess is that she is quite successful."

"Did you get along well with her?"

"She was not the most congenial individual I have ever met," Lucinda said dryly. "The only thing we had in common was our mutual interest in the medicinal properties of herbs."

"How did she come to learn of the specimens in your conservatory?"

Patricia looked at him, surprised by the question. "Everyone in the botanical world knows about Lucy's specimens, Mr. Jones. It doesn't seem odd that a successful apothecary would be aware of my cousin's collection, nor that she would be curious to see it."

"Mrs. Daykin has evidently been in the apothecary business for some time," Caleb said. He turned back to Lucinda. "Has she ever contacted you before?"

"No," Lucinda said. "There was only the one visit."

"Which occurred on what date?" Caleb asked.

Lucinda winced. "I was afraid you would ask that. I cannot recall the precise date, although I'm sure I made a note in my journal. I can tell you that it was not long before Hulsey's visit, however."

"Did you show her the fern?"

"Yes, along with a great many other specimens that I thought an apothecary would find interesting. She did not appear unduly curious about my *Ameliopteris amazonensis,* however."

Patricia lowered her coffee cup. "Perhaps she deliberately concealed her interest."

"Why would she do that?" Lucinda asked.

A strange heat lit Caleb's eyes. "Because she is connected to Hulsey," he said very softly. "She knew that he would be interested in your fern. In fact, he no doubt sent her here."

"Do you really think so?" Patricia asked.

"The timing of her visit coincides with the demise of the Third Circle. Hulsey would have been between patrons and desperate to renew his dream research. I suspect that he sent Daykin here on a sort of scouting mission. Probably sent her around to a great many botanical gardens, as well, in search of herbs and plants he could use." He looked at Lucinda. "But your collection would have been of special interest to him."

"Why?" Patricia asked.

"Because Hulsey is a member of the Society," Caleb explained. "He is no doubt aware that Miss Bromley's parents were not just any botanists, but botanists of talent. He had every reason to expect that the collection in this conservatory would likely include some specimens with psychical properties. He sent Daykin to inspect the specimens first, however, because he did not want to take the risk of coming here if it wasn't necessary. He must know that the Society is looking for him."

Lucinda thought about that. "When she reported that there was a certain fern with psychical properties in my collection, he requested a tour in order to ascertain for himself whether or not it would be useful to him and to work out how to steal it."

Caleb nodded once, very certain now. "It feels right."

"What happens next?" Patricia asked.

He closed the notebook. "I am going to pay a call on Mrs. Daykin as soon as I finish this excellent breakfast."

"I'll go with you," Lucinda said.

Caleb frowned. "Why the devil would you want to do that?"

"Something tells me that Mrs. Daykin might be a trifle uneasy about speaking with you. My presence will serve to calm her."

"Are you implying that I might make her nervous?"

Lucinda gave him her most gracious smile. "Rest assured that there is nothing amiss with your social polish and convivial personality, sir. It is just that some women

128

might be somewhat alarmed by the sight of a gentleman who looks as though he was recently in a fistfight." She cleared her throat meaningfully. "A gentleman who *was* in a fistfight."

His scowl darkened. "Hadn't thought of that."

"The implications of recent violence are difficult to ignore," she continued smoothly. "You would not believe it, but I have it on good authority that there are those with weak nerves who are quite shocked by that sort of thing."

Caleb glanced at the mirror again and exhaled in resignation. "You may be right. How very fortunate that your nerves are not so easily shattered, Miss Bromley."

Fifteen

*T*he narrow street was cloaked in fog. From inside the carriage it was difficult to make out the dark row of shops, let alone read the names on the signs. Anticipation flickered through Caleb's veins. He was going to discover something very important here today. He could feel it.

"You can't see more than a couple of yards in this stuff," he said to Lucinda.

She looked at him. "I gather you think that is a good thing?"

"Mrs. Daykin will not notice us until we open the door and walk into her shop."

"You're convinced that she is involved in this affair, aren't you?"

"Yes, and if I'm right she will have reason to be wary of both of us. Me, because I am a stranger to her and a stranger with a battered face, at that. You, because of the theft of the fern."

"But if you are wrong and she is innocent?"

"Then she will have no qualms about answering our questions, especially since you will be present to assure her that I am not a member of the criminal class."

He opened the door, kicked down the carriage steps and descended, trying not to jolt his ribs any more than necessary. He was feeling much improved today, thanks to Lucinda's tonics, but he was still sore in places.

The prospect of finding answers was also extremely therapeutic. The icy thrill of the hunt sleeted through his veins. When he reached up to assist Lucinda, he discovered that she was tense with excitement, too. Energy pulsed in the air around them. The intimacy of the shared sensation aroused him. He wondered if she felt the same sensual pull.

She lowered the veil of her hat to cover her face and gave him her gloved hand. He closed his fingers around hers, enjoying the contours of her delicate, feminine bones. He could feel the shape of her ring beneath the fabric of her glove, as well. When she gripped his hand a little tighter to steady herself on the steps, he was surprised by the strength of her grasp. All that gardening work in her conservatory, he thought. She was stronger than she appeared.

They walked to the door of the shop. The windows were unlit.

"One would think that she would have a light on inside, given the fog today," Lucinda observed. "It must be quite dark in there."

"Yes," Caleb said, cold certainty shifting through him, phantom-like. "Very dark, indeed." *The darkness of death,* his senses whispered.

He tried the door. It was locked.

"Closed," Lucinda said, dismayed. "We have wasted our time."

"Not necessarily." He reached into his coat pocket and retrieved a small lockpick.

Lucinda took a sudden, quick breath. "Good heavens, sir, surely you can't mean to break into the shop."

"There is no 'Closed' sign in the window," Caleb said. "You are a professional acquaintance of hers. It is only reasonable that out of concern that Mrs. Daykin might have had an accident or fallen ill, you would go inside to check on her."

"But there is nothing to indicate that there is anything wrong."

"One can't be too careful. Dangerous places, apothecary shops."

"But . . ."

He got the door open, gripped her arm, swept her inside and closed the door again before she could finish the sentence.

"Well, I suppose a little breaking and entering is nothing compared to the risk of being arrested for poisoning Lord Fairburn," Lucinda said. Her voice was a trifle thin and a bit higher than usual but otherwise gratifyingly cool.

"That's the spirit, Miss Bromley," he said. "Look for the silver lining, I always say."

"Something tells me you've never said that before in your entire life, Mr. Jones."

"Those of us blessed with a cheerful and positive temperament always say that sort of nonsense."

He could not see her eyes because of the veil but he could feel her watching him in that knowing way of hers.

"You are aroused, aren't you?" she said.

He felt as though he had just slammed into a brick wall. The breath was knocked out of his lungs. *Good Lord.* He had been aware from the outset of their association that she was an unusual female. Nevertheless, even for her, it was a very direct question.

"What?" he said when nothing more clever came to mind.

"Your psychical senses," she explained calmly. "They are aroused. I can feel the energy that is swirling around you."

"My senses. Right. *Aroused*. That is one word for it."
He concentrated on a survey of the room. "Not the one
I generally use, but accurate enough. In its own way."

"What word do you prefer?"

"Elevated. Heightened. Open. Hot."

"*Hot*. Hmm. Yes, that is a very good description of
what it feels like when one employs one's talent to the
fullest extent. There is a sense of heat involved, just as
there is when one walks or runs or climbs a flight of stairs
very quickly. Such exercise results in a sensation of
warmth. One's pulse beats faster. A person might even
perspire as a result of the internal heat."

His imagination conjured a riveting image of her
body damp from the heat of sexual desire. His own pulse
accelerated rapidly.

"Energy is energy," he muttered, "regardless of where
on the spectrum it is produced."

"I had never thought of it in terms of physics."

He felt his jaw clench. "Miss Bromley, I wonder if
we might continue this very interesting conversation
some other time. I find it distracting."

"Yes, of course. Sorry."

He refocused his attention on the interior of the
shop. The deep shadows formed a palpable gloom that
was as thick as the fog outside the windows. The atmosphere was clouded with the fragrance of dried herbs,
spices and flowers, as well as more acerbic, medicinal
scents.

"Oh, dear," Lucinda whispered. "My fern."

"What? Where?"

"I fear that Mrs. Daykin is dealing poison from these
premises." Her shoulders stiffened. "A poison made with
my fern."

"Are you certain?"

"I can sense it." She walked slowly through the shop

and went behind the front counter. "There are traces of it back here."

He watched her. "Is it the poison that killed Fairburn?"

"Yes." She began opening drawers and cupboards. "But I do not think she keeps a supply here. As I said, I can only detect the merest traces. In the past she has sold other kinds of poisons, as well. I can sense them, too."

"I expect that explains her business success."

He began to prowl through the room using what he thought of as his other vision to take in details in a way that would have been impossible if he had relied only on his normal five senses. Brick by crystal brick he added to the multidimensional maze that he was constructing in his mind.

"What are you searching for?" Lucinda asked.

"Things," he said absently. "Details. Elements that do not feel right and those that do. I'm sorry, Lucinda, I do not know how to explain my talent."

"What if Mrs. Daykin returns while we are on the premises?" she asked uneasily.

"She won't."

"How can you be so certain of that?"

He flipped through a stack of receipts. "I do not believe that Mrs. Daykin is among the living."

"She's *dead*?"

"I'd say that there is a ninety-eight percent probability that the answer is yes."

"Good grief, how can you know that?" Lucinda crumpled her veil on the brim of her hat and looked at him with an expression of stark wonder. "What is it about the atmosphere in this room that speaks of death to you?"

"There is a certain kind of psychical residue left by malevolent forces and acts of great violence."

"And you can sense them?"

"It is part of my gift." He opened a drawer and removed a sheaf of papers. "Or my curse, depending on one's point of view."

"I see," she said, gently. "It must be a difficult talent, given that there is so much violence in the world."

He looked at her across the counter and found himself compelled to tell her the whole truth even though he knew she might despise him for it. "You will no doubt be appalled to learn that I experience what can only be described as an exhilarating excitement at times like this."

She did not so much as flinch. "I understand."

He could only stare at her for a few seconds. Perhaps she had not heard him correctly.

"I doubt that very much, Lucinda."

"There is nothing strange about your reaction, sir. You are using your senses in the manner which nature intended. I experience a similar sense of satisfaction when I am able to concoct a healing tisane that will improve a person's spirits or even save a life."

"Unlike you, I am not in the business of saving lives or sanity," he said. "I seek answers to the riddles posed by violence."

"And in the process you save lives," she insisted, "just as you saved that young boy who was kidnapped by the cult."

He was not sure how to respond to that. "Trust me when I tell you that whoever came here with violence in mind left with the certain knowledge that his errand was successful."

"You can detect that, as well?"

"Yes."

She looked at a sheaf of papers he had removed from the drawer. "What have you got there?"

"Receipts. The latest are dated yesterday. There are none for today." He dropped the receipts back into the drawer and picked up the newspaper lying on a shelf behind the counter. "This paper is a day old. Everything came to a stop here in this shop sometime yesterday."

"You are quite certain that Mrs. Daykin didn't simply leave in a great hurry?"

He opened the cash register and removed a handful of notes and some coins. "If she had fled the premises, I'm sure she would have taken the day's profits with her."

Lucinda contemplated the money with a somber expression. "Yes." Shock flashed across her face. "Are you saying that she is still here?"

He examined a row of small, neatly labeled apothecary jars. "Upstairs, no doubt."

"You are strolling around down here, casually looking for clues, when you know that there is a dead woman at the top of the stairs?"

For the first time she sounded truly shocked; no, *outraged*.

He looked at her, frowning slightly. "It is how I work. I like to get the whole picture. I'll deal with the body in due course—"

"For pity's sake." She headed for the stairs. "We will deal with the body now. For your information, sir, the dead come first. Clues can wait."

"Why?" he asked, quite blank. "The woman passed hours ago. Very likely during the night. A few minutes' delay in our discovery of the corpse will make no difference."

But Lucinda was already on the stairs, skirts grasped in both hands. The street-sweeper ruffles at the hemline swished across the treads, revealing glimpses of her high-heeled boots.

"It is a matter of decency and respect, sir," she said sternly.

"Huh." He followed her up the stairs. "Hadn't thought of it in those terms."

"Obviously. You are too focused on gathering evidence and clues."

"It is what I do, Lucinda." Nevertheless, he kept following her up the stairs. He did not want her to discover the body alone. She might unintentionally disturb important evidence.

"Do you really believe we will find Mrs. Daykin's body in her rooms?" Lucinda asked when she reached the landing.

"Bodies are difficult to conceal and transport. Why would the killer bother to remove his victim from the scene of the crime?"

"Victim?" She paused, her gloved hand on the doorknob. "Then you think this is a case of murder?"

"Well, yes, of course. Isn't that what we have been talking about?"

Her hand tightened around the knob. "I thought perhaps she might have taken her own life."

"Suicide? Why the devil would she do that?"

"Guilt? For all the deadly poison that she has evidently sold?"

"It appears she was dealing the stuff for a long time. I very much doubt that she was suddenly stricken with remorse within the past twenty-four hours."

He was growing concerned. Lucinda appeared to have plunged into a very odd mood. Perhaps it was the fact that they were about to encounter a body. No, not just that, he decided. Something else. He was inept when it came to explaining strong emotions but he certainly recognized them when he saw them. Beneath the façade of cool composure, she was agitated.

He reached toward the knob and covered her gloved hand with his own. "What is it? What is wrong?"

She looked up at him, dread in her eyes. "What if Mrs. Daykin was killed because of me, Caleb?"

"Damnation, so that's the problem." He captured her face between his gloved hands, forcing her to meet his eyes. "Listen closely, Lucinda. Whatever happened inside that room is not your fault. If Mrs. Daykin is dead, as I believe, it is because she was somehow involved in this affair of poison."

"Perhaps she was merely an innocent bystander who made the mistake of telling Dr. Hulsey that I was in possession of an unusual fern."

"Stop, Lucinda. Whatever else she was, Mrs. Daykin was no innocent bystander. You said yourself she had been dealing poison for some time."

"What if the person selling the poison out of this shop was someone else? An employee, perhaps? It is possible that Mrs. Daykin never knew what was going on."

"She knew."

"She was an apothecary, a woman with a true talent for healing, surely she would never—"

"You know the old saying *That which is strong enough to cure is strong enough to kill.* The business of poison no doubt pays well. Greed is one motive I do comprehend."

Gently but firmly he removed her hand from the knob and opened the door. The miasma of death spilled out.

"Dear heaven." Lucinda yanked a dainty square of embroidered linen out of a pocket in her cloak and held it over her nose and mouth. "You were right."

He pulled out his own handkerchief to blunt the smell. Unfortunately, nothing could soften the psychical impact. The body no longer generated an aura or energy of any kind, but the act of dying left its mark on a room.

There was no indication of physical violence. The woman on the floor appeared to have simply collapsed. But her eyes and mouth were wide open in an expression of frozen horror.

"It is Mrs. Daykin," Lucinda said quietly.

"Poisoned?" he asked.

Lucinda moved closer to the dead woman. She stood looking down for a moment. He could feel a whisper of psychical currents and knew that she was heightening her senses.

"No," she said, very sure of herself. "But I do not see any signs of a wound, either. Perhaps she suffered a stroke or a heart attack."

"Bit of a coincidence, don't you think?"

"Yes. But if not by natural causes, how did she die?"

"I don't know but she was most certainly murdered. What is more, she let the killer into this room."

"You can sense that with your talent?" she asked, clearly impressed.

"No. I can deduce that from the fact that there is no sign of forced entry."

"Ah. Yes, I see what you mean. A lover, perhaps?"

"Or a business associate. In my brief career as an investigator, I have discovered that either can prove treacherous."

Keeping his senses open, he searched the room swiftly and methodically. Out of the corner of his eye he saw Lucinda move to a side table and pick up a framed photograph.

"This must be her son," she said. "The one she mentioned the day she visited me. There is something familiar about him."

Caleb straightened and studied the picture. The subject was a young man in his early twenties. He was stiffly posed in a dark suit. His hairline was already starting to recede. He gazed out at the viewer with a fixed intensity typical of photographic portraits.

"Do you recognize him?" Caleb asked.

"No. It was just that, for an instant, when I first saw the picture I had a fleeting notion that he reminded me of someone I have met." She shook her head and put the photograph on the table. "It is probably his resemblance to his mother that I noticed."

He glanced at Daykin. "He doesn't look much like her but I suppose there must be something of her in his looks."

"Yes." She watched him open the drawers of a small desk. "Anything of interest there?"

"Bills, letters to firms that supplied her with herbs and chemicals." He shuffled through another stack of papers. "Nothing of a personal nature." He started to close the desk but stopped when he saw the tiny scrap of paper tucked into the back of a cubbyhole. He withdrew it.

"What is it?" Lucinda asked.

"A series of numbers. It looks like the combination to a safe."

"I do not see one," Lucinda said.

A rush of certainty swept through him. "It is here, somewhere."

He found it moments later, hidden behind the headboard of the small bed. The combination written on the slip of paper opened it immediately. Inside was a notebook and three small packets.

He sensed energy flaring again and recognized it intuitively. Lucinda.

She reached down to stay his arm. "Be careful. Those

packets contain poison, the same kind that killed Lord Fairburn."

He did not question her conclusion. Satisfaction flashed through him.

"I told you that Mrs. Daykin was no innocent bystander," he said. He removed the notebook and thumbed through it quickly.

"What is it?" Lucinda asked, peering over his shoulder. "The writing looks like nonsense."

"It's a code." He studied the cryptic notes for a few seconds and then smiled a little when the pattern appeared almost immediately. "A very simple one. I believe we have found Mrs. Daykin's record of the transactions concerning the sales of poison. Spellar will be delighted. This notebook may well provide him with the information he needs to close the Fairburn case as well as a number of others."

"Why on earth would Mrs. Daykin have kept an account of such transactions? It is damning evidence."

Another whisper of certainty stirred his senses. "She must have concluded that the risk outweighed the business advantages."

"What do you mean?"

He held up the notebook. "This journal makes excellent blackmail material."

"Good grief. Mrs. Daykin profited coming and going. First she sold the poison and then she extorted money from those who used it."

"A businesswoman through and through."

Sixteen

*T*hree days later, at one o'clock in the morning, Lucinda sat with Victoria on a velvet cushioned bench. The bench was situated on a balcony overlooking a glittering ballroom.

Together they surveyed the brilliant scene. The reception for the recently engaged Mr. Thaddeus Ware and his fiancée, Leona Hewitt, was at its height. It was not the guests of honor Lucinda and Victoria were watching, however.

"They make a very attractive couple," Victoria said, peering through her opera glasses. "But I'm afraid a match is out of the question. Young Mr. Sutton won't do at all."

"What a shame," Lucinda said. "He seems a very pleasant gentleman."

"He is." Victoria lowered the opera glasses and fortified herself with a sip of champagne from her glass. "He's just not right for your cousin."

"You can tell that much from up here?"

"At this distance I can only get a vague sense of the resonating currents between them, but that is enough to assure me that he will not do for her." She made a small mark in a little notebook and raised the glasses to her eyes again with military precision.

Lucinda followed her gaze. Down below a vast

number of elegantly dressed couples, including Patricia and the unsuitable Mr. Sutton, danced to the sensual strains of a waltz. Patricia looked at once innocent and ravishing in a pale pink satin gown trimmed with a cascade of pink tulle. Long pink gloves sheathed her arms. Delicate pink flower ornaments sparkled in her hair.

Lucinda was well aware that she herself presented a decidedly different appearance. *Innocent* was not the word that sprang to mind. Victoria's dressmaker had chosen cobalt blue silk for her. *Perfect for* les cheveux rouge *and those blue eyes,* Madam LaFontaine had declared in an excruciatingly bad French accent that had likely originated near the docks, not Paris.

The gown was cut low to reveal what Lucinda considered a rather daring expanse of shoulder and bosom. Madam LaFontaine had refused to raise the neckline so much as half an inch. Victoria had agreed with her. *The secret to carrying off a notorious reputation is to flaunt it,* she had told Lucinda. *You must be bold.*

Lucinda was not entirely certain the woman-of-the-world approach was the correct one but there was no denying that Victoria knew what she was about when it came to matchmaking. Patricia's dance card was completely filled. She was going to be exhausted when the ball was over, Lucinda thought, smiling a little. Her dancing slippers would likely have holes in the soles. Each time she came off the floor Patricia barely had a chance to take a few sips of lemonade before the next young man appeared to claim his turn.

"What do you see when you look at a room full of people, Lady Milden?" Lucinda asked.

"A great many couples who should never have married and an equal number who are engaged in illicit liaisons."

"That must be rather depressing."

"It is." Victoria set the opera glasses aside and took another sip of champagne. "But I find that my new career as a matchmaker does a great deal to elevate my spirits. A successful match is an antidote, you see."

"According to my count, Patricia has danced with nine different candidates," Lucinda said. "How many more are there?"

"Two from my files but I spotted several more gentlemen who are not my clients who managed to get their names on her card. That is fine with me. I always like to allow for the unexpected. Sometimes two people simply find each other with no help from a matchmaker. One would not want to rule out that possibility. That is, after all, how Thaddeus and Leona met."

"At a ball like this?"

"Well, not exactly," Victoria conceded. "A museum gallery, actually."

"Ah, they have artistic interests in common."

"No," Victoria said. "It was the middle of the night and it wasn't a mutual interest in art that brought them together. They were both there to steal a certain artifact from a very bad man. Nearly got themselves killed."

"Good heavens. How very . . ." She stopped because she could not find the appropriate word. "Unusual."

"They are an unusual couple. He has a talent for mesmerism. She reads crystals."

Lucinda looked down at Thaddeus and Leona. She was no matchmaker but even from this distance she could sense the bond of intimacy between them. It was there in the way Thaddeus stood close to his fiancée and in the way she smiled at him.

"They are very fortunate to have found each other," she said quietly.

"Yes," Victoria said. "As soon as I saw them together I knew they were a perfect match."

"What will you do if none of the gentlemen here tonight proves to be right for Patricia?"

"I have scheduled a number of teas, lectures, museum and gallery visits as well as another ball next week. Never fear, I will find someone for her."

"You take a very positive attitude toward your work."

"That is easy to do when one has a client as charming as your cousin," Victoria said.

"What happens when you are faced with a potential client who is not particularly charming?"

Victoria gave her a sharp, searching look. "Why do you ask?"

Lucinda flushed. "It was merely a hypothetical question."

Victoria picked up the glasses and turned her attention back to the dance floor. "If you are talking about Caleb Jones, the problem is unlikely to ever arise."

"Why not?"

"Caleb Jones is a very complicated man and he gets more so by the day."

"Is that a polite way of saying that he will never find a good match?"

"I understand that you have spent some time with him lately. Surely you have realized that he does not view the world in what most people would call a normal manner. Nor is he at all predictable when it comes to the proprieties."

Lucinda thought about Caleb's habit of showing up at her front door every morning.

"He does not conform to the usual rules of etiquette," she said. "I'll give you that."

"Bah. He knows how to behave. He is a Jones, after all. But his manners are quite deplorable. He is impatient with others to the point of rudeness, and he avoids social

145

gatherings whenever possible. I have it on good authority that when he is at home he spends every waking moment alone in his laboratory and library. How many women could be happy with a man like that?"

"Well—"

"He will marry, of course. He's a Jones. It's his duty. But I doubt that he will ask me to match him." Victoria sniffed. "Thank heavens."

"You really don't believe that you could find him a good match?"

"Let's just say that I think it highly unlikely that Caleb Jones and the woman he finally weds will ever know true marital happiness. Not that such a situation would make them unique in any way. Indeed, it is the norm in the polite world."

"I agree that Mr. Jones can be somewhat brusque but I think that what you perceive as his difficult personality is merely a by-product of his talent and the self-control he employs to master it."

"That may be true but when you get to be my age, my dear, you will realize that such an extreme degree of self-mastery is not particularly desirable in a man. It tends to make one rigid, unyielding and inflexible."

It was not as if she had not made a similar observation to Patricia, Lucinda reminded herself. Nevertheless, it was depressing to dwell on all the reasons why Caleb would never find happiness.

"If you ask me, I doubt very much that Caleb will even notice his own lack of marital satisfaction," Victoria continued, as if she had read Lucinda's mind. "It is not in his nature to fall in love. He will put a ring on some woman's finger, get her pregnant and then retreat to his laboratory and library."

"Are you saying that Mr. Jones is immune to strong passions?" Lucinda asked, shocked.

"In a word, yes."

"No offense, madam, but you are quite wrong."

It was Victoria's turn to be surprised. "Never say you believe that Caleb Jones is capable of experiencing the more delicate sensibilities?"

"*Delicate sensibilities* may not be quite the right phrase but I assure you, he is capable of intense emotion and great depth of feeling."

Victoria's eyes widened. "Why, Miss Bromley, I do not know what to say. You are the only person I have ever met who would make such a statement about Caleb Jones."

"I suspect that he is a very misunderstood man, even within the bosom of his family."

"Fascinating," Victoria murmured. "Speaking of Caleb, I wonder where he is tonight. As I said, he avoids social affairs whenever possible but he does have a sense of responsibility toward the family. I did expect him to show up for a few minutes, at least. He and Thaddeus are cousins, after all."

"I believe Mr. Jones is very busy with his current investigation," Lucinda said.

Defending Caleb and explaining his actions was starting to become a habit, she thought, a bad one, no doubt. Entirely unnecessary, as well. If ever there was a man who could take care of himself, a man who could not have cared less about the opinions of others, it was Caleb Jones.

The truth was, she had no idea where he was or what he was doing. She had not seen him since breakfast that morning. He had arrived promptly at eight-thirty, downed a large helping of eggs and toast, said something about conferring with Inspector Spellar and then dashed off in a hansom.

Although he was obviously sleeping better, she was

growing concerned because the faint, unwholesome tension was still there in his aura. She wondered if she should change the ingredients in the tisane. But her senses assured her that she had prepared the appropriate tonic.

A sudden stirring of awareness brought her out of her reverie. She looked down into the ballroom and saw Caleb at once. He stood in a shadowy alcove, partially concealed by a decorative screen. He studied the dancers the way a lion at the watering hole might watch a herd of unwary antelope.

"There is Mr. Jones," she said.

"Which one?" Victoria asked vaguely. "There are any number of them here tonight."

"Caleb." Lucinda motioned with her fan. "Behind the palms."

"Yes, I see him." Victoria leaned forward to peer more intently through the opera glasses. "So like him to sneak in through a side door rather than use the main entrance and have to deal with the formalities. I told you, the man detests this sort of social affair. If past history is any guide, he'll stay for five minutes and then disappear."

He might not be planning to stay long but he had taken the time to change into black-and-white evening attire, Lucinda noticed. The elegantly cut coat and trousers and the snow-white linen shirt underscored the invisible aura of power that always seemed to shimmer around him.

He left the alcove and prowled around the outskirts of the crowd, inclining his head curtly once or twice at certain individuals he passed but managing to avoid conversation. He made his way to Thaddeus and Leona, spoke to them briefly and then looked up toward the balcony.

He saw her at once. She caught her breath. *It is as if he knew precisely where to find me,* she thought.

He said something else to Thaddeus, nodded quite civilly to Leona, and then he walked away, vanishing down what appeared to be a service hall. Lucinda sat back, firmly squashing the sharp twinge of disappointment. What had she expected? That he might actually seek her out for a moment or two of conversation?

Victoria snapped her fingers. "Poof, gone already. Typical. Imagine trying to find a good match for a man who cannot be bothered to even ask a lady to dance."

"It would certainly be a challenge," Lucinda agreed. *But I would far rather he left than be obliged to watch him take the floor with one of the ladies down there,* she thought. The realization was disturbing. She clenched the folded fan in her hand. She must not fall in love with Caleb Jones.

"Ah, Mr. Riverton is approaching Patricia," Victoria said. Enthusiasm laced her voice. "I have great hopes for him. A very scholarly type, young Riverton. And his notions on the rights of women are quite advanced."

Lucinda studied Riverton through the bars of the railing. "A nice-looking gentleman."

"Yes. Strong talent, as well." Victoria studied the pair for a moment. "It appears that the energy between them is at least somewhat compatible." She lowered the glasses and made a note in her little book. "Definitely worth a closer look."

Lucinda started to lean forward to get a better view of Riverton. She stopped when another shiver of awareness splashed through her. She turned and saw Caleb emerge from the shadows of a dimly lit hall.

"What the devil are you doing up here, Miss Bromley?" he said, not bothering with even a semblance of a polite greeting. "I thought you'd be downstairs."

"And a pleasant good evening to you, too, Mr. Jones," Victoria said dryly.

"Victoria," Caleb said, looking as if he had just now realized she was present. He took her gloved hand and bowed over it with surprising grace. "My apologies. Didn't see you there."

"Of course you did," Victoria said. "It was just that you were concentrating entirely on Miss Bromley."

Caleb's brows rose slightly. "I was looking for her, yes."

"Do you have some news?" Lucinda asked.

"Yes, as a matter of fact."

He gripped the balcony railing and looked down as though suddenly fascinated by the patterns the dancers were weaving on the ballroom floor. When he turned back to her, the controlled energy in his eyes seemed to burn a little hotter.

"If you will do me the honor of dancing with me, I will tell you what I have learned," he said.

Stunned, she could only stare at him, mouth open in what she suspected was a most unbecoming manner.

"Uh," she got out after an eternity.

"Run along," Victoria said. She rapped the back of Lucinda's gloved hand sharply with her fan. "I'll keep an eye on Patricia."

The sting of the fan broke Lucinda's trance. She swallowed and recovered her senses.

"Thank you very much, Mr. Jones," she said. "But it has been some time since I danced the waltz. I fear I am out of practice."

"So am I, but the pattern is a simple one. I'm sure we'll both manage not to trip over our own feet."

He took her hand and hauled her up off the padded bench before she could think of any more arguments. She glanced back once over her shoulder, but there was no help from that quarter. Victoria was watching them with a most peculiar expression.

The next thing she knew she was being led swiftly along a long, dim hall and down a narrow, cramped flight of servants' stairs. When they reached the bottom of the staircase Caleb opened a door and drew her out into the dazzling ballroom. He forged a path through the crowd with characteristic single-minded determination.

And then, in a heady instant, she was in his arms, just as she had been that day in the library when he kissed her.

He swept her into the sensual pattern of a slow waltz. She knew that heads were turning, both on the floor and off; knew that she and Caleb were drawing the sort of attention she had so hoped to avoid. But she no longer cared. Caleb's powerful hand was warm and strong at the small of her back and he was looking at her as though there was no one else in the room. Heat and energy enveloped them, inextricably entwined with the music.

"You see?" he said. "The patterns of the waltz are not the sort of thing one forgets."

She was not dancing, she thought. She was flying. "So it would seem, Mr. Jones. Now, tell me your news."

"I spoke with Inspector Spellar shortly before I came here. He has made an arrest in the Fairburn case based on the evidence in Daykin's little book of transactions."

"Lady Fairburn?"

"No, the sister, Hannah Rathbone. She collapsed and confessed immediately when Spellar showed her the notebook. Rathbone's name is in it."

"I see. I suppose she killed Fairburn because she wanted her sister to become a wealthy widow."

"That would certainly be the logical explanation. But according to Spellar, Rathbone murdered her brother-in-law because he'd just ended the affair that he was having with her."

"Good heavens. So it was a crime of passion, not of money."

"As I said, not the most logical of motives but there you have it. You are no longer in danger of being arrested for the Fairburn murder."

"Mr. Jones, I cannot thank you enough—"

"There is, however, still the problem of your fern showing up in the poison that Daykin sold."

Alarm jolted through her. "But with Mrs. Daykin dead, there is no one who knows that it was an ingredient in her poison."

"There is at least one person who knows," Caleb said.

"Oh, dear. You mean Dr. Hulsey."

"We can now say with great certainty that Hulsey was well acquainted with Mrs. Daykin. He made at least some of the poison she sold."

A thought struck her. "Do you think Hulsey might be the one who killed her?"

"No," Caleb said.

"What makes you so sure of that?"

"Hulsey specializes in dangerous chemicals. If he wanted to murder someone, he would have been inclined to employ a weapon with which he was familiar."

"Poison."

"Yes."

A chill went through her. "But I did not detect any on the body."

"Which tells us that someone else killed her."

"One of her blackmail victims?"

"Possible," Caleb allowed. "But according to that notebook of hers, she had been in the business for years. The fact that someone only recently decided to murder her is—"

"I know. Too much of a coincidence. I thought the same thing about my father's so-called suicide. I could not believe that he would put a pistol to his head immediately after his partner was found dead."

"What the hell?" Caleb came to an abrupt halt in the middle of the dance floor. "Your father did not take poison?"

Aware that those around her were staring in avid curiosity, she lowered her voice to a whisper.

"No," she said.

"Damnation. He was murdered. Why the devil didn't you tell me?"

He grabbed her wrist and hauled her off the floor, through the crowd and out into the night-darkened gardens. When they were alone he gripped her shoulders.

"I want to know exactly what happened to your father," he said.

"He was killed with a pistol," she said. "It was made to look as if he pulled the trigger himself. But I am convinced that someone shot him."

Energy whispered in the night. She could feel the force of Caleb's talent.

"You are right, of course," he said.

An incredible tide of relief swept over her.

"Mr. Jones, I do not know what to say. You are the only one who has ever believed me."

Seventeen

"It's all connected," Caleb said softly.

"What is?" she asked, a little breathless from the dancing and the cold fire of his energy swirling around her. "Have you had some sort of insight?"

"Yes, thanks to you." His jaw tightened. "I should have thought to ask the obvious question back at the start of this affair. I was too intent on tracking Hulsey."

"What is this obvious question?"

"How does your father's murder and the murder of his partner connect to the theft of the fern?"

"What?" Shaken, she searched his shadow-etched face. "I don't understand. How could there possibly be a link between those events?"

"That, Miss Bromley, is what I must discover."

"But you sense that there is one?"

"As I said, I should have observed it sooner. I can only say that I have been somewhat distracted."

"Well, it is not as if you have not had your hands full, what with destroying that evil cult and discovering that the man I knew as Dr. Knox was the mad scientist you have been searching for. Not to mention the little matter of finding Mrs. Daykin's body and making certain that I did not get arrested for murder. You have been rather busy of late, sir. One can understand why you might not have bothered with the murders of two men who died a year and a half ago."

"Those were only minor issues," he said. "It was the other thing that got in the way."

"What other thing?"

"While we are on the subject, I believe that your fiancé's death is also linked to this business. It has to be."

She was stunned anew. "You can't mean to connect Mr. Glasson's murder to this thing, too."

"It is all of a piece," he said. "The pattern is quite clear now. The problem, as I said, was the great distraction that has interfered with my thought processes."

"Indeed?" She raised her brows. "And just what was this astonishing distraction that is so powerful it caused the very talented Caleb Jones to make a mistake?"

"You," he said simply.

She was speechless.

"What?" she finally managed.

He caught her face between his strong hands. "You are the distraction, Lucinda. I have never known anyone who could disorder my thoughts the way you do."

"That does not sound like a compliment."

"It was not intended as a compliment. It was a statement of fact. Furthermore, I do not think I will be able to concentrate well until I know for certain that you find me to be equally distracting."

"Oh," she whispered. "Yes. Yes, I do find you distracting, sir. Extremely so."

"I am very pleased to hear that."

His mouth closed over hers.

Her senses were suddenly on fire, wide open to the night. The gardens came alive in the darkness, burning with an iridescent radiance that swept across the spectrum. Seconds ago the flowers blooming at the edge of the terrace had been invisible in the shadows. Now they were transformed into small fairy lanterns, pulsing light in a myriad of nameless colors. The grass produced an emerald aurora. The tall hedges were transformed into glowing green walls. The energy of life sang to her senses.

Caleb pulled her closer, tighter. His mouth slid heavily off hers and found her throat.

"Do you want me, Lucinda?" he asked roughly. "That is what I must know. I do not think that I will ever again be able to focus properly until the question is answered."

She had abandoned all hope of ever experiencing the power of passion. Now the awesome force of it swirled through her like a great tempest. She would betray no one if she let these powerful winds sweep her away. The only risk was to her heart, and it was a grave one. But the thought of never knowing the glorious sensations that she sensed awaited her in Caleb's arms was by far the more appalling alternative. *Better to have loved and lost.*

She raised her gloved fingers to his face. "I desire you, Caleb. Is that the answer you want?"

"More than I have ever wanted anything in my life."

His mouth closed over hers, again, searing and hungry. The music and muffled sounds of the ballroom seemed to fade into another dimension. Raw power pulsed hot in the night. The tide of bright, fierce energy drew her deeper into an intoxicating chaos.

She wrapped her arms around Caleb's neck and opened her mouth for him. The shimmering atmosphere shifted around her. It took her a few seconds to realize that Caleb had picked her up in his arms and was carrying her away from the terrace, deep into the phosphorescent gardens.

"I can feel the heat in you," he said. "Your senses are hot, aren't they?"

"Yes." She drew her fingertip along the line of his jaw. "So are yours."

"This garden is your world. What does it look like to you?"

"It is magical. Alive. Every plant, down to the tiniest blade of grass, gives off a faint luminescence. I can see a thousand shades of green in the leaves. The flowers shine with a light all their own."

"It sounds like a fairy-tale landscape."

"It is," she said. "What do you see?"

"Only you." He stopped in front of a low, darkened structure. "Open the door."

She reached down, found the knob and twisted it. The door swung inward. A pleasant warmth and a maelstrom of intense botanical scents flowed out. Her senses hummed with the potent energy of dried lavender, roses, chamomile, mint, rosemary, thyme and bay. In the moonlight she could see dark bunches of herbs and flowers suspended from the ceiling. On the floor were a number of baskets filled with more fragrant clusters.

"A drying shed," she said, enthralled. "I have one of my own."

"We can be private here."

He lowered her slowly to her feet and crossed the room to where a wooden chair stood. He picked up the chair and wedged it under the doorknob. Then he came back to her.

"You think of everything," she said.

"I try."

Very gently he removed her eyeglasses and set them aside. Then he took her back into his arms.

She was trembling so with anticipation and excitement

that she had to clutch his shoulders in order to keep her balance.

He kissed her again and then he turned her gently so that her back was to him. He began to unfasten the delicate hooks of her stiffened bodice. Within moments the gown was open.

He kissed her bare shoulder. "Thank the Lord you are not wearing one of those damned steel corsets."

"The Rational Dress Society considers them to be very unhealthy," she explained.

He laughed, a low, throaty growl. "Not to mention a great nuisance at times like this."

He turned her back to face him and gently lowered the bodice, taking the tiers of elaborately draped skirts with it, until the gown pooled around her feet. She was left in only her thin chemise, drawers, stockings and shoes.

Entranced, she unbuttoned his coat and pushed her hands inside, thrilling to the heat of his body. He shrugged out of the garment with quick, impatient motions, unknotted his tie and unfastened the front of his shirt. She flattened her palms against his bare chest.

"We need a bed," Caleb said.

He moved away from her, picked up the nearest basket and turned it upside down. A vast quantity of dried herbs and flowers tumbled out of it, geraniums, rose petals, eucalyptus, lemon balm. He emptied a second and then a third and fourth basket until there was a large, aromatic heap on the floor. Her wide-open senses were so dazzled by the heady essence of so much massed botanical energy that it was all she could do not to dive into the pile.

Caleb covered the fragrant mattress with his coat and drew her down onto the makeshift bed. The fragile, dried herbs and petals were crushed beneath their weight, releasing more ethereal, intoxicating energy into the atmosphere.

He stretched out alongside her, half covering her, and closed one hand over the curve of her breast. Something inside her was stirred to an even higher level of awareness. She heard a soft, choked cry and realized that it had come from her own throat.

"Hush," he ordered gently. He sounded as if he was swallowing laughter or possibly a groan. He brushed her lips in warning. "We have this place to ourselves but we do not want to risk drawing the attention of others who might decide to take a stroll through the gardens."

She surfaced momentarily from the delightful trance. Her reputation could scarcely sink any lower in the eyes of the world but it would be beyond mortifying to be discovered nude in a man's arms. Some things a woman simply could not live down.

"Never fear," Caleb said. "I will know if anyone comes near this shed. I am not a true hunter but excellent hearing is a family trait."

"Are you sure?" she asked.

"Will you not trust me to protect you?"

He was as solid as a block of granite. If he made a vow, he would keep it, she thought.

"I trust you," she whispered, amazed to hear herself say the words. The truth shook her to the core. "I *do* trust you, Caleb Jones."

He leaned over her and kissed her slowly, reverently. She knew that it was his way of sealing the promise he had made.

She softened against him, thrilling to his hard, heavy weight. He touched her as though she were a rare and exotic orchid. Energy flashed and pulsed between them, mixing with the potent essence of the dried herbs and flowers.

Shock snapped through her when she felt Caleb's hand slide between her legs. She froze.

"I need to feel your heat," he whispered.

She parted her thighs for him, hesitantly at first and then with a sense of pooling excitement. His warm palm moved along her stocking to the bare skin above her garter. The intimacy of the experience was almost unbearable. Heat pulsed deep within her.

"You hold everything a true alchemist could ever hope to find," Caleb said. The words were thick with wonder. "All the secrets of midnight and fire."

He stroked her gently, deeply, finding the sensitive places within and without, enchanting her. She drew in a sharp breath, every muscle tightening. The compelling tension twisting inside her somehow blended with the exotic energy of the drying shed until she could no longer distinguish between the normal and the paranormal.

Instinctively, wanting to know Caleb as intimately as he knew her, she slid her hand down his hard body. When she reached his trousers she discovered that he had already opened them. Her exploring fingers found the heavy, rigid length of his erection. Startled, she pulled back a little.

Caleb went very still.

"Do you find me . . . unacceptable?" he whispered. There was a terrible flat quality in the question. She sensed pain beneath the grim self-control.

"You are more than . . . acceptable." She pressed her face against his chest, grateful for the darkness that concealed her head-to-toe blush. "It is just that I was not expecting quite so much that was so . . . acceptable."

She felt his chest shake.

"Don't you dare laugh at me, Caleb Jones."

"Never," he said.

"I can feel you laughing."

"I'm smiling, not laughing. There is a significant difference."

She started to argue the point but he was stroking her again, sending ripples of delicious tension through her, and she could no longer think coherently. She sensed that she was about to fly into the very heart of the storm. Impulsively she circled him with her fingers, no longer worried by his size. She heard him suck in a harsh breath.

"I hurt you," she said, releasing him instantly.

"No," he grated.

Tentatively she touched him again. He groaned into her throat.

"Come for me," he said.

He moved his hand on her again but it was hardly necessary. The heat in the words generated more than enough power to fling her into the swirling currents. The tension inside her was released in a white-hot flash of energy that was unlike anything she had ever known.

Caleb moved on top of her and thrust heavily into her.

Pain and exquisite pleasure mingled for an unbearable moment, unleashing still more fire across the spectrum. Dark waves thundered through her. Caleb's energy, she thought, flowing at full strength. She understood then that he had freed it from the talons of self-control that he employed to restrain it.

It was as though floodgates had been opened. A torrent of power engulfed her, drowning the pain, threatening to swamp her senses. The irresistible currents pulsed stronger as Caleb thrust again and again into her. Somehow she knew that she had to respond in some fashion.

She dug her nails into his shoulders and summoned every bit of her own power. Opposing currents clashed violently in the night. The embrace became a battle of wills. Caleb had raw strength on his side but she soon discovered that she had her own feminine power.

For a harrowing moment, she feared that they would somehow destroy each other as the rivers of psychical energy clashed and crashed together.

But even as disaster loomed, she sensed the currents start to resonate between them, each enhancing and sustaining the other until the power she and Caleb generated together was stronger than what either could create alone.

"Lucinda." His voice was ragged, as though he was in great need or terrible pain.

She opened her eyes. He was watching her with such searing intensity she was amazed he did not set fire to the room.

"Lucinda."

This time he spoke her name in wonder.

The muscles of his back turned to granite. His mouth opened on a muffled shout of exultation. And then his climax was upon him, eliciting a second, gentler wave of pleasure deep within her. She felt their auras fuse for a bright, shining moment of shattering intimacy.

Together they rode the flashing, rippling, pulsing currents into the heart of the night.

Eighteen

$\mathcal{T}$he sound of low voices—a man's murmur and a woman's soft, sultry laugh—brought Caleb out of the harmoniously ordered realm where he had been drifting. He listened intently for a few seconds, fixing the location of the couple. The pair was some distance off but headed toward the drying shed.

He sat up, carefully untangling himself from Lucinda. The bed of dried herbs and flowers crunched and crackled beneath his coat. The fragrance mingled with the lingering scents of the lovemaking.

Lucinda stirred and opened her eyes. In the moonlight he could see her bemused, unfocused expression. She smiled, looking remarkably pleased with herself, and raised her fingertips to his mouth.

He caught her hand, kissed it quickly and then yanked his handkerchief out of his pocket. He cleaned her gently and hauled her to her feet and handed her the eyeglasses.

"We must get you dressed," he said into her ear.

"Mmm."

She did not seem to be in any great hurry, he noticed. Bending down, he scooped up the gown and set about trying to get her back into it. He had undressed a few women in his time, but he had never tried to reverse the process. Now he discovered that it was more complicated

163

than it appeared. His lack of experience showed immediately.

"Why in blazes do women wear such damnably heavy clothes?" he grumbled, fastening the hooks.

"Rest assured that this gown is considerably lighter than those many of the fashionable ladies are wearing back in that ballroom. And I'll have you know that, in addition to the fact that I am not wearing a corset, my underclothing and petticoats meet the requirements of the Rational Dress Society. They weigh less than seven pounds."

"I'll take your word for it," he said.

He sensed that she was fighting not to laugh. She was still oblivious to the risk of discovery. It occurred to him that she was not yet aware of the other couple.

"There are two people nearby," he said, putting his mouth very close to her ear. "They are coming in our direction, no doubt intending to use this shed for the same purpose we just did. The door is secure but they will be able to hear voices quite clearly through it."

That got her attention.

"Good heavens." Hurriedly she leaned down, hiked up her skirts and adjusted her stockings.

He concentrated on closing his trousers. Then he refastened his shirt and waistcoat and knotted his tie with the ease of long habit. No man in the Jones family had ever had the patience to employ a valet. He grabbed his coat off the heap of crushed flora and tugged it on quickly. He smiled a little to himself when he caught the rich, spicy scents of Lucinda's body.

"My *hair*," she whispered, aghast. Frantically she struggled to pin up the long strands that had come loose from the complicated chignon. "There is no way I can repair it."

He could hear the voices outside very clearly now.

He clamped a hand across Lucinda's mouth. She stilled instantly.

The doorknob rattled.

"Bloody hell," a man growled. "The damned shed appears to be locked. We'll have to find our privacy elsewhere, my dear."

"Do not even think of suggesting that we repair to some distant corner of the gardens." The lady's voice sharpened. "I am not about to ruin this gown with grass stains."

"I'm sure we'll find some suitable location," the man said quickly.

"Bah. We may as well return to the ballroom. I am out of the mood, in any event. I would much prefer another glass of champagne."

"But, my darling . . ."

The voices faded quickly as the couple retreated in the direction of the big house.

"I do not think that man's evening is going to end as pleasantly as my own," Caleb said.

Lucinda ignored him. "I cannot go back into the ballroom looking like this. You must get me to my carriage. Lady Milden will have to see Patricia home."

"There is no need to panic, Lucinda." Feeling supremely in command of the situation, he removed the chair from under the doorknob. "I will take care of everything."

Solving problems was what he did well, he thought, not without a degree of pride. He took her arm and guided her out of the drying shed.

He had the advantage of knowing the grounds of the Ware mansion as well as he knew those of his own house. It was no trick at all to steer Lucinda around the side, past the kitchen and the tradesmen's entrance and out into the drive.

There were a number of carriages and several hansoms arrayed in front of the big house. Shute broke off a conversation with two other coachmen when he saw Caleb with Lucinda. He tipped his hat in greeting.

"Ready to leave, ma'am?" he asked. After one quick glance he studiously looked away from Lucinda's hair.

"Yes," she said briskly. "Quickly, if you please."

He opened the door and lowered the steps. "What of Miss Patricia?"

"Mr. Jones will request Lady Milden to convey her home. Won't you, Mr. Jones?"

"Certainly," Caleb said, amused by her flustered air.

"Oh, and please ask her to collect my cloak from the footman, too."

"I'll do that," Caleb promised

Lucinda scooped up handfuls of her tiered skirts and flew up the steps into the shadows of the cab. Caleb gripped the edge of the door and leaned inside, enjoying one last dose of her scent and energy.

"I will call on you tomorrow at the usual time," he said.

"What?" She sounded somewhat breathless. "Oh, right. Your daily report."

"And my breakfast. A very important meal, I've been told. Good night, Miss Bromley. Sleep well."

He closed the door and stepped back. Shute nodded at him, climbed up onto the box and picked up the reins.

Caleb watched the vehicle until it disappeared into the light fog. When he could no longer make it out, he turned and went back into the house through a side entrance.

He was en route to the flight of servants' stairs that led to the balcony when a familiar voice in the hallway behind him brought him to a halt.

"Can we interest you in a glass of port?" Gabe asked. "I'd suggest you join us for some billiards but I know how you feel about games of chance these days."

He turned and saw his cousin lounging in the doorway of the billiards room. Behind Gabe stood Thaddeus, a billiard cue in one hand. Both men had removed their evening coats, loosened their ties and rolled up their shirtsleeves.

"What the devil are you two doing here?" Caleb asked. "I would have thought your presence was required in the ballroom."

"Leona and Venetia took pity on us and gave us leave to take a break while they entertain a flock of elderly matrons," Thaddeus said.

"A glass of port sounds like an excellent idea." Caleb walked back toward them. "And so does a game of billiards. I assume the wager is an interesting one?"

Thaddeus and Gabe exchanged unreadable looks.

"You haven't played billiards with us in months," Gabe said.

"I've been busy. There hasn't been any time for billiards." Caleb peeled off his coat and slung it over the back of a chair. "What is the amount of the wager?"

Again, Gabe and Thaddeus looked at each other.

"You never place wagers," Gabe said. "Something about the inherent unpredictability of random chance, I believe."

"Billiards is not a game of random chance." Caleb went to the rack on the wall and selected a cue. "I have no objection to the occasional wager when I can estimate the probabilities involved."

"Very well." Thaddeus looked at Caleb across the width of the table. "Say a hundred pounds? It's just a friendly game among us cousins, after all."

"Make it a thousand," Caleb said. "It will be an even friendlier game that way."

Thaddeus grinned. "You're that sure of winning?"

"Tonight I cannot lose," Caleb said.

Some time later Caleb replaced the cue in the rack. "Thank you, cousins. That was an invigorating interlude. Now, if you don't mind, I must go find Lady Milden and then I'm going home. I have to rise early these days."

"Because of your investigation?" Thaddeus asked.

"No," Caleb said. "Because of breakfast."

Gabe propped himself against the table. "You haven't played billiards in months yet you managed to take a thousand pounds off each of us tonight. What made you so sure you would win?"

Caleb collected his coat from the back of the chair and shrugged into it. "I was feeling lucky." He started toward the door.

"One thing before you leave, cousin," Gabe said.

Caleb paused in the doorway and looked over his shoulder. "What?"

"You may want to brush the dried leaves off the back of your coat before you return to the ballroom," Thaddeus said, straight-faced.

"Are those crushed flowers in your hair?" Gabe added. "I'm almost certain they are not in fashion for gentlemen this season."

Nineteen

Mrs. Shute opened the door to the town house before Shute had brought the carriage to a complete halt. She hurried down the steps garbed in her nightcap and wrapper, the black leather satchel in one hand. In the glow of the nearby gas lamp Lucinda could see the anxiety on her face.

"Here you are at last, Miss Bromley," Mrs. Shute said. "I thought you'd be home much earlier. I would have sent a message but there was no one to deliver it at this late hour."

"What is the matter?" Lucinda asked quickly.

"It's my niece in Guppy Lane," Mrs. Shute said. "She sent word an hour ago that the neighbor's boy, little Harry, is very feverish and having difficulty breathing. She says his mother is frightened half out of her wits."

"I'll go at once," Lucinda said soothingly. "Give me the satchel."

"Thank you, ma'am." Looking greatly relieved, Mrs. Shute handed her the satchel and stepped back. She paused, frowning a little. "Your hair, ma'am. Whatever happened to it?"

"Accident," Lucinda said crisply.

Shute snapped the reins. The carriage barreled off into the foggy night. Lucinda turned up the lamp, opened the satchel and quickly inventoried the contents. All of the usual vials and packets were there, including the ingredients she used to make the vapor that eased congestion of the lungs in children. If she required anything more exotic, Shute would be dispatched to the town house to fetch it.

Satisfied that she was prepared, she sat back and watched the eerie landscape through the windows. Buildings and other carriages loomed briefly in the fog before disappearing back into the mist. The swirling gray stuff muffled the clatter of hooves and wheels.

The summons to Guppy Lane had shattered the sense of unreality that had descended on her during the drive home from the ball. She could scarcely believe that she had engaged in an act of the most astonishing passion with Caleb Jones. In a drying shed, no less. She had read a great many sensation novels but she could not recall any scenes in which the hero and heroine had employed a drying shed for an illicit tryst.

Illicit tryst. She'd actually had one of those. The realization threatened to make her a little giddy.

But she knew that it was not the physical encounter among the dried herbs and flowers, exciting and exhilarating as it had been, that had played havoc with her senses. Her body had recovered from the delicious shock of her first sexual experience but she still felt disoriented and oddly dazzled. Her senses hummed at a pitch that seemed a little too high. It was as if a few currents from the storm of psychical energy that she and Caleb had unleashed still whispered through her. She sensed intuitively that they would remain, linking her somehow to Caleb. She wondered if he now felt the same strange resonance of a connection.

Shute brought the carriage to a stop in front of a small house. It was the only house in the lane in which a window was illuminated. All the other homes were dark, the occupants long abed. In another hour or two, at about the same time that the denizens of the social world were on their way home to bed after leaving their parties and clubs, the people in this neighborhood would be rising. They would eat a simple breakfast and set off to London's shops, factories and the large, wealthy households where they worked. The lucky ones, that is, Lucinda reflected. Work of any kind that paid a living wage was always in short supply.

Shute got the door open. "I'll wait out here with the horse as usual, Miss Bromley."

"Thank you." She picked up the satchel and gave him a wan smile. "It does not appear that either of us will be getting any sleep tonight."

"Won't be the first time, now, will it?"

The door to the small house flew open. Alice Ross, dressed in a cap and a faded wrapper, hovered anxiously in the opening.

"Thank God, it's you, Miss Bromley," she said. "I'm so sorry to bring you out at this hour but I haven't been this frightened since Annie took sick at Christmas."

"Please don't concern yourself about the time, Mrs. Ross. I regret that I am late. I was out when your message arrived."

"Yes, ma'am, I can see that." Alice gave the cobalt blue gown a shyly admiring look. "You look lovely, ma'am."

"Thank you," Lucinda said absently. She brushed past Alice and went toward the small figure on the cot in front of the fire. "There you are, Harry. How are you feeling?"

The boy looked up at her, face flushed with fever. "Been better, Miss Bromley."

His breathing was hoarse and labored in a way she had often encountered in children.

"And you soon will be again," she said. She set the satchel on the hearth, opened it and took out a packet. "Now then, Mrs. Ross, if you will boil some water for me, we shall very quickly have Harry breathing more easily."

Harry squinted up at her. "Ye look really pretty, Miss Bromley."

"Thank you, Harry."

"What happened to your hair?"

Caleb stripped off his coat, waistcoat and tie and then paused, looking at the big four-poster bed. The lovemaking had left him feeling more cheerful and more relaxed than he had been in months. He had intended to take advantage of the rare sensation and go straight to bed in the bedroom he rarely used.

Now he found himself hesitating. He wanted and needed sleep but the aftereffects of the physical release and the unfamiliar psychical lift of the buoyant spirits that had accompanied it were already fading.

Another sensation was stealing in to rob him of the all too brief respite from the omnipresent sense of urgency that gripped him these days. It was still faint and the feeling was very different from his usual nighttime spells of melancholia but he knew that if he did go to bed he would not sleep.

He left the bedroom and went down the hall to the library-laboratory. Inside he turned up one of the lamps and made his way through the maze of bookshelves to the vault. He worked the complicated combination and opened the door. Reaching into the dark opening, he took out the journal of Erasmus Jones and the notebook.

He sat down in front of the cold hearth, removed the

onyx-and-gold cuff links and rolled his shirtsleeves part-way up his forearms. For a while he sat there, looking at the two volumes. He had read each of them several times from beginning to end. Small slips of paper marked passages that might or might not be important.

At first he had approached the task with a sense of keen anticipation, the way he always did when he confronted a complex problem or puzzle. There would be a pattern, he had told himself. There was always a pattern.

It had taken him a month to decipher the complex code that his great-grandfather had invented for the journal. It had required almost as long to work out the encryption of Sylvester's notebook. The code in that book proved unlike any that the old bastard had used in his other journals and papers.

But in the wake of those hopeful breakthroughs he had found little to encourage him. Erasmus's journal described a steady descent into eccentricity, obsession and madness. As for Sylvester's notebook, it had become increasingly incomprehensible. It seemed composed entirely of mysteries within mysteries, an endless maze with no exit. To his dying day Erasmus had remained convinced, however, that it held the secret to curing his insanity.

He chose a page of the notebook at random and translated a short passage in his head.

. . . *The transmutation of the four physical elements cannot be accomplished unless the secrets of the fifth, that which was known as ether to the ancients, are first unraveled. Only fire can reveal the mysteries* . . .

Typical alchemical nonsense, he thought. The notebook appeared to be full of it. But he could not escape the feeling that he was missing something. What was it about the damned book that had so fascinated Erasmus?

The unpleasant restlessness was building fast within him, metamorphosing into a compelling sense of urgency. No longer able to concentrate, he closed the notebook and got to his feet.

He stood there for a moment, trying to focus his mind on the Hulsey investigation. When that did not work to settle his thoughts, he started toward the brandy decanter, the distraction of last resort and one which he had been resorting to rather frequently of late.

Halfway across the room he stopped. Maybe he would brew some of the tisane that Lucinda had given him for what she claimed was the tension in his aura. He was certainly tense tonight, he reflected. He was not entirely certain of her diagnoses but there was no question but that he always felt better for a time after he drank the stuff.

Lucinda. Memories of their time together in the drying shed no longer heated his blood. Instead he felt as if he had ice flowing in his veins.

Lucinda.

And suddenly he knew, in a way that his psychical nature never questioned, that she was in grave danger.

Twenty

*T*he inhaled vapors worked quickly, easing Harry's congestion in a matter of minutes.

"That should do it." Lucinda got to her feet, struggling a little against the awkward weight of her skirts. She smiled at Alice Ross. "I'll leave you a sufficient supply to see him through the crisis. But I believe he will recover quickly."

"I do not know how to thank you, Miss Bromley," Alice said. Weary relief softened her face.

"You can thank me by making sure that young Harry returns to school as soon as he is well."

On the cot Harry uttered a disgusted groan. "I can make more money selling the *Flying Intelligencer* on the corner."

"School is an investment." Lucinda closed the satchel. "If you attend now, you will make a lot more money in the future than you ever will selling newspapers."

Gilbert Ross, a mountain of a man who made his living as a carpenter, loomed behind Alice.

"He'll be back in school as soon as he's fit," Gilbert vowed. "Don't you worry about that, Miss Bromley."

Lucinda laughed and leaned down to ruffle Harry's hair. "I'm delighted to hear it." She straightened, picked up the satchel and walked to the door. "I'd bid you all good night but it seems it is almost morning."

Gilbert opened the door. "Thank you, ma'am. I'll be paying for your kindness in the usual manner. When you need a bit of carpentry work done, you have only to send word."

"I know. Thank you, Mr. Ross."

She went outside and discovered that the fog had thickened substantially during the time she had been attending Harry Ross. Her dainty carriage loomed in the mist.

Her senses stirred as she went toward the vehicle. She was intensely aware of the damp chill of the dawn air. *Should have taken the time to collect my cloak before I let Caleb hustle me away from the ball. What was I thinking?* Ah, but she knew the answer to that. She had not been thinking about anything except the exhilaration of the lovemaking and the strange sense of a psychical connection with Caleb.

Memories of the heated encounter flashed through her head again but they did not warm her. If anything, she felt colder, unnaturally so.

The heavily caped figure at the railing straightened and strode quickly to the carriage. He did not speak as he opened the door and lowered the steps.

Shute always greeted her. And he always had a few words to say to whomever she had been visiting. But he did not even lift a hand to acknowledge Gilbert Ross, who stood watching in the doorway.

The sense of wrongness grew stronger.

She heard the door to the house close behind her. Gilbert was evidently satisfied that she was now safely in Shute's hands. A panicky sensation twisted her stomach.

She had been looking forward to the comforting warmth of the carriage rug but for no logical reason she stopped less than two yards from the vehicle. There was something not quite right about Shute. The coat did not fit him properly, she thought. It was too tight across the shoulders and the hem was a bit too short. The hat was not correct, either. Shute wore his at an entirely different angle.

Whoever he was, he was not Shute.

She started to turn, intending to run back up the steps of the Ross house and pound on the door.

"No ye don't," the false Shute growled.

A powerful, gloved hand slapped across her mouth and hauled her back against a heavily muscled chest.

She struggled frantically, trying to kick at her captor's legs, but her foot was immediately tangled in her skirts and petticoats.

"Stop fighting, you stupid bitch, or I'll knock you senseless." The footpad kept his voice low. He dragged her toward the carriage. "Bloody hell, give me a hand here, Sharpy," he said to someone else. "Her damned skirts are in the way. I keep tripping on them."

"I'll get her feet," the second man said. "Watch ye don't frighten the horse. Last thing we need is a runaway carriage."

She realized that she still gripped her satchel in her left hand. Frantically, she struggled to open the bag. Neither man paid any attention. As far as they were concerned she had stopped struggling and that was all that mattered. The second man had her feet now. He lifted her off the ground. She got one of the two satchel straps undone.

"Hurry." The man wearing Shute's coat held the door open. "Get her inside and get a gag in her mouth before someone decides to take a look out the bloody window."

The second villain, the one called Sharpy, struggled to wedge her through the door of the small carriage. She managed to unfasten the second strap of the satchel.

Plunging her hand inside, she groped blindly for the packet she wanted, praying that she would get the right one.

"Her bloody damned skirts are caught in the door," the other man hissed.

"Never mind, I'll handle her, Perrett. Get on the box and get us out of here."

She had the packet in her hand now. She ripped it open, held her breath and squeezed her eyes shut.

She flung a handful of the contents toward the man who had her feet.

Sharpy yelped in surprise when the powdered, highly potent mix of dried, finely ground hot peppers struck his eyes, nose and mouth. He dropped her feet and shrieked. The yell was followed by a great deal of gasping and coughing.

"What the bloody hell—?" Perrett said, confused and impatient.

Her eyes still tightly closed, her lungs burning from the need to breathe, she flung more of the powder backward in the general direction of Perrett's face.

He cried out and abruptly let her go. Unable to get her feet under her in time, she went down hard on one shoulder and her hip. Her skirts cushioned some of the impact but not all. Pain jolted through her. Instinctively she took a breath, inhaling some of the misty powder. Her throat was on fire. She rolled under the carriage, seeking untainted air, and cautiously opened her eyes.

Her eyes did not water but everything looked blurry. She had lost her glasses in the struggle.

"The witch blinded me," one of the men screamed. "Can't breathe. *Can't breathe.*"

His companion howled.

She heard another voice in the night. Gilbert Ross.

"There's bloody footpads out here," Ross shouted.

"They're trying to kidnap Miss Bromley."

More doors opened. Men in nightgowns and caps appeared. At the sight of the familiar carriage, they surged forward.

The would-be kidnappers seemed to grasp the fact that they were now in mortal danger from the outraged householders of Guppy Lane. They stumbled away, running toward the corner.

Several of the men took off after the pair but quickly gave up the chase when they discovered that their bare feet were no match for the rough cobblestones.

"Miss Bromley," Alice Ross cried.

Hiking up her skirts, she ran down the steps toward Lucinda.

Lucinda sat up painfully and, thanks to the stiff little bustle, with considerable awkwardness. Ball gowns, she reflected, were not designed for such energetic activities. What with the lovemaking and an attempted kidnapping, the lovely cobalt blue silks would never be the same.

"Miss Bromley, are you all right?" Alice demanded anxiously.

"Yes, I think so." She did a quick assessment. Her pulse was racing and her throat was tight and burning from the bit of pepper powder she had inhaled. She was also sore from the rough landing on the pavement. But none of the problems were serious, she told herself.

Alice reached down with both hands. "Here, let me help you."

"Thank you." She managed to get to her feet, aware that she was shivering from the aftermath of the struggle. She forced herself to concentrate on the problem at hand. "Where's Shute? I'm afraid those two dreadful men did something terrible to him. One of the footpads stole his coat. They may have killed him."

Pounding hooves and the rumbling clatter of a fast-moving carriage interrupted her. She wiped her eyes with the back of her hand, trying to make out the blurred scene.

The hansom rolled out of the fog and halted. A figure vaulted down from the cab. She could not make out his face without her glasses but she knew him with all of her senses.

"Caleb," she whispered.

He strode swiftly toward her through the swirling gray mist of dawn. The long overcoat flared around him like a dark aura. He did not seem to be aware of the cluster of people milling around in the lane. They melted out of his way as if by magic.

When he reached Lucinda, he clamped his hands around her shoulders and pulled her tightly against him.

"Are you all right?" he rasped.

She nearly screamed when his fingers crushed her injured shoulder. "*Yes*. Please. My shoulder."

"Damnation." He released her quickly. "You're hurt."

"Just a little bruised. What are you doing here?"

"What happened?" he demanded, ignoring her question.

It was the first time she'd had a chance to try to make sense of the violence. She frowned, forcing herself to concentrate. "I think those two men tried to abduct me. I suspect their intention was to rob me."

"More 'n likely they planned to sell her into a brothel," the woman who lived next door to Alice declared in sepulchral tones. "You read about that sort of thing all the time in the press."

"Oh, I really don't think so," Lucinda demurred.

"Mrs. Badget is right," another woman announced. "Why, just the other day there was a piece in the *Flying*

180

Intelligencer about respectable ladies being abducted and ruined so shamefully that they had no choice but to enter a brothel."

Lucinda glared at her. "You may believe me when I tell you that being kidnapped and ruined, as you call it, would not induce me to take up a career in a brothel, Mrs. Childers. It would, however, make me angry. Very, very angry. And I am not without resources. Just ask those two villains."

The women stared at her, wide-eyed with admiration.

"She's right," Alice said briskly. "They were both crying like babies when they ran off."

"Where is Shute?" Lucinda asked again, searching the mists.

"I found him," someone shouted.

Everyone turned in the direction of the voice. Shute, accompanied by one of the neighbors, appeared from the mouth of a narrow alley. He was moving unsteadily but he was on his feet, Lucinda noted with relief.

She started forward, stumbled immediately and would have crumpled to the pavement again if Caleb had not caught her.

"You've injured your ankle, as well?" he demanded, as though it was her fault. He scooped her up into his arms.

"No, I seem to have broken the heel of one of my shoes. Kindly put me down, sir. I must see to Shute."

"You're certain you are not seriously hurt?"

"Yes, Caleb," she said. "I'm certain. Now, please put me down."

Reluctantly he set her on her feet. A woman hurried forward.

"I found your glasses, Miss Bromley," she said. "But they're broken."

"I have another pair at home." Lucinda limped toward Shute, aware of Caleb following close behind her. "What did they do to you, Shute?"

"My apologies, Miss Bromley." Chagrined, Shute gingerly touched his head. "Bastards came up behind me. Had me down before I even knew what hit me."

She examined him as best she could in the weak light. "Do you think you were unconscious?"

"No. Just dazed. Before I knew it they had me trussed up like a chicken with a gag over my mouth."

"You're bleeding and you are no doubt in shock. We must get you inside where it's warm. Then I'll treat your wound."

"Bring him into our house," Alice said. "It's plenty warm in there."

"Right." Lucinda urged Shute gently toward the doorway. "Would you please bring me my satchel, Mrs. Ross? It will be on the pavement near the carriage."

"I'll fetch it," Alice said.

With Caleb's assistance, Lucinda maneuvered Shute toward the door.

"Did you get a good look at the men who assaulted you?" Caleb asked.

"I'm afraid I cannot offer a good description," she said. "It all happened so fast. But both of them stank of cigarette smoke."

"That only describes three-quarters of the villains in London," Caleb muttered.

"One of them was called Sharpy and the other Perrett," she added.

"They weren't from this neighborhood," Gilbert Ross said. "I can tell you that much."

"It doesn't matter," Caleb said. "I'll find them."

"How?" Lucinda asked, not questioning the certainty

in his words, merely curious about the strategy he intended to employ.

"Gossip flows as swiftly in the criminal underworld as it does in the clubs and drawing rooms of the so-called better classes." There was something dark and feral in Caleb's eyes. "Trust me, Lucinda. I will find them."

Twenty-one

"What the devil did you do to those two men to make them flee like that?" Caleb asked. He sounded intrigued.

Lucinda looked at him across the rim of her teacup. She could see his face clearly now, thanks to the spare pair of glasses that she had located in her desk. His features were still set in cold, hard lines and there was an implacable expression in his eyes. But he had that other part of him, the chillingly dangerous part that she had glimpsed briefly a short time ago in Guppy Lane, back in hand.

They were in the library. Patricia, who had arrived home a short time earlier, had joined them, still in her ball gown.

Caleb stood with his back to the window. He had removed his long overcoat. Lucinda had been astonished to see that he wore the shirt and trousers he'd had on earlier at the ball. Evidently he had not gone to bed. The shirt was undone at the throat and the sleeves were pushed up on his arms.

He must have left his house in a great hurry, she concluded. Unfortunately, the informality brought back images of how he had looked bending over her in the drying shed, coming down on top of her, crushing her into the fragrant bedding. She had to work hard to concentrate.

It was Patricia who responded to Caleb's question.

"I expect she threw some of her pepper powder into their faces." She glanced at Lucinda. "Isn't that right?"

"Yes." Lucinda put her cup down on the saucer. "My mother and I always carried some when we traveled abroad with Papa. It became a habit. Mama concocted the original recipe but over the years I have changed the ingredients somewhat in order to enhance the effects."

"I also carry a supply," Patricia said to Caleb. "As does my mother. A lady can never be too careful."

"I usually carry the pepper somewhere on my person," Lucinda explained. She looked down at the stained and torn blue silk skirts of the ball gown. "But I neglected to instruct Madam LaFontaine to insert a pocket into this dress. That was why I had to struggle with my satchel, which complicated things no end."

Caleb shook his head. "I suppose I should be amazed but somehow I am not. It is obvious that the women in this family are a self-reliant lot."

"I still cannot believe that you were very nearly abducted tonight, Lucy." Patricia shuddered. "It does not bear thinking about. And in Guppy Lane, of all places. You have always said that you felt quite safe there."

"I *am* safe there," Lucinda said. "I assure you, those villains do not reside in that neighborhood. The Rosses and the others would have recognized them immediately. I expect the footpads were loitering in the vicinity, hoping to surprise an unwary victim. When they saw my carriage, they concluded that I would be an easy target. One might say that it was a crime of opportunity."

"No." Caleb's tone was low and grimly certain. "You were not selected by chance. What happened tonight was a deliberate attempt to kidnap you. If they had been successful, I have no doubt but that you would have been killed. The authorities would have pulled your body out of the river tomorrow or the next day."

Stunned speechless, Lucinda could only stare at him.

Patricia's cup clattered loudly in the saucer. She looked at Caleb, mouth open in shock.

Lucinda recovered first. "Why would those two want to murder me? I am sure that I have never met either one of them before in my life."

"Judging by the descriptions I got from the residents of Guppy Lane, they were a couple of ordinary footpads from the streets, employed for their muscle. They didn't give a damn about you one way or the other. Whoever hired them to grab you is the one who wants you dead."

A twinge of pain went through Lucinda's shoulder. "I was afraid you were going to say that."

"You haven't answered the question, sir," Patricia said. "Why would anyone want to kill Lucy?"

Caleb's expression was cool and steady. Lucinda could feel the energy in the atmosphere around him. In his own way, he was hunting.

"I think it is obvious that the person who commissioned the kidnapping has discovered that I am conducting an investigation on your cousin's behalf," he said. "He is afraid that she might provide the clues I need to locate Dr. Basil Hulsey. And if I find Hulsey, I will find those who are now financing his research into the founder's formula."

Lucinda sat very still on the sofa. "In other words, someone in the Order of the Emerald Tablet tried to have me abducted and murdered tonight."

Caleb inclined his head a little. "There is a ninety-seven percent probability that is exactly what happened."

She shivered. "Well, you certainly do not try to sugarcoat matters, sir."

"It is not my way, Lucinda. Would you prefer that I did?"

She smiled wryly. "No, of course not."

He nodded, satisfied. "I didn't think so. You are like me in that respect. You prefer truth."

"Most of the time," she said under her breath.

Patricia turned toward her. "But this means that you are in great danger, Lucy. Whoever hired those two dreadful men may well try to snatch you again."

"Probably not in broad daylight, though," Caleb said, very thoughtful now. "And very likely not from this house. It would be too risky, what with your neighbors watching and your staff about. Do not forget that they made no move to seize you tonight until you were in Guppy Lane."

"They must have been watching this house," Lucinda said. "They followed me, waiting for an opportunity."

"Yes," Caleb said. "But I doubt that you will ever see either of them again. The Order of the Emerald Tablet does not tolerate failure."

Lucinda shuddered. "Do you think they will be killed?"

Caleb shrugged. "Wouldn't surprise me, although it's possible they will survive at least for a time. Indeed, I'm hoping they will."

"Why?" Patricia asked.

"Because I have a great many questions for them. If they have any common sense, they will go to ground in the stews. From what I can tell, the Order draws its members from the upper classes. Such individuals are unlikely to have the sort of connections required to track down those from the criminal underworld who do not wish to be found."

Lucinda raised her brows. "But you do have connections of that sort?"

"One or two," he said. "Not nearly as many as I believe I'm going to require in the future. It is obvious the agency will need them."

"A chilling thought," Lucinda said.

"Meanwhile, I cannot be with you and Miss Patricia at all times," he continued, "so I am going to employ a bodyguard to keep an eye on both of you."

Panic shot through her. "You think Patricia is also in danger?"

"You are obviously the primary target," he said. "But if I were in the shoes of whoever was behind tonight's activities, I would see your cousin as an elegant way to lure you into a trap."

"Yes, of course," Lucinda whispered. "I never thought of that."

Patricia was clearly impressed. "No offense, Mr. Jones, but you do tend to think in a rather convoluted fashion."

"You are not the first to point out that unfortunate habit." He stopped and took out his watch. "It is nearly seven. I must send a message immediately. I want the bodyguard to come to this address as soon as possible this morning so that I can get on with other aspects of the investigation."

Lucinda put down her cup. "I have never dealt with a bodyguard. I am not entirely certain what one does with such an individual."

"Think of him as a footman," Caleb said. He opened a desk drawer and took out a sheet of paper. "In other words, make sure that he is always conveniently at hand."

Twenty-two

*I*ra Ellerbeck opened the delicately hinged lid of the tiny gold-and-emerald snuffbox. With a practiced motion, he took a pinch of the yellowish powder, raised it to his nose and inhaled.

Snuff was no longer a fashionable way of taking tobacco, having been replaced by cigarettes and cigars. Personally, he found *Nicotiana tabacum* repulsive in any form. It was not the powdered form of that particular herb, however, that he carried in the tiny container. The drug in the snuffbox was far more potent and infinitely more dangerous.

He felt the frisson of heightened awareness immediately and opened himself to the seething currents that swirled in the vast conservatory. An array of vision-inducing cacti, psilocybin mushrooms, belladonna lilies, Turkestan mint, henbane, opium poppies and so much more—all carefully cultivated and hybridized with the aid of his unique talent to enhance their toxic and intoxicating powers—whispered their dark energies into the atmosphere. At once his nerves steadied and his confidence trickled back.

He looked at his son. Allister lounged against the edge of a workbench with an elegantly languid air.

"What went wrong?" Ellerbeck asked, fully in control again, at least for a while.

"The pair of thieves that I hired failed." Allister's mouth twisted, his disdain obvious. "According to the rumors in Guppy Lane, Miss Bromley distracted them with some sort of noxious substance that burned their eyes and made it hard for them to breathe. In the confusion Bromley was able to summon assistance."

Rage surged. With great effort, Ellerbeck willed the distracting sensation back under control. The formula had some tedious side effects, one of which was that, in addition to temporarily enhancing his eroding psychical senses, it stirred certain violent emotions. Unfortunately, he had not discovered that particular problem until after he had started Allister on the drug. Now it was too late for both of them. Hope was fading fast. He had only a few months left, at best. If Hulsey did not come up with an improved version of the formula soon, all was lost.

"You must get rid of both of those men," he said. "If Jones tracks them down—"

"Do not concern yourself." Allister smiled, flushed with the prospect of two more kills. "I will take care of Sharpy and Perrett tonight. Meanwhile, they are hardly likely to go to the police. It would be tantamount to admitting that they took part in a kidnapping attempt. Even if they did talk to Jones, there is no danger to us. They have no way of knowing who I am. As far as they are concerned, they were employed to abduct Miss Bromley for the purpose of selling her into a life of prostitution. There really is no problem, I assure you."

"Damnation, don't you see? The *problem* is that Caleb Jones is now aware that someone attempted to abduct Bromley. He has gone so far as to install a bodyguard in the household."

He had been so certain that getting rid of the apothecary would put an end to the thing; so sure that once

Daykin's sideline in poison had been exposed, Jones would consider the investigation closed.

Instead, Jones appeared to be continuing his inquiries. In desperation the decision had been made to get rid of Lucinda Bromley. Now that plan, too, had failed.

Thaxter had sent word to him an hour ago. According to the rumors swirling in the clubs this morning, Caleb Jones was intimately involved with Lucinda Bromley. There could be only one logical explanation and it was highly unlikely that explanation was of a romantic nature. Jones was hunting.

"What makes you think Edmund Fletcher is a bodyguard?" Allister asked. "According to the maid I talked to in Landreth Square this afternoon, he is a friend of the family who will be staying with Miss Bromley and her cousin for a time."

Ellerbeck resisted the urge to throw a heavy watering can through the glass wall of the conservatory. He picked up a glass jar instead and walked a short distance along a path to his collection of carnivorous plants. He noted that one of the large, pitcher-shaped traps of his *Nepenthes rajah* was still digesting its last meal, a tiny mouse.

He stopped in front of an intensely green *Dionaea*.

"That would be too much of a coincidence by half," he said. "This is Caleb Jones we are talking about. He will have sensed what really happened last night. There can be no doubt but that Fletcher is a bodyguard."

"I could easily get rid of Fletcher for you."

Ellerbeck sighed. "Jones would simply install yet more guards around the Bromley household."

"I can take care of Jones, as well."

"Do not be so certain of that."

Allister tensed with anger as he always did when Ellerbeck implied that there were limitations to his talent.

"You told me that Jones is merely some sort of intuitive talent," Allister said. "He may be very good at chess but that ability will not protect him from what I can do."

Exasperation flooded through Ellerbeck, a hot acid that made him want to scream. He tried but he could not keep all of the emotion out of his voice. "Damn it to hell, don't you see? If you managed to kill Caleb Jones, we would be left with an even greater problem than we now face."

"What do you mean?"

Ellerbeck fought his frustration. To think that he had once believed that the drug might save his son. Allister had always been dangerous. The streak of madness had shown itself early in life. But for a few weeks after he had begun taking the formula, he seemed to become more stable. Within days, however, the side effects had appeared.

"Consider what you are suggesting," Ellerbeck said. "The murder of Caleb Jones would draw the attention of the Master, the Council and the entire Jones family. That is the very last thing we want."

"But no one would realize that Jones had been killed," Allister insisted. "You know how I work. It will appear that he died of a heart attack, just like Daykin."

"It is not common for a man in his prime to drop dead of a heart attack."

"It happens on occasion."

"Not in the Jones family. They are a healthy lot. Your methods might satisfy the members of the Council, but trust me when I tell you that without a very creditable explanation, no one in the Jones clan would believe that the death of Caleb Jones was due to natural causes. Not for a moment. The Master and everyone else on that damned family tree would turn over every stone in London until they found answers."

"They wouldn't find any."

"Do not be so sure of that. I doubt that either of us would survive the investigation that would be launched. Even if the Joneses did not succeed in discovering us, the First Circle would be furious. The leaders would see to it that our supply of the drug was cut off entirely."

"We have Hulsey. He can continue to brew the formula."

"The First Circle would take him from us in a heartbeat."

Allister began to prowl along one of the pathways. "So we come up with a creditable explanation. Bloody hell, where did you come by this unnatural fear of the Jones family?"

"There is a reason why every Master of the Arcane Society since the founding of the organization has been a Jones."

"Certainly there's a reason. The founder himself was a Jones. It is no mystery why his offspring have always wielded so much influence within the Society. It is simply the weight of tradition."

Tradition played a part, Ellerbeck thought. But so did power and talent. There was no denying that the bloodlines of the Jones family carried a great deal of both. Hunters, in particular, abounded within the clan. As it happened, Caleb Jones was not endowed with that signature talent, but many of those who would come looking for his killer would most certainly possess such preternatural predatory abilities.

If even a fraction of the legends that swirled around the family were true, it was a certainty that they would pursue their quarry to the gates of hell and beyond.

But there was no point trying to explain that to Allister. In addition to the whisper of insanity, he was imbued with the natural arrogance that was the hallmark of all young males in their early twenties. Nothing a father could say would shake that. The only hope that remained for either of them was that Hulsey would concoct an improved version of the drug.

I must buy us some time.

He thought about what Allister had just said. *So we come up with a creditable explanation.*

He contemplated the spider in the bottom of the jar. The insect stared back at him with its chillingly inhuman eyes. The members of the First Circle would exhibit a similar lack of pity if they discovered that things were going so badly wrong.

A creditable explanation. It would require a great risk but it just might work. And there was nothing left to lose. He was dying and his son was plunging back into madness.

"You may be right," Ellerbeck said finally. "Perhaps we should remove Caleb Jones."

"I know that you would prefer that we avoid any contact with the Society and with the Joneses," Allister said, sensing an opening. "But we no longer have a choice. Like it or not, thanks to Lucinda Bromley, Caleb Jones has been drawn into this affair. You claim that he is dangerous."

"He is a Jones," Ellerbeck said simply.

"Very well, unless you can think of a way to convince him to abandon the case, we have no choice but to get rid of him before he discovers any links that will lead him back to Hulsey. The doctor would not last five minutes under questioning."

"He has been the weak point in this business all along. But we need him, Allister. He is the only man of talent I know who might be able to reduce the side effects of the formula."

"The drug works very well as far as I am concerned."

194

That is because you are already insane, Ellerbeck thought. A great depression threatened to drown him. His only son was a madman with a talent for murder.

He set the jar on a workbench, took out the snuffbox and inhaled another pinch of the drug.

Immediately the crushing weight of his morbid thoughts lifted. Given time, Hulsey would perfect the formula and Allister would be saved. *And so will I.*

The key was time.

"You have given me an idea." A flicker of anticipation pulsed through him. "Perhaps we have been too timid in our approach. Desperate times call for desperate measures."

Allister was momentarily taken aback by the concession but he recovered swiftly. "Don't worry, I won't have any trouble getting rid of Caleb Jones for you."

"I believe you. But you will have to carry out the project in a manner that will satisfy the Jones family. They must be given the firm impression that there is no mystery to pursue. A death that appears to be a heart attack or stroke will not work."

Allister scowled. "You have a plan?"

"It occurs to me that if Caleb Jones is found dead, there is one thing that might keep his family from tearing London apart in the search for the killer."

"What?"

"The death of the murderer."

Allister's brow furrowed. "You intend to cast suspicion on someone else?"

"Yes." A very similar scheme had worked in the past, Ellerbeck thought. There was no reason it would not work again.

Allister looked skeptical. "I like the notion but if it is to be convincing, the evidence would have to point to someone who possesses a very strong motive."

"Not only a motive, but a history of having committed murder with poison. In other words, the perfect suspect."

Allister went quite blank for a few seconds. Then understanding dawned.

"Lucinda Bromley?" he said, voice rising a little in amazement.

"By all accounts Jones is involved in an intimate liaison with her. Miss Bromley poisoned her last lover. Why not another?"

Allister smiled his slow, cold smile. "That is bloody brilliant. It will be no problem to stage the scene so that Jones appears to have died of poison."

"I know you think that he will be an easy target but the thing must be planned carefully. We cannot afford any more mistakes."

"Don't worry, I'll take care of everything."

Ellerbeck picked up the jar again, removed the lid and turned the container upside down. The spider tumbled into the bloodred mouth of the Venus flytrap. The spiny-leafed jaws snapped shut faster than the eye could follow, sealing the insect's doom.

Ellerbeck watched the spider's useless struggles for a moment. The plan would work. It had to work.

Twenty-three

"*M*r. Fletcher is most certainly no footman," Patricia fumed in low tones the following afternoon. "What's more, he obviously doesn't know how to act like one, either. Look at him, lounging there against the wall, eating tea sandwiches as though he were a guest in this household."

Lucinda exchanged a quick, amused glance with Lady Milden. It was three-thirty in the afternoon and the drawing room was decorated with more than half a dozen elegantly dressed young men. Through the window she could see two more eager, rather anxious-looking gentlemen in their early twenties, coming up the steps, bouquets in their hands.

The room was already crammed with cut flowers and posies of every description. She had been forced to dampen her senses to suppress the reek of decay but Patricia and Lady Milden seemed to find the floral offerings delightful.

It was not just the underlying essence of the mass of dead flowers that rattled her senses. Faint currents of psychical energy pulsed lightly in the room. All of Patricia's admirers were members of the Society. That meant that each was endowed with some degree of talent. Put that many psychically gifted people in a confined space and even a person with minimal sensitivity would notice something in the atmosphere, she thought.

Mrs. Shute and two of her nieces who had been brought in to assist with the expected crowd of suitors bustled in and out continuously with fresh tea and an endless supply of sandwiches and small cakes. It was amazing how much food healthy young males could consume, Lucinda reflected.

The social rules that governed this sort of visiting between eligible young ladies and gentlemen were quite strict. Patricia was ensconced on the sofa in front of the teapot. Lucinda and Lady Milden were seated in chairs on either side, flanking her but allowing room for the admirers to approach Patricia and chat with her.

None of the young men should have remained for more than ten or fifteen minutes at most but half an hour had passed and thus far none had left and more were arriving by the minute. They took turns complimenting Patricia, but under the watchful eyes of Lady Milden and Lucinda, few of them could sustain a conversation for long.

"I will agree there is no way we could pass Mr. Fletcher off as a footman," Lucinda said calmly. "That is why Lady Milden and I decided to introduce him as a friend of the family."

"But he isn't a friend of the family," Patricia snapped. "He's supposed to be a servant of sorts but he doesn't take orders at all well. I told him to remain out in the hall. He would have had no trouble keeping watch from that location. Instead he insisted on coming in here."

Lucinda was forced to admit that Edmund Fletcher was not at all what any of them had been expecting in the way of a bodyguard. One assumed that men who chose such a career came from the streets. Mr. Fletcher, on the other hand, not only dressed like a fashionable young gentleman, he had the manners, airs and—hardest of all to imitate—the accent of a man who had been well bred and well educated. He was also, she sensed, a man of some considerable talent.

"Just ignore Mr. Fletcher," Lady Milden advised cheerfully. "I expect he is merely trying to carry out his responsibilities."

"Not only doesn't he take orders, he tries to give them," Patricia muttered. "He actually had the nerve to inform me that I was not to stand in front of the window. Can you imagine?"

A young man with a ruddy complexion and an empty teacup in hand approached hesitantly. Patricia gave him what Lucinda thought was an especially brilliant smile.

"More tea, Mr. Riverton?" Patricia asked.

"Yes, thank you, Miss McDaniel." Dazzled, Riverton held out his cup. "I understand from what you said at the ball that you are interested in archaeology."

"Indeed I am, sir." Patricia poured tea into his cup with a graceful flourish. "It is a passion of mine."

"I am positively passionate about the subject, myself," Riverton said eagerly.

"Is that so?" Patricia gave him another vivacious smile.

Across the room Edmund Fletcher rolled his eyes and downed the remainder of a sandwich. It seemed to Lucinda that his reaction caused Patricia to sparkle even more brightly.

Mrs. Shute loomed in the doorway. "Mr. Sutton and Mr. Dodson."

The new arrivals were ushered into the drawing room. Lucinda thought she sensed the level of energy rise as those already present took stock of the new competition. Lady Milden appeared supremely satisfied with what she had wrought. Edmund Fletcher ate another sandwich and appeared even more bored.

A flicker of awareness made Lucinda look out the window again. She saw Caleb alight from a hansom and start up the front steps. A few seconds later she heard his low voice in the front hall.

Mrs. Shute appeared again. "Mr. Jones."

Caleb entered the drawing room like a force of nature. The hum of masculine voices went abruptly silent. The young males moved out of the path of the new arrival, watching him with a mix of wariness, admiration and envy, the way young cubs might watch a full-grown lion. The level of power in the drawing room went up several degrees.

Caleb nodded once at Edmund Fletcher, who returned the silent acknowledgment with a respectful inclination of his head.

Ignoring the other males in the vicinity, Caleb stopped in front of Lucinda, Patricia and Lady Milden.

"Ladies," he said. "I wonder if I might borrow Miss Bromley for a while. I have a great desire to tour her conservatory."

"Yes, of course," Lady Milden said before Lucinda could speak on her own behalf. "Run along. Patricia and I will do very nicely on our own."

Lucinda rose and went toward the door with Caleb. She did not speak until they were out in the hall.

"A tour of my conservatory, Mr. Jones?" she said dryly.

"It seemed a reasonable enough excuse to remove you from the drawing room."

"I appreciate that. I'm happy to take a respite. It is painful watching all those eager gentlemen try to make polite conversation with Patricia."

"Matters appear to be proceeding well on the match-making front," he observed.

"Yes. Lady Milden is very hopeful of finding a match within days."

"What of Miss Patricia? Is she showing any signs of interest in any of the young men I saw back there?" Caleb asked.

"She is charming to all of them and appears to be enjoying their company but the only strong emotion of any sort that I have been able to detect is an incomprehensible animosity toward Mr. Fletcher."

"Why the devil has she taken a dislike to him?"

"I fear it is, in part, his own fault. He has made it clear that he doesn't think highly of any of her admirers or, indeed, of the entire project. I believe he feels that Patricia's approach to finding a husband is much too businesslike. He said something to the effect that he felt as if he was attending an auction of bloodstock at Tattersall's."

Caleb frowned. "Odd way to look at it. Using Lady Milden's consulting services strikes me as an extremely efficient and logical approach to the problem."

"Yes, Mr. Jones, you did make that clear." She led the way into the library.

"How is your shoulder today?"

"Still a bit sore but that is only to be expected. Shute is also recovering nicely. I assume you came here this afternoon because you have some news of the progress of your investigation?"

"No." He opened the French doors and ushered her ahead of him into the conservatory. "I came here this afternoon because, what with one thing and another, we have not had an opportunity to talk."

"About what?"

"The drying shed."

Horrified, she whirled to face him. She could feel the blush heating her face but she managed to keep her voice cool and composed; every inch a woman of the world. Which was, she thought, precisely what she had become thanks to what had transpired in the drying shed.

She cleared her throat delicately. "I hardly think that a conversation on the subject is necessary. That sort of thing happens occasionally between mature men and women."

"Not to me it doesn't. Never had an encounter of that nature in a drying shed in my life." He closed the doors very deliberately and looked at her with a disturbingly steady expression. His hard face was more dour than usual. "It was obvious that the experience was a novel one for you, as well."

"It is not as though I have had a great many opportunities of that sort, sir," she said crossly. "What is there to discuss?"

"Under normal circumstances, marriage."

"Marriage."

"Unfortunately, I am not in a position to offer it to you."

She was starting to feel quite unsteady. Automatically she gripped the nearest sturdy object, a workbench, and tried to breathe normally.

"I assure you I never held any expectation of such an offer." She waved one hand in what she hoped was airy dismissal. "It is not as if I am an innocent young lady like Patricia, who must guard her reputation. Heavens, mine was shredded beyond repair when my fiancé died."

"You were innocent," he said as though she had committed some grave crime. "I knew that even before I took you into the drying shed but I chose to ignore it."

Now she understood. He did not blame her. It was himself he was accusing of having committed a crime.

She straightened her shoulders. "I am twenty-seven years old, sir. Believe me when I tell you that there is a limit to the joys of innocence. At some point ignorance is no longer bliss. I found the events of last night extremely enlightening and . . . and *educational*."

"Educational?" he repeated neutrally.

"And enlightening."

"I am relieved to hear that you did not feel that our time in the drying shed was entirely wasted."

She blinked. His tone had not changed but something told her that she had offended him. Fine. Let him take offense. She was not feeling at all charitable toward him at the moment. She picked up a pair of shears and began snipping some dead blooms off a spray of orchids.

"Don't give our time in the drying shed another thought, Mr. Jones," she said.

"That will be a problem. I have not been able to stop thinking about it."

She was so startled she very nearly nipped off a young bud. Her pulse skidded. Very carefully she set the shears aside.

"What did you say?" she asked.

He shoved his fingers through his hair. "I have come to realize that the memories of last night will be with me always."

He did not appear thrilled by that discovery.

"I'm sorry if you consider that to be a problem, Mr. Jones." She was definitely starting to sound waspish now. "Perhaps you should have considered that possible outcome before you suggested that stroll to the drying shed."

"I did not say that the memories were a problem. But

203

it will take some time to accustom myself to them." He frowned. "I have always been able to put aside those sorts of intrusive thoughts when I wished to concentrate."

"Now I'm an intrusive thought?" She folded her arms beneath her breasts. "Mr. Jones, it may interest you to know that is not the sort of compliment a woman treasures from a man after an intimate encounter."

"I'm handling this rather badly, aren't I?"

"Yes," she said through her teeth. "You are."

"No doubt that is because I am trying to avoid the subject of marriage."

She chilled. "You were the one who brought up that subject. Not me."

"Lucinda, you have every right to expect an offer of marriage. I consider myself a man of honor. I should make that offer. I regret to say that I cannot." He paused. "Well, not yet, at any rate. Perhaps never."

Pain mingled with outrage, squeezing her heart so tightly she could hardly breathe. It was not that she wanted to marry him, she thought. But it would have been nice to know that the encounter in the drying shed had meant something more to him than a stain on his honor and a few intrusive thoughts.

She took refuge in pride.

"Look around you, Caleb Jones." She swept out her hand to indicate the conservatory and the large house beyond. "Isn't it obvious that I do not need to marry any man? I have survived great scandal on my own. I manage the inheritance I received from my parents very nicely and live a comfortable life. I have my passion for botany, and I take enormous satisfaction in helping the people who live in Guppy Lane. That is more than enough to fill a woman's life to the brim. I assure you, for a lady in my situation, an affair is far more convenient than marriage."

"Yes, I can see that." His dark brows came together in a fierce line over his eyes. "I do realize that I fail to meet most if not all of your requirements in a husband."

"That is not the point, sir."

"Hypothetically speaking, what would a man in my position need to offer you to induce you to marry him?"

She was coming to know that cold, intense look. Caleb had sensed another mystery to be solved.

"Love is what he would need to offer, sir." She angled her chin. "And I would need to be able to offer him a reciprocal emotion."

"I see." He turned away a little, as though he had just developed a keen interest in the odd *Welwitschia mirabilis* plant nearby. "I have always found love to be impossible to quantify or describe in any clear and meaningful way."

That was the logical, scientific mind for you. If one could not define something, it was easier to pretend it didn't exist. She could almost feel sorry for him.

Almost.

"Yes." She smiled coldly. "Love is impossible to define with words. Just as the paranormal colors of the flowers that I see when I open my senses are impossible to describe."

He glanced at her over his shoulder. "In that case, how does one know if one experiences it?"

That gave her pause. She could not confide her own feelings for him. He was, at heart, a man of integrity. That was why his sense of honor was gnawing at him this morning. She did not want to increase the weight of his guilt. After all, she shared equal responsibility for what had happened between them. What was more, she did not regret that incredible experience even though she was now paying a price.

She unfolded her arms, picked up the watering can and began industriously sprinkling a Lady fern. "Lady Milden says it is an intuitive thing, a matter of sensing a psychical connection of some sort." *Just as I did with you in the drying shed*.

His eyes narrowed. "Did you feel that type of connection with your fiancé?"

Thoroughly disconcerted, she set the watering can down rather forcefully. She opened her senses wide, taking comfort from the invigorating energy of the conservatory.

"No," she said, feeling more in control again. "But he seemed to be ideal for me in every regard. He met all of the requirements on my list. Every last one of them. I was certain that love would grow between us. How could it not? That is what all the guides to marital happiness promise, you see. Choose your husband carefully and love will follow."

"Good Lord. There are books written on the subject?"

His astonishment would have been amusing under other circumstances, she decided.

"Hundreds of them," she said blithely. "Not to mention the endless number of articles that appear in the ladies' magazines."

"Damn, I did not know that. I have never heard of such books and articles for men."

"Very likely because men would not bother to read them," she said. "Why should they? Marriage does not entail the same degree of risk for them that it does for women. Men enjoy so many more rights and freedoms. They need not worry excessively about being ostracized from the polite world if they are caught in a compromising situation. They can travel when and where they please without raising eyebrows. They can choose from any number of careers. An unhappy marriage can easily be compensated for with an expensive mistress. And if a man does decide to abandon his wife, he can be assured that the divorce laws will favor him in every regard."

"You can save the lecture, Lucinda," Caleb said dryly. "Rest assured every man in the Jones family has heard it often enough from the Jones women."

She flushed. "Yes, of course. Forgive me. I know that you hold very modern views on the subject of women's rights." *Probably one of the many reasons why I have fallen in love with you.*

He frowned. "You said your fiancé met *every* requirement on your list?"

She sighed. "You've got that look again."

"What look?"

"The one that tells me that you've picked up the traces of yet another mystery. In answer to your question, yes. Mr. Glasson seemed quite perfect. In hindsight, it was astonishing just how perfect he was. But it was not until after we were engaged that I realized the truth. He met only one of my requirements."

"Which one?"

"He most certainly possessed a fair amount of talent," she said grimly. "I could sense it when I was near him."

"A botanical talent?"

"No, although he did, indeed, have some knowledge of the subject. Eventually I discovered that almost everything about him was fraudulent. Yet somehow he managed to convince not only me but my father that he would make an ideal husband for me."

"In other words, he had a gift for deception."

"Yes, it was quite amazing, really." She shook her head, still baffled by how she had been taken in by Ian

Glasson. "Even Papa was deceived by him, and I assure you, my father was an excellent judge of character."

Caleb's expression became even more thoughtful. "Sounds as though Glasson was a chameleon talent."

She blinked. "What?"

"In my spare time I am devising a taxonomy for the various sorts of strong talents. The Society needs a more useful method of classifying and describing the ways in which powerful paranormal abilities are manifested."

"You astound me, sir," she said, amused. "I would not have thought that you had any spare time."

He ignored that, momentarily distracted by the new subject. "In the vast majority of people with talent, the psychical ability does not rise above the level of a vague, generalized sensitivity."

"Intuition."

"Yes. But my research of the Society's historical records as well as my observations indicate that whenever a very strong talent appears, it is almost always highly specialized."

Now she was starting to become intrigued. "Such as my talent for analyzing the energy of plants?"

"Exactly. Or a talent for hypnosis or aura reading. Chameleons have an ability to not only sense what someone else desires but, for short periods of time, generate the illusion that they can fulfill those desires."

She frowned. "Why the time limitation?"

"It takes a great deal of energy to maintain the illusion, especially if the intended victim is intelligent and if he or she possesses a fair amount of sensitivity. Sooner or later, the image is shattered and the chameleon's true nature is revealed."

"That probably explains why Mr. Glasson was rarely in my company for long periods of time." She hesitated. "Although there were occasions when we attended the theater or a lecture and were together for several hours."

"Those were situations in which your attention was directed at other things. He would not have been required to exert a high level of energy for an extended period." Caleb regarded her with a considering expression. "What caused you to suspect that he was not what he appeared?"

She blushed and turned away slightly. "You must understand that at the start of our association I was very impressed by his restraint."

"Restraint?" Caleb sounded baffled.

Caleb was a brilliant man, she decided, but sometimes he could be amazingly thickheaded.

"Mr. Glasson was very much the perfect gentleman," she elaborated.

"I don't see why that would arouse your suspicions."

She turned on her heel to face him again. "For pity's sake, sir, Ian Glasson kissed me as though I were his sister or his maiden aunt. Chaste and passionless does not even begin to describe it. Need I make myself any more clear?"

Caleb looked dumbfounded as comprehension struck. "Good Lord. He kissed you as though you were his *aunt*?"

"I assure you, he was extremely respectful of the proprieties." She closed the hand on which she wore the ring into a small fist. "Right up until the afternoon he attempted to rape me in the Carstairs Botanical Society gardens."

Twenty-four

*I*n an instant, Caleb saw it all with perfect clarity.

"He assaulted you because you tried to end the engagement that day," he said.

"In the wake of my father's death, something changed in our relationship," she said quietly. "I began to see the flaws in Ian. Once my eyes were opened, many things soon became obvious. I discovered that he was having an affair with a certain widow."

"When he realized that he was about to lose you, he did the only thing he could think of. He tried to compromise you so thoroughly that you would have no choice but to marry him."

She was startled by the quick summation of events but she nodded once, warily. "Yes, that is precisely what happened. It transpired that all he really wanted from me was my inheritance."

"You were seen fleeing from the remote corner of the gardens where he had tried to force himself on you. You were disheveled and your gown was torn. That sort of behavior could be ignored if there had been a wedding. But when word got around that the engagement had been terminated, you were suddenly notorious."

"Congratulations, sir. You did your research well."

Something in her tone told him that her words were not intended to be complimentary but he was too immersed in the maze that he was constructing to pay close attention. He started down the nearest graveled path, moving deeper into the jungle.

"Did you use your pepper powder on him?" he asked.

"No, it wasn't necessary."

"How did you escape his clutches?"

"I rammed my fan first into his midsection and then toward his eye. He was quite surprised, I think, or at least unprepared for that response. He released me in an instinctive movement to protect his eyes and I escaped."

Caleb contemplated the image of the stout length of a folded fan. "Never considered how dangerous one of those things could be." Admiration welled up inside him. "Very clever, Lucinda."

"Yes, well, I expect it was all those plant-hunting expeditions. One learns things."

"They do say travel is broadening," he said. "Within days after the engagement was ended, Ian Glasson was found dead of poison."

He heard her dainty, high-button boots crunching on the graveled walk behind him.

"Everyone assumed I was responsible," she said.

"Everyone was wrong."

Her footsteps came more swiftly on the gravel as she tried to keep up with him. "What makes you so sure of that? There is no doubt but that Ian was poisoned."

"By cyanide, according to the reports in the press."

"Yes."

"Not a poison you would have used." He looked around at the massed greenery. "You would have employed a far more subtle, undetectable substance. I'm sure there is no lack of raw material in this conservatory."

There was a short, tense silence behind him.

"I think I'll take that as a compliment," she said without inflection.

"It was merely a statement of an obvious fact."

"A fact that no one else ever noticed."

He stopped, lowered himself onto an iron bench, stretched out his legs and contemplated a large palm with fan-shaped fronds. "Just as no one paid any attention to the fact that your father supposedly committed suicide with a pistol and that his partner was also murdered with cyanide, not a botanical-based poison."

She sank down beside him. The intricately draped skirts of her gown brushed against his leg. He opened his senses to her energy.

"What are you implying, Mr. Jones?" she said quietly.

He could feel the new tension in her. She had already guessed what he was about to say. Sometimes it seemed as if she could almost read his mind. No one else had ever been able to sense the direction of his thoughts as she did.

"In all three instances the killer wanted to make the deaths appear suspicious. He intended that the finger of blame point at someone. But he used the wrong method to murder your father."

"The pistol? Well, it would have been next to impossible to poison Papa. His talent was similar to mine. He would have sensed a toxic substance, even cyanide, no matter how well concealed."

"But if your father truly had intended to kill himself, he would likely have taken poison."

"Almost certainly."

"The killer used cyanide on the other two victims because it is both fast and dramatic. Bound to be noticed."

"He even left bottles of the stuff at the scene," she said.

"When your father's partner was discovered dead of poison, your father was the obvious suspect. And when Glasson was found in similar circumstances, suspicion fell on you." He nodded once. "One must admire the symmetry of the plan."

"It is rather neat and quite tidy," she agreed, sounding quietly stunned.

"Yes, it is."

It was very satisfying to be able to discuss the logic of the case with her. In fact, it was more than satisfying, it was extremely helpful. Something about talking to Lucinda clarified his own thoughts.

"But there is one thing missing from your theory," she said.

"The identity of the killers?"

"Well, yes, that, too. But I was thinking of motive."

"When we find that, we will find the killer."

She studied him intently. "You believe that a single person killed all three men?"

"Given the time and techniques involved, I would estimate the probability that whoever killed your father and his partner is also responsible for the death of your fiancé to be in the neighborhood of ninety-seven percent."

Her brows rose. "You're sure it isn't ninety-five or ninety-six percent?"

It was a reasonable question, so he recalculated swiftly.

"Definitely ninety-seven," he said.

The faint gleam of amusement vanished from her expression. "You're serious, aren't you?"

"Yes."

"But that makes no sense. What possible link could there have been between my fiancé's death and the deaths of my father and his partner?"

"I don't know yet, but whatever it is, it is connected to the theft of the fern and the death of Mrs. Daykin." He studied the foliage in front of him. "This conservatory is the thread that runs through the entire affair. The answer lies here somewhere."

"Hmm."

He turned his head sharply to look at her. "What is it?"

"I don't know how it could possibly be significant but shortly before my father and his partner were murdered, there was another theft."

Energy crackled across his senses.

"A plant?" he asked, wanting to be certain.

"Yes. It was a strange, unidentified species that we found on that last expedition to the Amazon. I sensed that it had some unusual hypnotic properties. I thought it might prove therapeutic. But it disappeared shortly after we returned. There wasn't even time to name it."

"How long after your return was it taken?"

"A couple of weeks, I think. When I noticed that it was missing, I immediately told my father. He was extremely upset by the theft but as far as I knew that was the end of the matter. One can hardly call in Scotland Yard to investigate a stolen plant."

"No, of course not. Such a case would be far beyond the abilities of the police. Plant theft is best left to expert investigation firms such as the Jones agency."

She smiled. "Why, Mr. Jones, was that a small attempt at humor?"

"I have no sense of humor. Ask anyone."

"Very well, let us assume you are correct in your deductions."

"I usually am."

"Yes, of course," she said dryly. "Assuming you are infallible, how do you explain the fact that the first three murders occurred almost a year and a half ago, well before the theft of my fern and the death of Mrs. Daykin?"

"I don't know yet." He looked down at his hand wrapped around hers. "But there's a pattern. It is becoming more obvious by the day."

He was searching for the words to explain what he perceived so clearly with his talent when Mrs. Shute called from the far end of the conservatory.

"Mr. Jones? Are you in here, sir?"

Lucinda rose quickly and started along the path toward the French doors. "We're back here, Mrs. Shute. I was just showing Mr. Jones the medicinal herbs."

Caleb got to his feet, wondering why she had felt it necessary to invent a small lie to explain their presence in the rear of the conservatory. He noticed she was looking rather flushed, as well. Belatedly it occurred to him that she was concerned lest Mrs. Shute conclude that her employer was engaged in some improper activities among the foliage. His liaison with Lucinda was becoming complicated.

He rounded a corner and saw the housekeeper. She looked unusually tense and anxious.

"What is it, Mrs. Shute?" he asked.

"There's a young boy at the kitchen door, sir. Says his name is Kit Hubbard. Claims he's got an important message for you. Something about a dead man."

215

Twenty-five

The body was sprawled in a narrow alley near the river. It was a small realm of perpetual twilight even on a sunny day but in the fog it reeked of an unnatural, unwholesome atmosphere. A suitable setting for death, Caleb thought. The hair lifted on the nape of his neck. He opened his senses to the currents of recent violence that swirled in the vicinity.

"Young Kit tells me that he was known as Sharpy on the streets," he said. "Evidently he was an expert with a knife."

"He is definitely one of the kidnappers," Lucinda said.

"You're certain?" he asked, not doubting her statement but curious, as always, to hear her reasons.

He had not intended to allow her to accompany him. The argument had been short, terse and he had lost. But then, he'd always had a devil of a time going against logic. When Lucinda had coolly reminded him that she'd had some experience with violent death and that her expertise could be helpful, he had been forced to concede defeat.

Truth be told, the part of him that responded to the hunt was excited by the prospect of sharing the venture with her. Furthermore, he sensed that the intense reaction was not all on his side. Energy resonated between

Lucinda and himself. He had never experienced anything like this with anyone else.

"I'm sure of it," Lucinda said. "I did not get a good look at either man but I could sense the particular blend of *Nicotiana tabacum* that each man smoked."

He looked at her over the corpse. Her face was shadowed by the hood of her cloak but he could make out the serious expression on her intelligent face.

"Yours is an astonishing talent, Lucinda."

"Tobacco is a poison, after all. A slow-acting one, but a poison, nonetheless."

"Huh. I've heard it's good for the nerves."

"Do not believe everything you read in the press, sir."

"I never do." He focused his attention on the dead man again. "Well then, I doubt that Sharpy died from smoking. But, as in Daykin's case, there is no sign of violence. Any thoughts?"

"He did not die of poison." Lucinda looked down at the dead man. "I can tell you that much."

Caleb crouched beside the body and studied the expression of wide-eyed horror etched on the face. "It appears he was in a state of great fear when he collapsed."

"Like Mrs. Daykin?"

"Yes. That would account for the screams that Kit says were heard in the tavern."

"And why his companion was seen fleeing from this alley *as though all the demons of hell were after him*," Lucinda said, repeating Kit's exact words.

"But who or what did they see?" He went swiftly through Sharpy's clothing. "There is no question but that this was murder." He drew a knife out of a concealed sheath strapped to the dead man's leg. "But by what means? He was a hardened man of the streets but he did not even have time to draw his blade in self-defense."

"Do you think that he was literally frightened to death?"

Caleb rose. "I suspect that the cause of death was of a psychical nature."

Lucinda looked at him through the shadowy mists that pooled in the alley. He sensed her astonished shock.

"There are those who can kill with their talents and leave no trace?" she asked, sounding quite horrified.

"The ability is extremely rare," he assured her. He studied the body. "But I have occasionally come across descriptions of such talents in the journals and records of the Society. In essence, the killer induces a level of panic so great that it causes a stroke or heart attack."

"But it would appear that this man did not even try to flee."

"Neither did Daykin. According to my research, the victim is literally paralyzed with fear and cannot even raise a hand to defend himself, let alone run for his life."

"My parents were registered members of the Society. I was born into it. But I have never heard of such ghastly talents."

"For the very good reason that the Council and my family have always gone out of their way to suppress the information." He took her arm and drew her back toward the mouth of the alley. "Just as they do their best to relegate the founder's formula to the status of myth and legend."

"I suppose I can understand why."

"For the most part, the public considers the paranormal as a source of amusement and wonder. The vast majority of those who claim to possess psychical talents are viewed as magicians and entertainers or, at worst, frauds. But imagine how the citizenry would react if it got out that some people could actually commit murder without leaving any clues or evidence."

Lucinda shuddered. He felt it because he had his fingers wrapped around her elbow.

"The perfect poison," she said softly. "Undetectable and untraceable."

"Yes."

She turned her head to study him from the mysterious darkness beneath her hood. "The police will be helpless in this matter. They will find nothing to indicate that this was a case of murder. There will be no justice for that poor man unless we find his killer."

He tightened his grip on her arm. "That *poor man* recently attempted to kidnap and murder you."

"I will allow that he most certainly tried to abduct me but we cannot be positive that he intended to kill me. It is your theory and it is only a theory."

"Trust me on this. I have had far more experience with the criminal mind than you, Lucinda."

"Given the nature of my consulting work with Inspector Spellar, I think it is unlikely that your expertise is vastly more extensive than my own."

"Declaring whether or not a man has been poisoned is not the same as investigating the death."

"And just how long has the Jones agency been in business?" she asked far too sweetly. "A little less than two months? I have worked with Inspector Spellar for nearly a year."

"I cannot believe we are arguing about this." He smiled ruefully. "If either of us gave a damn about respectability or propriety, we would doubtless be shocked by our mutual fascination with the criminal mind."

"Everyone finds the criminal mind fascinating," she said briskly. "Although most are reluctant to acknowledge it. One need only count the number of newspapers and penny dreadfuls available for purchase on any day of the week on the streets of London. And all of them feature the most lurid accounts of crime and violent death."

"I will concede the point." He glanced over his shoulder at the body in the alley. "But I doubt that this murder will garner much attention."

"No," Lucinda said somberly. She looked back, too. "The press prefers that the stories be accompanied by a titillating scandal. The death of a lowly street villain who evidently died of natural causes will not raise any brows at breakfast tomorrow morning."

Twenty-Six

The headline on the front page of the *Flying Intelligencer* the following morning had nothing whatsoever to do with the discovery of a dead body in an alley. Lucinda gasped and promptly choked on a sip of coffee. She grabbed her napkin to cover her mouth while she tried to catch her breath.

Patricia, seated across from her, frowned in alarm. "Are you all right, Lucy?"

Edmund Fletcher, in the middle of his second helping of scrambled eggs, put down his fork, pushed back his chair and walked swiftly around the table. He thumped Lucinda quite briskly between the shoulder blades.

"Thank you." She waved the napkin, shooing him back to his chair. "I'm fine, Mr. Fletcher," she sputtered. "Really."

Patricia raised her brows. "Something in the morning paper upset you?"

"I am ruined," Lucinda said. "For the second time, I think, although I admit I may be losing track."

"It cannot be all that bad," Patricia insisted. "Whatever it is, you must read it to us."

"Why not?" Lucinda said. "The rest of London is no doubt doing precisely that at this very moment."

She began to read the piece aloud. Patricia and Edmund listened, transfixed.

REPORTS OF ATTEMPTED KIDNAPPING IN
GUPPY LANE
VILLAINS INTENDED TO SELL VICTIM TO A BROTHEL
by
Gilbert Otford

A lady whose name once figured prominently in this newspaper in a case of murder by poison barely escaped a shocking fate in Guppy Lane earlier this week.

Miss Lucinda Bromley, daughter of the infamous poisoner Arthur Bromley and later suspected in the death of her fiancé, was nearly abducted by a pair of villains who make their living selling respectable women into a life of shame. Witnesses claim that only the heroic action of a number of persons at the scene saved Miss Bromley from a fate worse than death.

Propriety and a profound regard for the delicate sensitivities of our readers forbid this correspondent from providing details of the grim future that awaited Miss Bromley had the kidnappers been successful. Suffice it to say that there is little doubt but that the lady would have found herself ensconced in one of those despicable establishments that cater to the unnatural desires of the most debauched and degenerate of the male gender.

Your humble correspondent wonders, however, if the would-be kidnappers would have selected a different victim if they had known the identity of the one they chose. After all, a lady whose fiancé died of poison after he drank a cup of tea that she had poured for him might be deemed something of a risk to her intended employer, not to mention the patrons of the establishment.

"I disagree," Caleb said quite seriously from the doorway. "In my opinion, an interesting past always adds a bit of spice."

Startled, Lucinda slapped the paper down on the table and glared at him. A stunned silence gripped the morning room. Caleb's expression was that of a man who has just made an entirely reasonable comment on the morning news. But there was a gleam in his eyes. This was, Lucinda thought, a rather poor time for him to exhibit what could only be described as his extremely odd sense of humor.

"Good morning, Mr. Jones," she said brusquely. "I did not hear you knock."

"Sorry I'm late. One of the maids saw me arrive a moment ago and very kindly opened the door for me." He went to the sideboard and studied the array of dishes. "The eggs look excellent this morning."

"They are," Edmund said quickly. "And do try the gooseberry jam. Mrs. Shute makes her own."

"Thank you for the suggestion."

Caleb selected a large serving spoon and heaped scrambled eggs onto a plate.

"Coffee, sir?" Patricia asked, picking up the pot.

"Yes, thank you, I could use some." He sat down at the head of the table. "I was up most of the night doing research in my library."

Lucinda tapped a finger on the damning headline. "You read Gilbert Otford's piece, I take it?"

"I never miss an edition of the *Flying Intelligencer*," Caleb assured her. "Best source of gossip in town. Would you mind passing the butter?"

"It is outrageous," Lucinda fumed. "I vow, I am tempted to go to the offices of the *Intelligencer* and give Otford's editor a piece of my mind."

"It could have been worse," Patricia said quickly.

Lucinda narrowed her eyes. "I do not see how."

There was another short silence while everyone tried to imagine a more notorious story.

"The kidnappers might have been successful," Edmund offered finally.

The others looked at him.

He reddened. "I was merely concurring with Miss Patricia. The story could have been far worse."

Patricia made a face. "Mr. Fletcher does have a point. I cannot bear to contemplate what would have happened had those dreadful men succeeded in snatching you off the street, Lucy."

"Well, they did not succeed," Lucinda said darkly. "And now you will likely find yourselves dealing with the results of Otford's story. Or perhaps I should say Lady Milden will. This news is bound to reawaken the old scandal."

Caleb reached for a slice of toast. "I think you underestimate Victoria's power within both the Society and the social world, Lucinda."

"You refer to the power of the Jones family?" Patricia asked.

"In a word, yes." He was neither proud nor apologetic, simply stating the facts as he viewed them.

Lucinda shook the folded paper at him. "There are some things that not even a Jones can fix."

"True." He glanced at the newspaper with little interest. "But that story by Otford isn't one of them."

She sighed, dropped the paper on the table again and smiled a little.

"You never fail to astonish me, Mr. Jones," she said wryly.

"I hear that a lot." He picked up the jam knife. "But generally speaking, the comment is not uttered in an approving manner."

"If neither Mr. Jones nor Lady Milden is worried about the effects of that newspaper story on your reputation, Lucy, I do not think that we need concern ourselves, either," Patricia said. She looked at the tall clock. "Speaking of Lady Milden, she will be here any minute. We have a very full schedule today, beginning with a shopping expedition this morning."

Edmund grimaced. "How thrilling. I cannot wait."

Patricia glowered. "No one said you had to accompany us."

"Yes, someone did say that he had to accompany you." Caleb forked up a bit of his eggs. "Me."

"Oh. Yes, of course." Patricia cleared her throat and continued down her list. "This afternoon we are to attend an archaeological lecture."

"Where that idiot Riverton will no doubt put in an appearance," Edmund muttered.

Patricia angled her chin. "Mr. Riverton assured me that he is quite passionate about the subject."

Edmund was coldly amused. "The only thing Riverton is passionate about is acquiring your inheritance."

"Lady Milden would never have introduced me to him if she believed that to be the case," Patricia shot back. A muffled knock sounded from the front hall. "That must be her now."

"What's so fascinating about archaeology?" Edmund demanded. "Just a bunch of ancient relics and monuments."

"Pay attention at the lecture today and you might find out what is so intriguing about artifacts." Patricia returned to her list. "Tonight there is another large social affair, the Wrothmere ball."

Edmund scowled and looked at Caleb. "How am I supposed to keep an eye on Miss Patricia at a ball?"

"Obviously you will have to attend, as well," Victoria announced, sweeping into the room. "And in your role as a friend of the family you will, of course, be obliged to dance with Miss Patricia at least once or twice to maintain the illusion."

Caleb and Edmund got to their feet to greet her. Edmund pulled out a chair. He looked stunned.

"What is the matter?" Victoria seated herself. "Don't you have any evening attire, Mr. Fletcher? If not, I'm sure Caleb's tailor can outfit you."

"I, uh, have evening clothes," Edmund said in a low voice. "I required them in my previous occupation."

"When you were a stage magician, do you mean?" Victoria said. "Excellent. Then that won't be a problem, will it?" She turned to Lucinda. "Did Madam LaFontaine deliver the second ball gown that we ordered for you?"

"It came yesterday afternoon," Lucinda said. "But surely you have seen the unfortunate story in the morning paper?"

"Hmm?" Lady Milden glanced at the copy of the *Flying Intelligencer*. "Oh, yes, the one about those men who attempted to kidnap you and sell you into a brothel. Very exciting stuff, I must say. I'll wager that every gentleman in the room will be lined up to dance with you tonight."

Twenty-Seven

An hour later Lucinda was still torn between irritation and utter bewilderment.

"I simply cannot comprehend why Lady Milden is
convinced that my reputation as a notorious female will
be an asset at the ball tonight," she fumed.

"Do not expect me to explain it," Caleb said. "The
nuances of polite society escape me."

They were standing in a mysterious realm she had
never expected to enter: Caleb's library-laboratory.
When he had invited her to accompany him to his residence after Lady Milden, Patricia and Edmund had
departed on the shopping venture, she had been first
startled and then intrigued. It was true that her status as
a spinster allowed her a degree of freedom equal to that
of a widow. She no longer had to guard her reputation
as carefully as Patricia did. Nevertheless, paying a call on
a single gentleman in his own home was a decidedly
daring thing to do.

Then again, when it came to her reputation, there
was virtually nothing left for her to lose, she thought.

She turned away from the nearest shelf of dusty,
leather-bound volumes and looked at Caleb.

"No, Mr. Jones, the nuances do not escape you," she
said. "Nothing escapes your powers of observation. The
proprieties dictated by society may bore you or they may

annoy you but I do not believe for one moment that you are unaware of them. You know very well how things operate in the highest social circles but I suspect that you simply choose to ignore the rules unless it suits your purposes to accommodate them."

He closed the door and turned, one strong hand still wrapped around the knob. His mouth curved faintly.

"And that, my dear, is the real secret of power in the polite world," he said.

"Does your entire family hold that view?"

"It might as well be the family motto." He watched her turn back to the ancient volumes. "That shelf is filled with alchemical treatises. Are you interested in the subject?"

"The old alchemists were primarily concerned with the elements, were they not? Mercury, silver, gold. I am more inclined toward botany, as you know."

"My ancestor Sylvester Jones thought of himself as an alchemist but in truth his interests ranged across the scientific spectrum. He did a lot of botanical research. In fact, most of the ingredients in that damned formula of his were derived from herbs and plants of various kinds."

"Do you keep the founder's journals and records here in this library?" she asked.

"I have several but by no means all of them. There are a lot more in the Great Vault at Arcane House. Gabe wants to institute a project aimed at copying the old bastard's writings so that we will have duplicates in the event some are lost or destroyed. But it will not be a fast or simple venture."

"Because of the quantity of work that he left behind?"

"That and the fact that he wrote everything in his own private code. We also suspect that several volumes are still missing. We found a large library when we excavated Sylvester's tomb but there were some significant gaps in terms of dates."

"What happened to the missing books?"

"Who can say? I think it is very likely that some of them ended up in the hands of the three women with whom he is known to have produced offspring. Others may have been stolen. He had a great many enemies and rivals."

"Where do you keep the founder's journals that are in this collection?"

He looked toward a heavy steel door set into one of the thick stone walls. "They are in that vault, along with some . . . other books."

A flicker of intuition told her that whatever those *other books* were, he did not want to discuss them.

"What a fascinating place this is." She replaced the volume on the shelf and wandered slowly down an aisle created by two long bookcases, pausing occasionally to read the titles stamped into the leather spines. "It is rather like my conservatory, a world unto itself. Every time one turns a corner one finds something unique and fascinating."

There was silence behind her. She glanced at Caleb over her shoulder and saw that he was studying the library as though he had never seen it before.

"I had not thought of it that way," he said eventually. "But you are right. This is my conservatory." He reached out and touched one of the ancient books. "Most people find this chamber oppressive. They wonder how I can bear to spend so much time here. Hell, the whole damn house makes them uneasy."

She smiled. "You are not like most people, Caleb."

"Neither are you."

She turned down another aisle of books. He followed.

"Are you still concerned about that piece in the morning paper?" he asked.

"Not as much as I was when I first read it," she admitted. She plucked another book from a shelf. "The thing that worried me the most was the effect it might have on Patricia's husband project. But if Lady Milden believes that an attempted kidnapping of her client's cousin with the intent of selling said relation into a brothel is the merest frippery, who am I to argue?"

"What about being here alone with me?" Caleb said. "Does that concern you?"

The darkness was back in his voice and in him, stirring the tiny hairs on the nape of her neck. And suddenly the atmosphere was charged with the kind of energy only he could generate, the sort that elevated and compelled all her senses. The intimate currents of power that pulsed between them, especially when they were in close proximity, seemed to be growing stronger by the day. Did he feel *it,* too? she wondered. Surely he could not be oblivious.

Impulsively she tried to lighten things.

"You forget that I barely escaped a career that would have forced me to endure the most lustful and depraved desires of the male gender," she said, opening the book in her hand. "I assure you that, compared to such a fate, being alone with you is not of any grave concern to me."

"I am male," he said. There was nothing in his voice. It was perfectly neutral.

"Yes, I noticed." She turned a page. The Latin seemed to blur a little. She had to concentrate in order to translate it. *A Historie of Alchemie.*

"And whenever I think of you I am filled with lustful desires," Caleb said in that same too-even voice.

She closed the book very slowly and turned to face

him. The heat in his eyes was as powerful and as intimate as the invisible currents of energy swirling around her. She realized her pulse was beating very quickly.

"Would those desires also be of a depraved nature?" she asked softly.

"I don't think so," he said, unnervingly serious, as usual. "Depraved implies an unnatural quality, does it not?"

She clutched the book tightly. "I think that is a fair definition, yes."

"What I feel when I am with you seems entirely natural." He walked to where she stood and gently removed the heavy volume from her fingers. "And very necessary."

"In that case, I do not think I need be overly concerned," she whispered.

Twenty-Eight

The indescribable rush of exhilaration and certainty slammed through him again, as it always did when he was close to her. He knew that when he touched her he would forget about the other damned books in the vault and the impending sense of doom that always came over him when he studied them. His hand shook with the force of his desire when he put *A Historie of Alchemie* back on the shelf.

He drew her into his arms. She came willingly, a sultry, intoxicating heat in her eyes.

"The other night in the drying shed you set me free for a time," he said against her mouth. "I want to feel that way again."

Her fingers tightened on his shoulders. "Caleb, what are you talking about?"

"Nothing. It's not important. You are all that is important."

Shadows veiled the sweet warmth in her eyes. He knew that she was about to argue with him and demand answers he did not want to give. So he kissed her, instead.

The embrace started out slow and deliberate. He wanted to make things last as long as possible, wanted to savor the sense of rightness and the deep certainty that flooded through him when he was with her. But when she sighed and put her arms around his neck, his passion burned with a fierceness that threatened to consume him. His intuition was screaming at him: *It is possible that you will have very little time with her. You must not waste any of it.*

He picked her up and carried her to the cot in front of the hearth. It seemed to take forever to remove her high-heeled boots, the heavy gown and the layers of underclothes beneath it.

When she was wearing only her stockings he put her down on the rumpled quilt that covered the narrow bed.

For a moment he could only stand there, drinking in the sight of her. In the moonlit darkness of the drying shed he had relied on his sense of touch and the energy they generated together to tell him that she was perfect for him. But now he could see her, too, and the vision of her lying there, waiting for him, dazzled him.

"You are so beautiful," he said.

She gave him a shy, tremulous smile. "You make me feel beautiful."

"You make me feel free."

Free from the cage that was slowly closing around him.

He wanted to tell her about the journal and the notebook but he feared that to do so would ruin the magic between them. The last thing he wanted from her was pity. There was still the possibility that he would escape his fate. When he was with her, hope flowered inside him. Damn it to hell, he *would* escape.

He peeled off his coat, yanked at the knot of his tie and shrugged out of his shirt. His shoes and trousers were the next to go. He tossed everything into a careless heap on the floor. Then he stopped, awkwardly aware that she was studying him the way he had looked at her a moment ago.

It occurred to him that it was quite likely that the only nude men she had ever seen in her life would have been classical statues. He was no *David* fashioned of cold, polished marble and perfect in every detail. He was a man with all the rough edges and the hard planes and angles that came with the gender. And he was fully, achingly erect.

"Men are not nearly so delightful to look upon as women," he warned.

She smiled slowly. "I find you very satisfying to look upon, Caleb Jones."

She held out her hand. Relief soared through him. He gripped her fingers and allowed her to pull him down onto the cot beside her, right where he wanted to be. He kissed her again, easing her onto her back and trapping one of her legs beneath his own so that he could explore her more thoroughly.

Enthralled by the soft, delicate curves of her breasts, he bent his head to take one nipple between his lips. She shivered in his arms. When he stroked a palm over the delightful spheres of her buttocks, she murmured something inaudible and flattened her hand against his bare chest. It seemed to him that the warmth of her fingers went straight to someplace deep inside him, to his heart.

He touched her elsewhere, seeking the hot, damp secrets between her thighs, wanting to feel the full brilliance of her energy. She twisted against him and uttered a small, choked cry.

Slowly, cautiously, she began a tactile study of her own. He shuddered at her touch.

The gathering storm of their mutual desire stirred the atmosphere, enveloping them. The intimacy of the moment thrilled him as nothing else ever had. He might have very little time with her but what he had he would savor with all of his senses. Without knowing it he had been seeking this sensation all of his life.

At last, when he could bear the desperate need no longer, he entered her, thrusting slowly, deeply, claiming her with his own power even as he abandoned himself to hers.

With Lucinda he was free to unleash all of the dangerous heat that burned at the core of his being. The currents clashed and resonated. The aurora of their fused energies lit up the space around them with colors and fires that could only be truly appreciated when all of his senses were flung wide open.

For an instant, caught up in the heart of the storm, he glimpsed the power of raw chaos and laughed at the patterns he saw there.

Some time later he felt her stir against him. He tightened his grasp. She struggled harder to disentangle herself from his arms. He opened his eyes and reluctantly released her. She sat up quickly and then she got to her feet and started to dress with a speed and determined efficiency that sent a jolt of alarm through him.

"What's wrong?" he asked, eyeing the tall clock. Less than forty minutes had passed. He sat up and reached for his trousers. "Have I made you late for an appointment?"

"Yes." She pulled her chemise down over her head, plopped her glasses on her nose and regarded him with a stern expression. "The appointment is now. With you. It is past time you told me whatever it is that you have been concealing from me."

His stomach knotted. The golden afterglow evaporated as if it had never existed.

"What the devil makes you think that I've got secrets?" he asked.

She stepped into the pooled skirts of her gown and pulled the bodice up to cover her breasts. "Do not try to evade the question, Caleb Jones. You have more secrets than most men. I told myself that you are entitled to your privacy but I find that I cannot endure the mystery another moment. We are lovers now. I have rights."

"We have made love exactly twice." He grabbed his trousers and started to dress, inexplicably angry. "What makes you think that gives you any rights?"

"I may be somewhat inexperienced in these matters but I am not naive." She fastened the front of her gown, watching him with narrowed eyes. "Lovers do not keep secrets from each other."

"I did not know that there was a rule. I have certainly never had any trouble keeping secrets from—" He broke off, clearing his throat.

"Other women with whom you have been intimate?" she finished crisply. "I am not other women, Caleb."

He could feel himself reddening. "You do not need to remind me of that." He was suddenly on the brink of losing his temper, something that rarely happened. He snatched up his shirt and concentrated fiercely on fastening it.

"I cannot go on like this," Lucinda said quietly.

He was so cold inside now he thought he might remain frozen forever.

"I understand." He concentrated on fastening his shirt. For some reason the pattern of the buttons and buttonholes seemed extraordinarily complicated. "You have every right to demand marriage. But I told you that is the one thing I cannot give you."

"Rubbish. This is not about marriage. It is about something far more important."

236

He planted his hands on his hips. "And just what the hell would that be?"

"The truth."

He exhaled slowly, deeply. "I cannot give you that, either."

"Why not?"

He shoved his fingers through his hair. "Because it will destroy what we do have together, and I cannot bring myself to do that. I need you too much."

"Oh, Caleb, whatever it is, it cannot be so terrible that we cannot face it." She rushed around the cot and grabbed handfuls of his shirt. "Don't you understand? We must confront this together."

"Why?"

"Because it affects us both."

"It affects me, not you. Do not concern yourself, Lucinda."

"Stop it." She was very fierce now. "Do not try to tell me that you are unaware of the connection between us. Even if you were to sail away to the farthest corner of the world tomorrow I would never be free of you."

The anger overwhelmed him then. He seized her wrists, imprisoning her.

"Nor would I ever escape you," he said. "No matter what happens to me, no matter how far I sink into madness, I will never forget you, Lucinda Bromley. I swear it on my soul."

"Madness?" Her eyes widened. "What are you talking about? I realize that you are inclined to become very intense and single-minded, perhaps a trifle obsessive at times. But you are certainly not mad."

"Not yet."

He released her and plunged into the maze of bookshelves. When he reached the door of the vault he worked the combination that opened the massive lock.

By the time Lucinda caught up with him, the steel door was opening ponderously to reveal the pool of night behind it. Palpable energy pulsed from the shadows, the result of so many paranormal objects massed together. He felt his senses stir and knew that Lucinda was equally aware of the disturbing currents.

As the opening widened, light from the nearest lamp spilled into the yawning darkness, illuminating the shelves of ancient volumes and strange artifacts. He reached up and took down the heavily worked steel box that contained the journal and the notebook.

Lucinda's brows crinkled together above the rims of her eyeglasses. She hugged herself and shivered, as though chilled by a cold draft of air.

"What on earth is that?" she asked, wary now.

"The reason I am inclined to be somewhat tense these days." He strode back through the maze of shelving and set the chest on the table in front of the hearth. Raising the lid, he took out the two leather-bound volumes inside.

She studied the books with an expression of intense curiosity. "What are those?"

"You will be interested to know that the Jones agency has recently solved a rather old case of murder. The killer's name is Barnabus Selbourne and he has been dead for nearly a century. But Selbourne is not one to allow a little thing like death to stop him. There is a very high probability that he is about to kill again."

"Dear heaven, who?"

"It appears that I am the next person on his list."

Twenty-Nine

*C*omprehension lit Lucinda's face. Behind the lenses of her eyeglasses her eyes were very blue and very intense. "You believe that little notebook can kill?"

"I believe it has already done so. The victim was my great-grandfather, Erasmus Jones."

He dropped the book back into the steel chest and picked up the brandy decanter. "You say you want the truth?" He splashed the brandy into a glass. "Very well, sit down and you shall have it."

She sank slowly into one of the chairs, watching uneasily as he tossed back half the contents of the glass in a single swallow. Then he sat down and removed the notebook from the steel chest again.

"First, the details of our clever little case of murder," he said. He held the notebook with both hands and contemplated the leather cover. "The motive became clear as soon as I had finished deciphering the code Erasmus employed in his journal. It begins with a love triangle." He gave her a derisive look. "I did tell you that I am not a romantic, did I not?"

"Yes, I believe you mentioned that once or twice."

"I'm not at all certain that Erasmus Jones believed in love, either. But he did comprehend desire and the wish to save a young woman from a hellish marriage. Isabel

Harkin's father intended to force her to wed our villain in the piece."

"Barnabus Selbourne?"

"Yes. It seems Selbourne was known for a violent temper. He had already been widowed three times before he offered Isabel's father a king's ransom for her hand. All three of the previous wives had died untimely deaths after what were rumored to be very short and very unhappy marriages."

"Selbourne murdered them?" she asked quietly.

"That is what Erasmus concluded. As I said, he was determined to save Isabel from the same fate. They eloped. When they returned, Isabel's father was furious but that was nothing compared to Selbourne's rage. My great-grandfather wrote in his journal that it was as if Selbourne had been deprived of his chosen prey."

"What a ghastly expression."

"Erasmus observed that Selbourne's previous wives had all had a superficial but nevertheless striking resemblance to each other and to Isabel. Same color hair, eyes, proportions, age and so forth."

"In other words, Selbourne was obsessed with women who looked like Isabel."

"In the year following the wedding, two attempts were made to kill my great-grandfather. He suspected Selbourne was behind the attacks but could not prove it. Then Selbourne tried to murder Isabel. At that point, Erasmus considered that he had no alternative. He had to kill Selbourne."

"How did he plan to do it?" Lucinda asked, fascinated.

"The old-fashioned way. Pistols at dawn. Selbourne was grievously wounded and died two days later. But he had already prepared his revenge in case he did not survive the encounter. He intended it to be a dish served very cold indeed."

"What happened?"

"A few weeks after the duel, this little volume came into my great-grandfather's hands. It was rumored to be a lost notebook of none other than Sylvester Jones. Erasmus was, of course, intrigued with it and immediately set about trying to decipher the code."

"Did he succeed?"

Caleb set the book on the table. "After spending some weeks working on it he was able to translate portions but they made no sense. He concluded that there was another code concealed within the first and began trying to find the patterns. In the ensuing months he became increasingly obsessed with deciphering the notebook. He very quickly went insane. Shortly thereafter he died."

"What happened to him?"

"In the end he set fire to his own laboratory, jumped out a window and broke his neck." Caleb tilted his head against the back of the chair. He closed his eyes. "But not before he made certain that his journal and the notebook would be preserved for those who came after him who possessed his talent."

Lucinda shivered. "What a great tragedy."

Caleb opened his eyes and drank some more brandy. He lowered the glass with great precision. "And thus was a family legend born."

"Jones men who are born with your sort of talent are condemned to be driven mad by their psychical abilities? Is that the legend?"

"Yes."

"Do you really believe that there is something about that notebook that drove your great-grandfather mad?"

"Yes."

"Do you believe that the notebook was written by Sylvester?"

"No. It is most certainly a forgery created by Barnabus Selbourne."

"How could a book drive a man insane?" she asked.

"I think there is something about the code." Caleb turned the brandy glass in his hand. "Deciphering it became a compulsion for Erasmus. He sank deeper and deeper into the maze, seeking the pattern, but he never found it. He knew that he was going insane but somewhere along the line he became convinced that the secret to avoiding his fate was in the damned notebook. In the end, however, he was lost."

She leaned forward and put a hand on his thigh. The warm touch had a miraculously calming effect on his senses.

"You speak as though the book cast some sort of spell over your great-grandfather," she said gently. "Surely you do not believe in magic, Caleb."

"No. But I do believe in the power of obsession. God help me, Lucinda, for months now I have felt myself being sucked into the chaos inside that abominable notebook."

"Burn it," she said forcefully.

"If only I could. I think of that option every day and every night. I have lost track of the number of times I have built a fire on the hearth and tried to throw the notebook into the flames. I have not been able to make myself do it."

"What stops you?" she asked.

He looked at her. "The same thing that stopped Erasmus. I know it sounds bizarre and irrational, but my talent tells me that I dare not destroy the book before I discover its secrets."

"Why not?"

"For some reason I cannot explain I am certain that, although the notebook may be the death of me, it is also my only hope of escaping the curse."

"Hmm."

He finished the brandy and set the glass on the table. "I do not know quite what sort of reaction I expected from you but *hmm* definitely isn't it."

He felt oddly crushed. He had told himself he did not want her pity but she could have shown a bit more sympathy. Before he could come to terms with his own reaction to that little *hmm*, she picked up the notebook and opened it.

"Well, well, well," she said, turning the pages slowly. "How interesting."

He gripped the arms of his chair and shoved himself to his feet. He needed another brandy.

"I'm glad you find the bloody thing *interesting*," he said. He picked up the decanter and poured himself another stiff dose. "Especially since I doubt that you can even read the title page. It is written in the same damned code Selbourne used throughout the notebook."

"I cannot read it," she said, calmly turning another page. "But I can tell you that it certainly is not going to drive you mad."

He nearly dropped the decanter. For a moment all he could do was stare at her, transfixed.

"How do you know that?" he said finally.

She riffled through a few more pages. "You are right about the notebook. It did drive your great-grandfather mad but not by luring him into a chaotic universe created by an undecipherable code."

He forgot about the brandy, just stood there, staring at her, mesmerized.

"How, then?" he asked. Even to his own ears his voice sounded harsh and raw.

"Poison, of course."

"*Poison?*"

She wrinkled her nose. "It is infused into the very pages of the book. The paper was no doubt dipped into the toxic substance and then allowed to dry before the author took up his pen. Every time your great-grandfather turned a page he absorbed a little more of it. I suspect that Selbourne used gloves to protect himself when he wrote the nonsense in the notebook. Fortunately for you, the stuff is now nearly a century old."

It dawned on him that she was holding the notebook in her bare hands. "Damn it to hell, Lucinda, put it down."

She gave him a quizzical look. "Why?"

"You just said it was poisoned." He snatched the notebook from her fingers and hurled it into the cold fireplace. "You must not touch it."

"Oh, it won't affect me or most other people, for that matter. The poison is psychical in its effects but it is finely tuned to work only on an individual with your particular talent. I can sense it but it will not harm me."

"Are you certain?"

"Positive." She looked at the book. "Selbourne must have been something of a genius with poisons to have prepared such an elegantly lethal substance. I suspect his talent was quite similar to my own."

"He was nothing like you. Selbourne was an alchemist rumored to have dabbled in the occult."

"I think it more likely he dabbled in some very exotic hallucinatory substances. I recognize a few of the ingredients in the poison but not all. I suggest you burn the thing."

"An excellent idea." He went to the hearth and set

about making a fire. "It is strange but even now that I know that it was poisoned, part of me resists the notion of destroying the notebook."

"Your unnatural interest in it is perfectly understandable. The stuff has lost most of its potency but there is still more than enough to rattle your senses and create that unhealthy fascination you feel for it. Your great-grandfather would have stood no chance against the power of the poison when it was fresh."

He watched the flames take hold and start to lick at the little book. "I was right about one thing, that damned notebook was the murder weapon."

"Yes."

He rose, gripped the mantel with one hand and used the iron poker to prod the leather covers open so that the flames could more easily reach the pages. He had to fight the urge to pull the damned thing out of the fire.

"I would advise you to move away from the flames," Lucinda said. "It is quite possible that the smoke contains traces of the poison."

"Should have thought of that myself." He went back to the chair, sat down and watched the book burn. "I owe you my sanity and my life, Lucinda."

"Rubbish. I do not doubt but that you could have continued to resist the effects of the poison."

He looked at her. "I am not at all sure of that. Even if it did not succeed in driving me mad, it would certainly have made my life a living hell."

"Yes, well, I will allow that it is extremely fortunate that you are so singularly strong-minded. I fear that a man endowed with a weaker psychical constitution would likely have been fitted with a straitjacket by now."

He forced himself to look away from the burning

book. "Will I feel this damned mesmeric fascination for the thing the rest of my life even though the book has been turned into ashes?"

"No, the effects will fade quite quickly. But a few more cups of the tisane that I prepared for you will hurry the recovery process along, especially now that you are no longer being exposed to the poison." She gave him a suspicious look. "You *have* been drinking the tisane, have you not?"

"Yes." He glanced at the pot and the small packets on a nearby shelf. "I did notice that I felt better after a cup or two. But as soon as I picked up the journal again, I was plunged back into the obsession."

"Every time you opened the book you gave yourself another dose of poison." Lucinda smiled. "Congratulations on solving the case, Mr. Jones."

"No," he said. "You solved it. I do not know how to thank you, Lucinda. I owe you more than I can ever repay."

"Don't be ridiculous." Her tone was suddenly quite brusque. She clasped her hands together very tightly in her lap and gazed steadily at the burning book. "You do not owe me anything."

"Lucinda—"

She turned her head and fixed him with a cool, unreadable expression. "I did no more for you than you did for me when you solved the Fairburn case. I believe the score is even, sir."

"I did not know we were keeping score." He was starting to get irritated again. "The thing is, it strikes me that we make a good team."

"I agree. We both appear to take great satisfaction from the process of solving crimes. When this affair of the fern is over, I would be quite happy to consult on future cases for the Jones agency."

He steepled his fingertips. "Actually, I was thinking of a somewhat more formal alliance."

"Were you?" Her brows rose. "Well, I suppose we could draw up a contract but it hardly seems necessary to involve lawyers. I think we will do very well together if we keep things more informal, don't you?"

"Damn it, Lucinda, I'm talking about us. You and me. We just agreed that we make a very good team."

Her eyes widened. "Yes."

He allowed himself to relax. "Well then, why not make it legal?"

Excitement brightened her expression in a very satisfactory manner. She glowed.

"What a wonderful notion," she said enthusiastically. "I will have to think about it, of course."

"You always seemed the decisive sort to me."

"Yes, but this decision is so binding. So formal. So *legal*."

"Well, yes. That's the whole point, isn't it?"

"But I'm almost certain I can promise you that my answer will be yes."

He allowed himself to relax a little. "Good."

"After all, the chance to be a full partner in your agency is simply too thrilling to pass up."

"What?"

"I can see it now." She held up both hands, framing an invisible image. "Bromley and Jones."

He sat forward, unable to believe what he had just heard. "What the hell?"

"I understand, you would prefer Jones and Bromley. You did found the firm, after all. But one must consider the marketing aspects of these arrangements. Bromley and Jones has a certain ring to it. It is somehow more rhythmic."

"If you think for one minute that I'm going to call

this firm Bromley and Jones, you can damn well think again. That is not what I'm talking about and you know it."

"Oh, very well, if you're going to be difficult about it, Jones and Bromley it is. But that is my last offer."

"Bloody hell."

"Oh, dear, I'm afraid we will have to continue these negotiations some other time." She rose quickly. "It is getting late. I must go home."

"Damn it, Lucinda—"

"There is the Wrothmere ball tonight. So many details to see to. I believe Victoria said the hairdresser would arrive at two." She gave him a vivid smile. "Don't worry, I'm certain that once you grow accustomed to the sound of Bromley and Jones, you will like it."

Thirty

"The thing is, Miss Patricia is such an intelligent woman," Edmund said. Seething frustration underlined every word. "Why can't she see for herself that none of that bunch of fawning dandies is right for her? Half are only after her inheritance, and the other half are dazzled by her looks. Not one of them is truly in love with her."

"If you're asking me to explain what a woman wants in a husband and why she wants it, you've got the wrong man." Caleb splashed some sherry into a glass. "Ask me something simple such as the probability that a deranged scientist named Basil Hulsey is at this very moment working on a new version of the founder's formula. I'm good at things like that."

He braced himself to drink some of the sherry. He disliked sherry intensely, especially the cloyingly sweet sort that Lucinda evidently preferred. But his choice of beverage was limited. He and Edmund were in Lucinda's library and sherry was the only option available. Lucinda and Patricia were upstairs dressing for the ball. Victoria was with them, supervising the last-minute details.

Edmund had been prowling the room. He paused, momentarily distracted. "Have you had any luck at all in tracking Hulsey?"

"Some." Caleb lounged on the side of Lucinda's desk.

249

"But not nearly enough." He pulled out his pocket watch and checked the time. "I'm hoping for a little more tonight."

"What do you expect to learn this evening?"

"I have an appointment with the second kidnapper."

"You found him?" Excitement briefly replaced the simmering irritation in Edmund's eyes. "He agreed to meet with you?"

"Not exactly. Young Kit came to see me an hour ago. He said the man has been seen in a certain tavern drinking himself into a stupor every night since his associate died. My plan, such as it is, is to confront him this evening. I'm hoping that the element of surprise will work in my favor."

Edmund frowned. "You should not go alone. Take me with you."

"No. I need you to keep watch over Patricia and Lucinda."

"Then take someone else along. One of your cousins, perhaps."

"According to Kit, the man is a nervous wreck, as it is. Evidently the experience of watching his partner die has greatly unnerved him. Having two strangers approach him would very likely send him fleeing into the night and then I'd have to track him down all over again. No, this kind of situation is best handled with a degree of delicacy."

"If you say so." Edmund was not entirely satisfied but he did not pursue the issue. He resumed his pacing. "Do you really believe that Lady Milden knows what she's about with her matchmaking?"

"I have no notion." He drank a little more of the bad sherry and then gave up on it altogether. He set the glass aside. "She's only been in the business for a very short time. There hasn't been time to judge her skill."

"It could take years to find out if she actually does have a talent for it. In the meantime, Miss Patricia might very well find herself wed to a brute or a fortune hunter. Her life will be ruined. Riverton, especially, strikes me as a nasty piece of work. I doubt he'd stop at anything to marry an heiress."

Caleb thought about that for a couple of minutes while he watched Edmund wear a path in the carpet.

"Miss Patricia is not exactly an heiress," he said neutrally. "My understanding is that she will inherit a comfortable income but certainly not a great fortune."

"All I know is that her income, whatever it is, looks very enticing to Riverton. I swear, if I have to listen to him tell her one more time how passionate he is about archaeology I will make him disappear out the nearest window."

"You seem to be very concerned with Miss Patricia's future happiness," Caleb observed. "I was under the impression that you thought her approach to marriage was rather cold-blooded."

Edmund's expression darkened. "That's just it, Miss Patricia is not a cold woman. Quite the opposite, in fact. I fear that in her anxiety not to be misled by her emotions, she is going against her own warmhearted nature. This so-called scientific approach to finding a suitable husband is nonsense. Have you seen that damned list of requirements she gave Lady Milden?"

"I believe she did mention her criteria, yes." He narrowed his eyes, thinking about it. "Evidently she got the idea from Miss Bromley."

Bromley & Jones. How in blazes had Lucinda come up with that? She was far too intelligent to have misunderstood his offer this afternoon. If she did not want to marry him, why not come right out and say so? Why all that silly chatter about becoming a partner in his firm?

Unless she *had* misunderstood him. Good Lord. Was it possible that he had not been clear?

"The man she is looking for does not exist," Edmund announced.

"What?" Caleb forced himself to pay attention to Edmund. "Right. The list. Evidently Lady Milden had no trouble collecting a sizable number of suitable suitors."

"But they are all wrong for Miss Patricia, every last one of them," Edmund insisted.

"You're certain of that?"

"Positive. I feel it is my duty to save Miss Patricia but she will not listen to me. I swear, she treats me as though I were a guard dog. She is forever either giving me orders or patting me on the head."

"She pats you on the head?"

"Figuratively speaking."

"I see," Caleb said.

He got the uneasy feeling he was supposed to come up with something mature and helpful in the way of masculine advice but nothing sprang to mind. Possibly because he was still trying to come up with some good advice for himself on the same subject.

Bromley & Jones.

Perhaps that damned list was the real problem. He was willing to concede that he did not meet all of Lucinda's requirements in a husband but she had admitted that they made an excellent team. She certainly appeared to be physically attracted to him, as well.

Was it possible those factors were not enough to convince her to compromise? Did he have to exhibit every single damned characteristic she had enumerated on that bloody list? Devil take it, was he going to have to develop a cheerful and positive temperament? Some things were beyond the grasp of even the most powerful talent.

An affair was all very well in the short term but he did not care for the element of uncertainty in such a relationship. What if a man who met Lucinda's precise specifications showed up someday and swept her off her feet with seductive talk of the mysteries of fern reproduction or the sensual aspects of pistils and pollination?

Victoria swept into the room, Lucinda and Patricia in her wake.

"We are ready, gentlemen," she announced with the air of a commander about to order troops into battle.

Caleb automatically straightened away from the desk. He was vaguely aware of Edmund coming to an abrupt halt and turning to face the women.

There was a short period of stark silence while both of them gazed at the ladies.

Lucinda frowned. "Is there something wrong, Mr. Jones?"

He realized he was staring. He could not help it. She was enthralling in a deep violet gown trimmed with velvet ribbons and discreetly placed crystals that caught the light. Long, snug-fitting gloves emphasized the graceful shape of her arms. A velvet band at her throat was trimmed with more of the brilliant crystals.

He knew then that he was destined to feel this thrill of energy and intimacy whenever she entered the room for the rest of his life. *This is right. You belong with me. To hell with your perfect husband. If he is ever foolish enough to show up, I'll make certain he disappears.*

Good Lord, he was starting to sound like Fletcher. But he meant every word. This was probably not the right time to say as much aloud, however.

When in doubt, fall back on good manners.

He pulled himself together, crossed the room, took Lucinda's gloved hand and bowed.

"No," he said. "There is nothing wrong. I was momentarily stunned, that's all. You and Miss Patricia look quite spectacular this evening. Don't you agree, Fletcher?"

Edmund gave a small start as though he, too, had just recovered from a trance. He went forward to take Patricia's hand and managed a formal bow.

"Lovely," he said. He sounded as though his throat had suddenly become tight. "You look like a fairy-tale princess in that aqua gown."

Patricia blushed. "Thank you, Mr. Fletcher."

Victoria cleared her throat to get everyone's attention. "Mr. Fletcher, you will accompany Patricia and me in my carriage. Mr. Jones will escort Lucinda in her vehicle. In the wake of that recent piece in the *Flying Intelligencer*, it is critical that he is seen conducting Lucinda into the ballroom tonight."

Lucinda made a face. "Really, I don't think this is necessary."

"Never argue with an expert," Caleb said. He used his grip on her hand to tuck her arm under his.

They went into the front hall where Mrs. Shute opened the door. The two carriages waited in the street. Caleb followed Lucinda into the shadowy interior of her small vehicle and sat down across from her.

"What has happened?" Lucinda asked immediately.

"What?"

"I can tell that something has occurred," she said. "There is a new kind of tension in your aura. You did take another cup or two of the tisane this evening as I instructed, did you not?"

"I fear your tisane, remarkable though it is, will have little effect on the current source of my tension."

"But you told me you found it soothing."

"It certainly is when it comes to dealing with poison.

What I am feeling now, however, has nothing to do with that damned notebook."

"What is it, then? Perhaps I have another remedy."

He smiled. "As it happens, you do. Unfortunately, I don't have time to take more than a small dose."

He leaned forward and kissed her; a fast, hard, possessive kiss.

"That will have to do for now," he said, sitting back before she could even begin to respond. "I have some news."

He told her about the message from Kit and his intention to meet with the kidnapper. She was immediately alarmed.

"You must not go to see him alone," she said. "Take Mr. Fletcher with you."

"He made the same suggestion. I will tell you the same thing I told him. His job is to watch over you and Miss Patricia. I will be fine on my own."

"Are you armed?"

"Yes. But I'm sure there will be no need to resort to a weapon. Don't worry about me. I will escort you into the ballroom. We will take a turn on the floor so that everyone can see us, and then I will slip away for an hour or so. I'll be back in plenty of time to take you home."

"You are dressed for the ballroom, not for meeting a villain in a dockside tavern."

"Believe it or not, I gave that matter some thought," he said. "I have an overcoat and a hat that will conceal my formal clothes."

"I don't like this plan." In the light of the carriage lamps her face was shadowed with concern. "I have a bad feeling about it."

"Credit me with some talent, my sweet. I estimate the probability that the meeting with the kidnapper will prove uneventful to be upward of ninety-three percent."

"That leaves a seven percent margin for error." She gripped her fan very tightly. "Promise me you will be careful, Caleb."

"I will do better than that. You have my word that I will show up in time to dance another waltz with you before I take you home from the ball."

Thirty-One

"He's a demon, I tell you." Perrett paused long enough to take another swig of gin. He wiped his mouth with the filthy sleeve of his coat. Leaning a little farther across the table, he lowered his voice. "Straight from hell. Wouldn't have believed it if I hadn't seen it with my own eyes. Wings like a giant bat. Claws instead of fingers. Eyes glowed like hot coals, they did."

Caleb doubted the description was entirely accurate but it was clear that Perrett had been badly frightened. He was also surprisingly desperate to talk about his terrifying experience to a stranger. Caleb got the impression that the kidnapper's associates had concluded that their comrade had lost his wits and now treated him like a lunatic. When Perrett had discovered someone who was willing to take his tale seriously, the floodgates had opened.

They were seated in a booth at the back of the lightly crowded tavern. Caleb was well aware that the heavy scarf, low-crowned hat, long coat and boots he wore were an imperfect disguise but they would serve. He was certain that no one on the premises would be able to describe him in any detail later. That was all that mattered.

"You say this demon hired you to kidnap Miss Bromley?" Caleb asked.

Perrett scowled. "Here now, who said anything about kidnapping? It was just a simple, straightforward business arrangement. The bastard told us he was a recruiter for a certain establishment that provides respectable women to entertain gentlemen. You know the sort. There's a demand for genteel ladies amongst a certain clientele."

"I see."

"Never understood it, myself. Give me a lusty girl who learned her trade on the streets. A wench like that knows what she's about when it comes to pleasuring a man. Respectable females are, generally speaking, unskilled labor. Waste of money, if you ask me."

"The man who employed you didn't want just any respectable female, though, did he? He paid you to bring him Miss Bromley."

Perrett shrugged. "That's generally how it works. The customer selects a particular female, usually one who doesn't have much in the way of family or money or a husband who might go to the police. Standard contract. We got half up front, the rest payable upon delivery of the merchandise."

"Why did you meet with your customer a second time when you knew you couldn't produce Miss Bromley?"

"Figured he'd understand the problem when we told him what had happened and give us a commission for some other female to replace Bromley. It wasn't our fault we couldn't snatch her. The witch threw some kind of burning powder in our faces. Sharpy and I thought we were going to go blind and choke to death right there on the street."

"But the customer wasn't interested in giving you any more commissions, I take it?"

"No." Perrett shuddered. "Got all worked up about it. Said something nonsensical about death being the

258

price of failure when you worked for the Circle. Sharpy and me, we figured he was a bit mad, if you want to know the truth. Then he went and used some kind of magic to kill Sharpy." Perrett's eyes watered. "Weren't no call for that. Not like we'd done him any harm. Hell, we were the ones who was injured on the job."

The sharp thrill of *knowing* swept through Caleb. Deep within the crystal maze he had constructed an entire passage suddenly glowed. He was headed in the right direction.

"The demon used the word *Circle*?" he asked carefully.

"Aye." Perrett's broad shoulders quivered. He drank some more gin to steady his nerves and then lowered the bottle. "Some kind of gang, I reckon." His mouth twisted in disgust. "Gentlemen form partnerships for business purposes same as the rest of us. The only difference is that they meet in exclusive clubs instead of taverns and alleys to make their plans, and they use fancy words like *consortiums* and *societies* instead of *gangs* to describe their operations."

"Yes," Caleb said. "They do." Lately the word that came to mind when he contemplated Basil Hulsey and the small group of traitors he was convinced were operating within the Arcane Society was *cabal*.

"But Sharpy and me, we didn't know we were employed by any gang of gentlemen called the Circle. Bloody hell, we thought we were working for one man, the demon. Except we didn't know he was a demon, of course. Never would have done business with him if we'd known that."

"Did he tell you anything else about the Circle?"

Perrett shook his head. "No. Nothing. Just looked real hard at Sharpy. That's when poor Sharpy started to scream. I was suddenly more scared than I've ever been in my life. I knew for sure that whatever the bastard was doing to Sharpy, he was going to do to me next. I swear, I could feel something in the air. Like little shocks of electricity. I knew I couldn't help Sharpy, so I ran for my life."

"Did the demon touch Sharpy? Give him anything to eat or drink? Was there a weapon of any kind?"

"No, that's what I'm trying to explain." Perrett peered around the quiet tavern and lowered his voice all the way to a whisper. "Nobody will believe me. They think I'm crazy. But I'm telling you, the monster never even pulled a knife or a gun. He must have been at least ten paces away from us when he used his sorcery on Sharpy."

"What else can you tell me about the demon?" Caleb asked. "Aside from the glowing eyes and the wings and the claws, that is."

Perrett shrugged and drank more gin. "Not much else to tell."

"Did he speak like a well-educated man?"

Perrett's broad face tightened. "Aye, he sounded a bit like you, come to that. Told you, he was a gentleman. You wouldn't expect a demon to pretend to be a work-ing-class cove, now would you?"

"No, probably not. Was he dressed like a gentleman?"

"That he was."

"Did you get a good look at his face?"

"No. Both times we met him it was at night in a dark lane. He wore a hat and a scarf and a coat with a high collar." Perrett broke off, frowning in confusion. "Like you."

"Did he arrive in a private carriage?"

Perrett shook his shaggy head. Anxiety was starting to pierce the fog created by the gin.

"Hansom," he said. He squinted. "See here, why do you care about the kind of carriage he used?"

Caleb ignored the question. "Was he wearing any jewelry?" No matter how drunk he was, a professional criminal would be unlikely to forget any details when it came to valuables.

Perrett's eyes glittered with a brief flash of excitement. "Had a very nice little snuffbox. Saw it gleam in the lantern light when he took it out of his pocket. Looked like real gold. Some kind of stones on top. Too dark to tell what sort. Not diamonds, though. Maybe emeralds. Could have been sapphires, I suppose. The thing would have fetched a nice price from a fence I know."

"The demon took snuff?"

"Aye. Took a pinch just before he used his magic to kill Ned."

"Interesting."

Perrett sunk back into a haze of drunken despair. "You're like all the others. You don't believe me."

"I believe every word you said, Perrett." Caleb reached inside his coat and withdrew some notes. He tossed them onto the table.

Perrett was immediately riveted by the sight of the money. "What's that for?"

"Payment for a most informative tale." Caleb got to his feet. "I'll also throw in some free advice. I would avoid any future encounters with the demon, if I were you."

Perrett flinched. "Don't worry. I'll make sure he never finds me."

"How will you do that?"

Perrett shrugged. "He may be a demon but like I said, he's also a gentleman. That sort never comes into this part of town. They don't know their way around neighborhoods like this one, y'see. I'm safe here."

261

"Don't be too certain of that," Caleb said softly. "A man might find his way to this street if he wanted something very badly from someone like you."

Perrett froze. His gin-bleary eyes widened first with shocked comprehension and then with panic. There was a beat or two of silence while Caleb waited for him to digest the fact that one particular gentleman had found his way into the Red Dog tavern that night.

"Who are you?" Perrett whispered.

"You will recall the lady you attempted to abduct in Guppy Lane?"

"What of her?"

"She is mine," Caleb said. "The only reason you are still alive is because I needed information from you. But I give you my oath that if you go anywhere near her after this moment, I will find you again, just as easily as I did tonight."

He smiled.

Perrett's mouth opened and closed several times. No words emerged. He started to shiver uncontrollably.

Satisfied, Caleb walked toward the door. He might not possess the more dramatic predatory talents that were so prevalent on the Jones family tree but he was, nevertheless, a hunter at heart. He could send that message with a smile.

Thirty-two

An hour later Lucinda stood with Victoria, Patricia and Edmund in a small alcove off the main ball-room. Together they contemplated the elegant crowd.

"It is just as you said, Lady Milden," Patricia declared with relish. "It seems that every gentleman in the room wants to dance with Lucinda. I do believe she has been out on the floor more often than I have."

"I don't understand it." Lucinda seized another glass of lemonade from a passing tray. She was parched. The only reason she had accepted so many invitations to dance was because the physical activity served as a temporary distraction from her growing sense of impending disaster. She could not escape the sensation that Caleb had made a grave mistake by meeting with the kidnapper. "What on earth is the attraction of a woman everyone believes was nearly sold into a brothel?"

Victoria smiled a serenely satisfied smile. "Never underestimate the appeal of a notorious lady, especially one who has been claimed by a member of the Jones family."

Lucinda choked on her lemonade. "Claimed?" she sputtered. "Claimed? What on earth are you saying? Mr. Jones danced one dance with me tonight and then took his leave."

"You may believe me when I tell you that the rumors about your association with Caleb Jones have been flying for days," Victoria said cheerfully.

Lucinda felt the heat rush into her face. "I hired him in his professional capacity to look into a private matter for me. Our association is a matter of business."

Victoria chuckled. "No one who saw him dancing with you the other evening and again tonight could possibly conclude that your relationship is limited to a matter of business."

"This is getting awkward," Lucinda said.

"Nonsense." Victoria waved the entire thing aside with a flick of her fan. "Nothing awkward about it." She raised a brow at Edmund. "I think it is past time you took Patricia out onto the floor, Mr. Fletcher. We must maintain the impression that you are a friend of the family."

Lucinda could have sworn that Edmund flushed a dull red. Patricia turned a warm pink and suddenly became very busy adjusting the hooks that pinned up the train of her gown.

Edmund stiffened and inclined his head very formally. "Miss Patricia, if you will do me the honor?"

Patricia stopped fussing with her gown, took a deep breath and gave him her gloved hand. Edmund led her away through the crowd.

Victoria glowed with enthusiasm. "Don't they make a lovely couple?"

Lucinda watched Edmund and Patricia move onto the dance floor. "When they aren't bickering. Honestly, I have never heard two young people squabble more than that pair. It's enough to make you . . ." She stopped and turned her head to look at Victoria. "Oh, good grief, surely you aren't going to tell me that they are a match?"

"A perfect match. Knew it the moment I saw them together, of course. Now we shall see what happens. Nothing like the waltz to quicken the pulse of romance."

Lucinda saw Edmund pull Patricia a little closer and spin her away into a long, whirling turn. Even from this distance it was easy to see that Patricia was practically effervescent.

"Hmm," she said. "Well, I suppose that explains the squabbling and the giggles. But I foresee problems. Mr. Fletcher seems very nice and he has certainly devoted himself to protecting Patricia but I fear he does not meet her requirements in a husband. He does not appear to have a steady, respectable income of his own, for one thing. As I understand it, his work for Mr. Jones is of a somewhat erratic and unpredictable nature. And he knows nothing of archaeology."

"Mere trifles, I assure you."

"I'm not so sure that Patricia or her parents will view those issues as trifles."

"When the energy is right, love finds a way."

Lucinda looked at her. "Love might find a way but it could lead to disaster. It is one thing for a woman of a certain age to engage in an illicit relationship, quite another for a young lady like my cousin to do so. You know that as well as I do."

"I assure you, I am not in the business of promoting illicit affairs." Victoria was genuinely offended. "I'm a matchmaker and I take my professional responsibilities very seriously. Mark my words, Patricia and Mr. Fletcher will be properly wed."

"In spite of the obvious obstacles?"

"No," Victoria said. "Because of them. Growing love is rather like growing good wine grapes."

"Meaning that the fruit is sweeter when the vines are forced to struggle under somewhat difficult conditions?"

"Precisely."

Thirty-three

No hansoms or hackneys prowled the dark streets in the vicinity of the Red Dog tavern. It was not the heavy fog that kept them away. It was the fact that the drivers were well aware that few of the denizens of the poorly lit neighborhood could afford the luxury of traveling by carriage.

Caleb walked toward the corner where a single gas lamp glowed in the mist. The glary light served as a beacon but it did not penetrate far into the night. His intuition warned him that he was being followed even before he heard the footsteps echoing behind him. The door to the tavern had not opened again. Whoever was back there in the shadows had been watching the entrance from across the street, waiting for him.

He had been followed from the Wrothmere ball, he thought. That certainly explained the edgy sensation he had been experiencing for the past hour.

Heat and energy pulsed through him, the same arousing sensations he experienced when previously dark sections of the maze were suddenly illuminated. It was always possible that his follower was an ordinary footpad seeking a convenient victim to rob but his talent told him otherwise. He estimated there was a ninety-nine percent probability that he was about to meet Perrett's demon.

He kept his own pace steady and deliberate as though unaware of the man behind him. The footsteps drew closer. There was no point in turning around to try to catch a glimpse of his pursuer. Only a true hunter endowed with psychical night vision would be able to see anything more than a dark shadow in the thick fog.

He removed one glove, put his hand into the pocket of his over-coat and took out the gun. Keeping the pistol out of sight alongside his leg, he moved into the glowing mist that surrounded the streetlamp.

The shocking blast of fear came out of nowhere. It stopped his breath for an instant, scattering his senses and flaying his nerves. There was a sharp clang. He realized in a rather vague way that he had dropped the gun.

He stumbled to a halt, frozen with a nameless dread that, in some small corner of his brain, he knew had no basis in logic or reason. His pulse thudded. His lungs tightened. It was all he could do to breathe.

He was suddenly plunged into his ultimate nightmare, teetering on the brink of the abyss that was chaos. Raw panic scorched through his veins.

Instinctively and intuitively he heightened all of his senses in response to the assault. His talent flared. The sense of impending chaos receded slightly, enough to allow him to pluck a few certainties from the swamp of incomprehensible darkness that threatened to engulf him.

He is doing this to you. This is how he murdered Sharpy and Daykin. He sends his victims into a great panic. You must push back or you will drown in chaos.

He would not leave the world like this, a victim of a maelstrom of utterly random, meaningless energy. He would find the patterns of clarity, reason and stability. That was his gift and he would use it to make the center hold even if he died in the process.

It took every fiber of willpower that he possessed but he managed to turn around to confront the killer. The process seemed to take an eternity because he had to concentrate so fiercely to make his muscles respond.

Perrett's demon materialized out of the fog and moved into the misty light. There were no flames in its eyes, no long claws or giant bat wings, but Caleb did not doubt but that he was confronting a monster.

"I'm surprised to see you here tonight, Jones." The creature came to a halt a few feet away. "Not the sort of neighborhood where one expects to find a gentleman of your station, is it? What brings you to these streets? Some amusing lust that cannot be satisfied in a better part of town, perhaps? A favorite opium den?"

Caleb said nothing. He was not sure he could speak. The searing energy assailing his senses seemed to have paralyzed his tongue. But his talent was responding to his will. Deep in his mind, a maze grew sharper, clearer, more comprehensible. A crystal wall glowed here, a floor there. Now all he had to do was find ways to link the illuminated portions.

"Allow me to introduce myself," the demon said. With a leisurely gesture he stripped off a glove, reached into his coat pocket and took out a small object that gleamed gold in the hazy light. "My name is Allister Norcross."

He opened the snuffbox and took a pinch of the powdery contents. Holding the mixture to his nose, he inhaled sharply.

An instant later another sharp blast of panic scorched Caleb's senses. It was all he could do not to collapse to the pavement in shivering, mindless terror.

"Ah, yes, the new version of the formula is working very well, indeed," Norcross said. "Hulsey was right."

Inside the maze more corridors glowed. Caleb forced

back the tidal wave of fear and focused on the pattern. He could do this. He knew how to hold his emotions at bay while he engaged his talent. He had spent most of his life learning how to control the core of wild, dangerous energy that was the source of his psychical power.

"I must say, I'm disappointed in you, sir." Norcross closed the snuffbox and dropped it back into his pocket. "I expected more from a member of the legendary Jones family."

"What do you want from me?" Caleb got out.

"So you found your tongue, did you?" Norcross was pleased. "Very good. Now I am somewhat impressed. Very few people can manage a coherent sentence when I demonstrate my talent."

Caleb said nothing.

"I will tell you what I want from you, Caleb Jones." Excitement crept into Norcross's voice. "I want to watch you go mad with fear, and then I want to watch you die of sheer fright."

"Why?"

"Because I enjoy such entertainment, of course. If it is any consolation, you will make a suitable test subject for the latest version of the formula. Hulsey gave it to me this afternoon and I have not yet had an opportunity to experiment. I will be an audience of one, however. Sadly, the truth of what I can do with the power of my mind must remain known and appreciated only within a very small circle."

"One of the Circles within the Order of the Emerald Tablet."

For a couple of seconds the pressure of fear let up. Caleb realized that the statement had surprised Norcross into losing his focus for a short time. Generating fear at such a high level would require great energy and intense concentration.

A second later, however, another wave of panic struck. Even though he was prepared for it, Caleb sensed chaos drawing closer.

"So you have learned something of the Order," Norcross said. "More than certain parties have realized, perhaps. Very good, Mr. Jones. In answer to your question, I am a member of the Seventh Circle of Power. But that is about to change. Those of us in that Circle will soon be elevated to a much higher level."

"Killing me is the price of promotion?"

Norcross laughed. "No, Jones, killing you has become necessary because you have been deemed a threat to my Circle. We have no choice but to get rid of you now that it has become obvious that you have discovered Hulsey's trail. Can't have you finding him, you see. That would ruin everything. After you are gone, I will see to Miss Bromley and then all the loose ends will have been snipped off."

And with that a dozen more corridors glowed in several different dimensions within the maze. A new kind of fear shuddered through Caleb. This was no longer a matter of hanging on to his sanity until his last breath. He had to survive this encounter in order to protect Lucinda. That realization allowed him to focus with renewed intensity.

"Miss Bromley is not a threat to you," he said.

"Perhaps not, but we really can't take any more chances. The public and the press will not be unduly surprised to learn that she poisoned you, just as she did her fiancé. Then she will take her own life, just as her father did. All very neat, don't you think?"

"Lucinda knows nothing about your damned Circle."

"You, of all people, will surely understand the need to be thorough. Now then, this conversation has been amusing but it is finished. Goodbye, Mr. Jones."

Chaos rose up out of the abyss, a dark wave of uncontrolled power. Caleb took refuge in the most brightly lit section of the maze in the dimension where the single most important truth glowed with the strength of the sun. He had to survive because he was all that stood between the demon and Lucinda. The answers, when one finally saw them, were always so astonishingly simple.

The whirling darkness crashed over and around the psychical construct in his mind. Caleb watched the scene from within the safety of the crystalline structure. A strange exhilaration swept through him. It was not often that one was given a chance to observe the raw power of pure chaos. He was enthralled.

He thought he heard a man scream somewhere in the night but he ignored it, his entire attention fixed on the raging currents. He concentrated harder, certain now that he could perceive the faintest glimmerings of a pattern in the very heart of the energy storm.

He knew then that all the answers were there, waiting for him. He also understood with complete certainty that no man could fully comprehend such grand truths and still remain sane. Nevertheless, a glimpse or two would be enough to thrill him to the end of his days.

"Stop, damn you."

The shriek that accompanied the words was distracting. Caleb ignored it. Who would have dreamed that there was such dazzling beauty in chaos? He would never be able to analyze it, let alone control it. But surely he was entitled to savor the raging power of the fiery energy that fueled his talent.

"My heart. *My heart.* You can't do this. *Stop* it."

The last word ended on another terrified scream.

He could no longer tolerate the distraction. Something had to be done about Norcross. Caleb looked away from the hypnotic currents of chaos.

Norcross had pulled out a gun. Although he gripped it with both hands, the pistol shook wildly. His face was a twisted mask of terror.

"What are you doing to me?" he gasped. "I'm going to explode. You're killing me." He tried to level the pistol at Caleb's heart. "You're the one who's supposed to die, you bastard, not me."

Norcross intended to hurt Lucinda. There was only one thing to be done.

Caleb seized a handful of chaos and swatted Norcross the way he would have squashed an annoying insect.

Allister Norcross opened his mouth one last time but no scream emerged. He crumpled to the pavement and went very still.

Thirty-four

"You're sure he's dead?" Lucinda asked.

"It's not the sort of condition one is likely to misdiagnose," Caleb said. There was no emotion whatsoever in his voice.

"Sometimes a state of unconsciousness can mimic death."

"Trust me, he's dead, Lucinda. You'll soon see for yourself."

They were in her carriage on their way to the scene of the confrontation. A short time ago she had been so relieved to see Caleb walk into the ballroom that it was all she could do not to break down, weeping in relief. But the moment he had reached her side she sensed the volatile energy of violence shimmering in the atmosphere around him.

She knew then that her anxiety throughout the evening had not been a product of her imagination. Caleb had nearly died. It would, she thought, take a long time for her nerves to recover from that shattering realization.

But she was more concerned for Caleb. Something was very wrong. She could feel it. He had just been in a battle for his life, she reminded herself, and he had killed a man. Such things took a terrible toll.

"He said his name was Allister Norcross?" she asked.

"Yes."

"Were you acquainted with him?"

"No."

"What did you do with the body?"

"I was obliged to leave it in an abandoned building." He looked out the window into the fog-shrouded night. "There was no choice. It is difficult enough to find a hack or a hansom in that part of town if one happens to be alive. I did not think I'd turn up any drivers willing to accept a dead passenger."

"Why do you want me to look at the body?" she asked.

"Because you may be able to discern things with your talent that are unclear to me." He turned back to face her. "I am sorry to put you through this, Lucinda. But I think it is important."

"I understand." She pulled her cloak more tightly around her shoulders. She was shivering, not from the chill of the night but in response to the ice-and-fire currents of his aura.

Shute brought the carriage to a halt in an empty street outside a darkened building. Caleb got out first. Lucinda followed quickly.

"Stay here and keep watch," Caleb said to Shute.

"Aye, sir," Shute said. "Here, you'll be wanting the lantern."

Caleb took the lantern and lit it. The splash of fiery light turned his eyes into pools of fathomless shadow. Another chill went through Lucinda. The sense of wrongness deepened.

Without a word, Caleb turned and led the way down a narrow alley. He stopped at a door and pushed it inward. She collected her nerve and her senses the way she always did when she knew she was about to encounter death and moved cautiously into the room.

So much for the possibility that Norcross might be in a coma. There was no question but that the man on the floor was dead.

"Do you recognize him?" Caleb asked.

"No."

"He is not a botanist or a scientist you might have met? Perhaps at a lecture or a talk? Someone your father knew?"

She shook her head. "I do not know him, Caleb."

"What can you tell me about his death?"

She looked up, startled by the question. "You said you killed him."

"Yes."

"I ... assumed you used your gun," she said hesitantly.

"No."

"A knife?"

"Take a good look, Lucinda," he said very softly. "There is no blood."

Reluctantly she went closer to the body. "Perhaps he struck his head in the course of the struggle?"

"No," he said again in that same flat and deadly tone.

Cautiously she opened herself fully to the psychical residue that clung to the body. At once the lingering energy of strange and dangerous herbs splashed across her senses. She sucked in a sharp breath and took a step back.

"What is it?" Caleb asked.

"There is poison here," she said quietly. "But it is unlike anything I have ever encountered. It is definitely of a psychical nature, however, and would have affected this man's talent in unpredictable ways. It is highly corrosive in its effects, destroying even as it temporarily intensifies the senses."

"The founder's formula." Caleb sounded very certain. "He said Hulsey gave him a new, improved version this afternoon."

"I can assure you that if you had not killed him, the drug would have. And quite soon, I think."

He took out a handkerchief and crouched beside Norcross. His hands were protected by his leather gloves but he used the square of heavy linen to remove a small object from the dead man's coat.

The lantern light gleamed on an elegant gold snuffbox decorated with a triangle fashioned of small green stones.

"He used snuff?" She frowned. "I did not sense any tobacco on him."

"There is a powder inside this box. I think it is the drug."

She adjusted her eyeglasses and peered more closely at the lid of the box. "Those look like emeralds."

"I'm sure they are." Caleb studied the snuffbox as though it were a tiny explosive device. "The design itself is alchemical, the symbol for fire."

She heightened her senses again.

"Whatever is inside that snuffbox contains the ingredients in the poison that the dead man was taking," she said.

"Is it safe to handle the box?"

"Yes. I very much doubt that merely coming into contact with the powder would have any serious or lasting effects. One would have to inhale at least a dose or two before it began to affect the psychical senses in a permanent manner. Initially, at least, the effect would actually be quite stimulating. The victim would no doubt think that the drug was heightening his powers."

"When, in fact, it was killing him."

"Yes." She hesitated, trying to judge the lethal essence

of the powder. "A strong young man like Norcross might last as long as three or four days at most. An older or weaker one would succumb more quickly."

Caleb contemplated the tiny emerald-and-gold object. "How do you suggest we destroy the powder inside that box?"

"Almost anything will render it harmless. I can sense that the composition of the formula is extremely fragile and unstable. An acidic substance such as vinegar will destroy its power. So would alcohol or strong spirits. Heat would also disrupt its harmful properties."

"What would happen if one ate it?"

"Very little, I should think. The digestive process would destabilize it. But I would not suggest ingesting it."

"I wasn't planning to do so." Caleb wrapped the snuffbox very carefully in the handkerchief and got to his feet. "I will get rid of this as soon as possible."

She looked at Norcross. "What of him?"

"I will notify Inspector Spellar. He will deal with it."

"But how will you explain the manner of death?"

"That is Spellar's problem, not mine." Caleb scooped up the lantern. "Which is fortunate, under the circumstances."

She followed him toward the door. "I can understand that you do not wish to be involved in a murder investigation but it was, after all, a matter of self-defense."

"That is not the problem, Lucinda."

"What do you mean?"

"The problem is that I do not know how I killed that man."

Thirty-five

They stood together in Caleb's laboratory, looking at the crystal goblet sitting on a workbench. The goblet was filled with brandy that glowed warmly in the firelight. The snuffbox was at the bottom of the glass, open and empty, an emerald-and-gold jewel trapped in liquid amber.

Caleb had diluted the powdered drug and rendered it harmless by a process that involved dousing the little box in several immersions of the brandy. Lucinda had assured him that the formula had been entirely destroyed by the first round of strong spirits but he had not wanted to take any chances. After each immersion, he had emptied the used brandy into an iron pan and burned it off in the heat of the roaring fire.

"You're sure it is safe to handle now?" Caleb asked.

"Oh, yes," Lucinda said. "It was safe after the first dunking. I told you, the drug is extremely unstable. Once it breaks down, it loses the properties that enable it to affect the senses. Even without interference, I doubt that it would retain its potency for more than a few days at most."

He looked at her across the width of the workbench. "You can sense that?"

"Yes. That powder is like a cut flower. It starts to decay immediately. But why would anyone deliberately take a formula that is so lethal and works so quickly?"

"I told you, Norcross said it was a new version of the drug. Maybe there had been no time to carry out experiments."

"Or perhaps Norcross was the experiment?" she suggested.

"You may be right. He certainly seemed quite pleased with the effects. He obviously didn't realize that it was killing him."

Caleb fell silent for a moment. She watched him sink into his private place.

"Do you think you could create an antidote to the drug?" he asked after a while.

She shook her head. "I'm sorry. I know of no plant or herb that would effectively counteract the strange energy of whatever was in that snuffbox. That does not mean that a remedy could not be created someday, but it is beyond my abilities. I suspect it will require advances in the field of chemistry as well as a great deal of research and experimentation."

"Do not apologize. Sylvester claimed to have found an effective antidote for the original version of the formula. He went so far as to etch the ingredients on a sheet of gold that covered his strongbox. But he noted that it must be taken simultaneously with the drug. For obvious reasons, there has been no practical way to test its effectiveness."

Curiosity fizzed through her. "Do you have the recipe for the antidote?"

"The original is at Arcane House but I made a copy."

He disappeared into the maze of shelving. A moment later she heard the vault door open. When Caleb reappeared he had a notebook in one hand.

"I inscribed the recipe exactly as it was etched into the sheet of gold foil," he said.

He opened the book, turned a page and then moved aside so that she could see his notes. She adjusted her glasses, leaned down slightly and read swiftly through the Latin names of the various plants and herbs.

"Hmm," she said.

"What is it?"

"I recognize most of these ingredients and I am familiar with their normal and paranormal properties. I'm quite sure that none of them would have any effect against the powder that we found in the snuffbox or any other poison, for that matter. Quite the opposite, in fact."

"What do you mean?"

She straightened. "A cup of this so-called antidote would kill a person in a matter of minutes."

He exhaled slowly and nodded once. "I had a feeling that might be the case. It was too damned obvious. The wily old bastard left one last trap for his enemies and rivals."

"You say he etched that formula on a strongbox?"

Caleb flipped the notebook shut. "Sylvester knew that someday someone might steal his precious formula. So he left the warning that it was a slow-acting poison and ever so helpfully provided the antidote. Inscribed in gold, no less. What alchemist would have been able to resist?"

"I see what you mean."

He went to stand in front of the hearth and contemplated the flames.

"It is imperative that we discover Norcross's address and his connections as quickly as possible," he said. "It is our only hope of finding Hulsey and the other members of the Seventh Circle."

A chill went through her. "What will you do with them when you find them, Caleb? I doubt that you will discover any proof that they committed murder."

He did not take his attention off the fire. "I will discuss that issue with Gabe but I think the answer is clear. Hulsey and the people who employed him to brew the drug must be stopped."

She folded her arms and watched him closely. "You mean killed, do you not?"

Caleb said nothing.

"*No.*" She uncrossed her arms and hurried to his side. "Listen to me, Caleb. It is one thing to conduct investigations on behalf of the Arcane Society. But you cannot allow the organization to turn you into some sort of executioner for hire. Such work will destroy you as surely as any deadly poison."

He gripped the mantel. "What the hell am I supposed to do about men like Hulsey and those who hired him? What of the monsters the formula creates?"

"I agree such madmen must be stopped. But given the allure of the formula, I fear there will always be those who will seek its power. You cannot undertake the terrible task of killing them all. I will not allow it."

He looked at her, his eyes stark. "You won't *allow* it?"

She raised her chin. "I realize that you think it is not my place to tell you what to do. But I cannot stand by and say nothing while you talk of transforming yourself into a professional killer."

"Have you got a better solution?"

She took a deep breath. "I think the answer lies in the very nature of the formula. From what you have told me, those who take any version of it cannot survive long if they are deprived of it."

"Destroy the drug whenever and wherever I find it and those who use it will also be destroyed. Is that your answer?"

"I accept that the Society has a duty to stop those who

are intent on re-creating the drug. I also understand that there may be times when you will be forced to act as you did tonight. But whenever possible, I believe that you must let the drug do its deadly work for you."

He watched her very steadily. "Do you think that approach will make me any less responsible for the deaths that may result in the years ahead?"

"Yes," she said, very fierce now. "I do believe that. It is not a perfect solution. No death, regardless of how it is caused, will be easy for you. All will trouble you. But those who concoct the drug are not innocents, Caleb. They are well aware that they are dabbling in dangerous and forbidden research. If they die as a result of their work, so be it. Let the punishment fit the crime."

"You are a formidable woman, Lucinda Bromley."

"And you are a formidable man, Mr. Jones."

He released his death grip on the mantel and captured her face in his hands.

He kissed her with a hot, compelling urgency that caught her by surprise. Energy flared but it felt different than it had on the previous occasions when he had made love to her. There was the sensual power that she had sensed before but also a desperate hunger. The healer in her rose to the surface.

"Caleb, are you ill?"

"I think so. I'm not sure. All I know is that I need you tonight, Lucinda."

He began to strip the violet gown from her. She heard delicate fastenings pop and fragile silk tear.

Alarmed, she reached up to frame his face with her hands. The heat in him made her gasp. It emanated not just from his body but from his aura.

"You feel feverish," she whispered.

But even as she said the words, she knew that the

fever raging in him had its origins in the metaphysical, not the physical realm. And suddenly she understood.

"That man you believe you killed tonight—"

"I *did* kill him. What is more, I would do it again without a moment's hesitation. But I am discovering that there is a price to pay for using my talent in such a manner."

Shocked, she searched his face. "Caleb, are you telling me that you used your *talent* to kill that man?"

"Yes."

She suddenly understood. The psychical fever raging in him was an aftereffect of what he had done tonight. If he had indeed killed Norcross with his talent, he had no doubt been forced to push himself to his very limits. He would likely soon collapse in exhaustion. But in the meantime he was trying to contain and control the unsettling whirlwinds and dissonant energy patterns that would be the result of such an enormous effort.

"It's all right, Caleb. You are with me."

"Lucinda." His eyes were those of a man standing on the edge of endless night. "I need you more than I have ever needed anything in my life."

She wrapped her arms around him, trying to infuse him with her own light and energy.

"I'm here," she whispered.

He pushed her down onto the cot and opened his trousers with quick movements. He did not bother to fully undress. The next thing she knew he was falling on her, crushing her into the thin mattress. The cot creaked and groaned beneath his weight.

There were no tender, preliminary caresses this time. Caleb handled her with a ruthless desperation. She knew he was exerting enormous control in an effort not to hurt her. But his hot need generated a new and different kind of excitement.

284

She clutched his shoulders. "I'm not fragile."

"I know." He put his fevered face against her breasts. "I know. You are strong. So strong."

He slid his hand between her legs, cupping her, making sure that she was damp, and then he entered her in a searing rush of energy that seemed to set their very auras ablaze.

He thrust once, twice, a third time and then he went rigid above her, pulsing his essence into her.

When it was over he collapsed, suddenly, deeply asleep.

Thirty-six

She waited several minutes before she wriggled out from beneath his heavy weight. He stirred a little but he did not open his eyes. She touched the pulse at his throat. The strong, steady beat reassured her. He was cooler now, too.

She got to her feet and began to dress. The gray light of dawn lit the windows. She knew she should go home but she dared not leave Caleb until he awoke. She settled down into the chair in front of the fire and waited.

Eventually he opened his eyes. She was relieved to see no sign of the psychical heat.

"What time is it?" he asked.

"Nearly five. I'm glad I sent Shute home after he brought us here. I would hate to think of him having spent the night in the carriage waiting for me."

Caleb sat up and swung his legs to the floor. "No need to be concerned. In the polite world it is nothing to return home at dawn after a ball. Your neighbors will hardly notice."

"You are obviously unacquainted with my neighbors."

He got to his feet and looked down, evidently surprised to discover that he was still wearing most of his clothes. He grimaced and fastened his trousers.

"Do you really give a damn about your neighbors?" he asked.

"No," she said.

"Didn't think so." He finished adjusting his clothes and looked at her. "I apologize for my lack of finesse, Lucinda. Did I . . . ?"

"You did not hurt me," she said gently. "You would never hurt me."

He exhaled heavily. "It was like a sudden fever. I cannot explain it."

"I have been thinking about it. I believe the explanation lies in whatever you did to that madman last night."

He went very still. "I told you, I don't know what I did to him."

"But you are absolutely certain that you somehow caused his death with your talent."

"There is no doubt about it." His jaw hardened. "I . . . felt it when it happened."

"Did you *think* about killing him before you did it? Did you somehow *will* his death?"

"Such a thing is impossible. One cannot *will* another's death."

"It appears he was doing something very much like that to you."

"No, he did not will my death." Caleb rubbed the back of his neck. "He used his enhanced talent in some fashion to disrupt my aura. Everything that happened last night can be explained by psychical physics, not sorcery."

"Tell me exactly how it occurred."

Caleb lowered his hand. "I knew I was being murdered. I also knew that if I died he would go after you. I could not allow that to happen. I could barely move, not even to pick up the gun that I had dropped. Some instinct told me that my only hope was to call on the full force of my talent. I think I had some notion of trying to use it as a sort of shield against the currents of his energy."

"In other words, you tried to fight fire with fire?"

"I suppose that was the general idea. But when my senses flared to their fullest extent, I suddenly *knew* what to do. It was like reaching into the heart of a storm, Lucinda. It felt as if I had seized a fistful of chaos. In some way I cannot explain, I managed to hurl the energy at that man, disrupting his aura. He died instantly. What's more, I knew, even as I did it, that he would die."

She thought about that for a while.

Caleb waited.

"Hmm," she said finally.

Caleb scowled. "What the devil is that supposed to mean?"

"Well, it sounds to me as though you managed to channel your talent in such a way that it could be used as a weapon."

"Believe it or not, I figured that much out all by myself," he said grimly. "The questions are, how did I do it and why didn't I know I could do it until the moment was upon me?"

"I don't have all the answers but I could hazard a guess."

"What is that?"

"I suspect that the reason you didn't know you could manipulate the energy of your talent in such a way until that moment was that you've never been engaged in a life-or-death struggle where there were no other weapons available." She spread her hands. "You were at death's door. Your instincts took over."

He contemplated the dying fire. "It is a strange thing to know that one is capable of killing in such a fashion."

"I think what really worries you is that, in that

moment, you did not feel in control of yourself or your talent. You relied entirely on instinct and intuition rather than logic and reason."

There was a long silence. When he looked up from the fire, his expression was one of solemn wonder.

"As I have noted before, you are a very insightful woman, Lucinda."

She gestured at the maze of bookshelves that surrounded them. "You told me that there have been other instances of powerful talents who could kill with their psychical energy."

"Yes, but the records of such individuals in the Society are so rare as to be the stuff of myth and legend."

She smiled. "You are a Jones, sir. A direct descendant of Sylvester the Alchemist. That makes you the stuff of myth and legend."

"But I do not possess any of those unusual talents. My gift is merely a very keen sense of intuition combined with a knack for spotting patterns. How can such an ability be made to act as a weapon?"

"I do not know," she said. "But power is power, regardless of how it is channeled, and you possess a great deal of it."

He thought about that for a long while.

"You are right," he said eventually. "It is an incomplete explanation but it will have to do. We will keep this information to ourselves, Lucinda. Do you understand? I do not want even the members of my family to find out what really happened last night."

"In other words, this newly discovered ability of yours is going to become a deep, dark Jones agency secret?"

"You may as well become accustomed to keeping secrets," he said. "Something tells me that the agency will accumulate a great many in the years ahead."

Thirty-seven

"You are going to become Mr. Jones's business partner?" Patricia hurried along the conservatory path,
trying to keep up with Lucinda. "But you are a botanist
and a healer, not a private inquiry agent."

"I said I am considering becoming his partner in the
firm." Lucinda stopped to tilt her watering can over
some bromeliads. "You know that I have a talent for
detecting poison. That ability is very useful in the investigation business."

"Yes, but to become a real partner in the Jones agency?
How absolutely thrilling." Patricia brimmed with admiration. "You have always been such an inspiration to
me, Lucy."

"Thank you." A little rush of satisfaction swept
through Lucinda. "Mr. Jones feels that my talent will be
of particular importance to the agency in the years ahead
due to the problem of this new Cabal."

"I can certainly understand that. Edmund mentioned
to me that he expects to be doing a great deal of consulting for the agency, as well."

Lucinda raised the spout of the watering can.
"Edmund?"

Patricia blushed. "Mr. Fletcher."

"I see. I could not help but notice at breakfast that you
and Mr. Fletcher seem to be on much better terms today."

290

"He is a very interesting gentleman," Patricia said. "I find his conversation quite stimulating."

"Do you, indeed?"

"I realize that he does not meet all of my requirements, of course," Patricia said quickly.

"Hmm."

"He possesses a rather unusual talent."

"So Mr. Jones told us."

"And a somewhat extraordinary past."

Lucinda looked at her. "How extraordinary?"

"Well, before he became a stage magician, he was obliged to make his living by helping himself to the odd valuable here and there."

"Good grief, he was a *thief*?"

"He confided everything to me, Lucy. He only stole from other criminals and fences. He was careful to take only very small items that would never be missed."

"In other words, his victims were people he knew would not call in the police."

Patricia brightened. "Precisely. He has a talent for getting through locked doors and for sensing where valuables are concealed. Those are the very abilities that will make him so useful to Mr. Jones."

"You appear to be quite concerned with Mr. Fletcher's future with the Jones agency."

Patricia straightened her shoulders. "I intend to marry him, Lucy."

"Oh, Patricia." Lucinda put aside the watering can and opened her arms. "What will your parents say when they find out that you are marrying a man who was once a thief and a magician?"

Patricia's eyes watered. She flung herself into Lucinda's arms.

"I don't know," she sobbed. "But I love him, Lucy."

"I know." Lucinda hugged her. "Lady Milden is equally aware of your affections."

Patricia raised her tearstained face, startled. "She knows?"

"She told me last night at the ball that you and Mr. Fletcher are an ideal match."

"Oh, my." Patricia pulled out a dainty handkerchief and blotted her eyes. "What am I to do? How will I convince Mama and Papa that I should be allowed to marry Mr. Fletcher?"

"We hired Lady Milden to guide us through this business of finding you a husband. As Mr. Jones says, one must put one's faith in experts. We will leave the problem of dealing with your parents to your matchmaker."

Patricia stuffed the damp handkerchief into the pocket of her gown and raised her chin. "If Mama and Papa do not give their consent, I vow I will elope with Mr. Fletcher."

"Hmm."

"Do you really think Lady Milden can convince my parents to accept him?"

"I think she is capable of achieving whatever she sets out to do."

Patricia smiled and blinked away the last of her tears. "Oh, Lucy. I do love him so."

"I understand," Lucinda said gently. "More than you can possibly know."

Thirty-eight

Edmund materialized out of the shadows behind the jeweler's shop. Caleb could feel the energy sizzling in the atmosphere. Fletcher might have honest intentions but the man did enjoy employing his talent. *Don't we all?*

"You'd think a jeweler would have better locks," Edmund said. Triumph and cool satisfaction hummed in the words.

"Did you get it?" Caleb asked.

"Of course." Edmund held up a leather-bound volume. "Ralston's record of jewelry commissions. This covers the last year."

"Good work." Caleb took the book. "We can study it in the carriage. Then you will replace it precisely where you found it. With luck, in the morning the jeweler will never notice that it was ever touched."

"Depend upon it, Mr. Jones." Edmund was clearly offended by the implication that he might not be able to handle such a task. "Tomorrow morning no one will notice anything amiss."

"I believe you. Let's go."

They made their way back along the alley to where Shute waited with the carriage. Earlier that evening Caleb had called upon one of his many relations, a young hunter, to take over the duties of bodyguard in Landreth

Square. He could have handled the task of breaking into the jeweler's shop but there was no question but that Fletcher's skill in this sort of thing was superior to his own.

Edmund had been the one who recognized the jeweler's hallmark on the bottom of the snuffbox. Caleb had refrained from inquiring how a magician had come to be so familiar with the signatures of very expensive jewelers. He had a fairly good idea of how Fletcher had survived before he went on the stage.

Inside the cramped vehicle, Caleb secured the curtains, turned up the lamps and opened the journal of accounts. It did not take long to find what he was looking for.

"One gold snuffbox to be decorated with the design of a triangle picked out in emeralds of good quality," he read. "To be identical to previous two commissions."

"There's more than one of those snuffboxes?" Edmund asked.

"Three at least, evidently."

"Who was the client?"

Caleb moved his finger across the page. Now it was his turn to feel the exhilarating rush of energy as more of the maze was suddenly illuminated. "Lord Thaxter. The address is Hollingford Square."

"You know him?"

"Not well but we have met." Caleb looked up. "He is a wealthy member of the Arcane Society. Some sort of botanical talent, I believe. I told Gabe this conspiracy reaches deep into the organization. One can only guess how many others within the Society are involved in the Order of the Emerald Tablet."

"What is the next step?"

"We pay a visit to Hollingford Square."

"It is after midnight."

"We are not going there to take tea with Thaxter."

Hollingford Square was drenched in moonlight. Caleb and Edmund left Shute and the carriage in the deep shadows and went around to the gardens behind the big house. Edmund made quick work of the locked gate.

"No lights on in the place," he observed quietly. "Everyone is abed. We are fortunate. There don't appear to be any dogs so we won't need the slice of roast that we picked up at the tavern."

"In that case, you may consume it later. Consider it a benefit of working for the Jones agency."

Edmund did not respond. He was utterly focused on the business ahead.

"The biggest risk will be the servants," he continued. "You never know when one of them will suddenly decide to go to the kitchen for a late-night snack. In addition to that, one must be concerned with the possibility that the owner of the house is an overly anxious sort who keeps a pistol in a bedside table. But, generally speaking, no one ever wakes up."

"Thank you for the tips," Caleb said. "Always good to work with a professional."

"Yes, well, I should probably tell you that I have done this sort of thing before a time or two, Mr. Jones."

"I assumed as much."

"I know you come from a long line of hunters and that you can move quietly but I still say it would be best if I went in alone."

"No." Caleb studied the darkened house, anticipation crackling through him. He could sense answers waiting. "I need to go inside."

295

"Tell me what you hope to discover. I'll find it for you."

"That's the thing," Caleb said. "I won't know what I am looking for until I see it."

"Yes, sir." Edmund looked around. "These gardens are astonishing."

"I mentioned that Thaxter's talent has something to do with botany. It strikes me that if one set out to re-create the formula, it would be very logical to recruit at least some individuals with that sort of psychical ability."

"Doesn't sound like Allister Norcross took a keen interest in botany."

"No, I don't think he did. I suspect his role in the Seventh Circle was of a somewhat different nature."

"He killed the apothecary and one of the kidnappers, didn't he?" Edmund asked quietly.

"Yes."

They entered through the kitchen. Both of them halted immediately. Caleb knew that Edmund was picking up the same sensation of eerie not-quite emptiness.

"No servants below stairs," Edmund said quietly. "I'm sure of it. But there is someone here. I can feel it."

"So can I."

"Reminds me of the sensation I got the night I let myself into Jasper Vine's mansion and found him dead. His staff was gone that night. The house was empty and there was a very strange atmosphere."

"You robbed the most powerful underworld lord in London?"

"A number of times. I don't think he ever noticed. I made a habit of taking only small things, you see, the odd pocket watch or a ring."

"The sort of items a very wealthy man might think he had simply misplaced."

"Right," Edmund said. "Not that Vine would have called in the police. Just didn't want him to come looking for me."

"Where did you find the body?"

"In the library. I don't mind telling you, it was a very unsettling encounter. He looked as if he'd seen a ghost just before he died. His face was all twisted up in fright. I helped myself to a very nice clock and a string of pearls he'd bought for one of his women and then I left."

"Son of a bitch," Caleb said softly. Another section of the maze glowed. "That sounds like Allister Norcross's work."

"How could Vine have been involved in this affair?"

"I don't know yet. But he was. I can feel it."

They moved through the kitchen and out into a long hall. Caleb paused at the door to the library. The drawers of the desk stood open. Most were empty of whatever papers and files they had once contained.

"Someone got here before us," he said.

"Sloppy work," Edmund observed.

"Whoever he was, he was in a hurry."

The morning room and drawing room were silent and still. Moonlight and the glow of the streetlamps shafted through uncovered windows. The servants had departed without bothering to close the curtains.

They started up the wide staircase. A faint voice became audible from somewhere in the heavy stillness above.

A man, Caleb thought, speaking to someone else. But there was no response.

He took his gun out of the pocket of his coat and went quietly along the hall. Edmund followed close behind.

The voice grew louder as they approached the last

bedroom on the left. A cold draft of air whispered from the room. Someone had opened a window.

"... I have been poisoned, you see. That is why I can talk to ghosts. Hulsey has murdered me. He blames me for her death. Really, how was I to know . . . ?"

The words were spoken in an eerily normal, conversational fashion, the same tone that a man might have employed in his club to comment upon the weather.

"... It wasn't as though I had any choice. Not after Jones got involved. There was no telling, you see. No telling what the apothecary knew. No telling what Hulsey might have said to her . . ."

Caleb stopped at the open door of the last bedroom and flattened himself against the wall. Edmund drifted past, a silent shadow, and took up a post on the opposite side of the doorway.

Caleb looked into the room. A man sat in a reading chair in front of a cold hearth. His legs were casually crossed at the knee, his elbows propped on the arms of the chair. He put his fingers together and spoke to the swath of moonlight that sliced through the open casement window.

"... Looking back, it was a great mistake to bring him into the Circle. Should have known better. But I was convinced I'd need his talent, you see. Didn't know about the insanity in the family, of course. Would never have agreed to make him a member if I'd been aware of that, I can assure you . . ."

Motioning Edmund to remain out of sight, Caleb lowered the gun to the side of his leg and moved into the room.

"Good evening, Thaxter," he said, keeping his voice very even and unthreatening. "Sorry to interrupt."

"What's this?" Thaxter turned his head, showing mild surprise but no alarm. "I say, are you another ghost, sir?"

"Not yet," Caleb said. He walked into the patch of moonlight and stopped. "My name is Jones. We have met."

Thaxter peered intently at him and then nodded. "Yes, of course," he said in the same too-casual tones. "Caleb Jones. I've been waiting for you."

"Have you, sir? Why is that?"

"I knew you would show up sooner or later." Thaxter tapped the side of his head with a forefinger. "Those of us with talent can sense these things. But I expect you know that as well as I do. You are a man of considerable power, yourself. Well, it is too late now, I'm afraid. I've been poisoned, you see."

"By the founder's formula."

"Nonsense. By Dr. Basil Hulsey. Gave me a fresh supply of the drug last night, you see. Told me it would be far more stable than the previous version. Don't mind saying I'd been having a few problems with the old one. We all have."

"Hulsey gave you a new version of the formula?"

"Yes, indeed." Thaxter moved one hand impatiently. "It transpired that he was most upset because we removed Daykin. But, really, what else could one do? It was his own fault."

"How is that?"

"Hulsey should never have taken the fern from Miss Bromley's conservatory and made the poison for Daykin. That brought you into the situation. There was a risk that you would eventually find your way to the apothecary. It was obvious she had to be removed. Didn't tell Hulsey but of course he found out immediately."

Caleb remembered the photograph in Daykin's rooms. "Daykin and Hulsey were lovers. She was the mother of his son. Hulsey poisoned you to avenge her death."

"Should have known better than to become involved with someone of Hulsey's background and station. That sort tend to be unreliable. They don't know their place. Problem is, Hulsey's combination of talent and skill is extremely rare. Not like one can just trot down to the workhouse and hire a scientist with psychical abilities, now is it?"

"You didn't murder Daykin, did you, Thaxter? You sent Allister Norcross to do it for you."

"That was his talent. The reason I agreed to bring him into the Circle. Knew he'd be useful to have around."

"You weren't concerned about his background?"

"Of course not. Norcross was a gentleman. As I said, I wasn't aware of the streak of insanity. Well, what's done is done, eh? We all make mistakes." He pulled out a gold pocket watch and studied it closely. "Not much time left, I see."

"Where is Hulsey?" Caleb asked.

"What's that?" Thaxter sounded distracted. He pushed himself up out of his chair and went to the chest of drawers that stood near the open window. "Hulsey? He and his son stopped by earlier tonight. Said something about wanting to see how the experiment was progressing. Evidently the poison takes a couple of days to kill. Hulsey explained he wanted me to have some time to think before I went on to the Other Side."

"Hulsey and his son were here tonight?"

"Took all my journals and records with them when they left. Told you, that sort can't be trusted."

"Do you know where they went?"

"Expect you'll find them in that laboratory of theirs over in Slater Lane. Hulsey practically lives there. Well, I must be going. Entire project is a failure. One doesn't survive such disasters when one is a member of the Order of the Emerald Tablet. That has been made quite clear."

"Tell me about the Order," Caleb said.

"The Order is for gentlemen and there is only one proper way out for a gentleman in a situation like this, isn't there?"

Thaxter reached into the drawer.

"No, damn you." Caleb launched himself across the room.

But fast as he was, he wasn't quite fast enough. Thaxter took the pistol out of the bureau, put it to his temple and pulled the trigger in one swift, efficient move.

Miniature lightning flashed in the darkness. The roar of the gun was deafening.

And then there was only the acute and sudden silence of death.

Thirty-nine

The laboratory had been stripped of any valuable instruments or notebooks that it might once have contained. All that remained was some shattered glass and a few bottles of common, readily obtainable chemicals.

"Hulsey and his son would have been in a great hurry to disappear after they gave Thaxter and Norcross the poisoned drug," Edmund said.

Caleb turned up the lamp and studied the chaotic scene. "Something died in here quite recently."

"There's a cage at the back of the room." Edmund walked forward cautiously, nose wrinkling in disgust. "Rats. Half a dozen of them." He turned away. "Well, it appears that the Jones agency has two mad scientists to track down now."

"Both of whom will no doubt soon be looking for someone to finance their research. That is the thing about science. It is impossible to pursue it without money. Sooner or later Hulsey will find a new patron. When he does, we will find him."

"It strikes me that you will be needing assistance in tracking down Hulsey and his son and the other members of the Cabal."

"You do not need to remind me of the enormity of the project that lies ahead," Caleb growled.

"I would just like to take this opportunity to let you know that I stand ready to offer my professional services to your firm at any time in the future."

"This isn't an employment agency, Fletcher."

"Right." Edmund cleared his throat. "Just thought I'd mention it. What do we do now?"

"Search the place. The last time Hulsey was forced to flee, he left behind some of his papers. With luck he might have left us something that will tell us where he went."

"I wonder if he had Miss Bromley's fern here," Edmund said, looking around. "I see no sign of it."

"I will bring Lucinda here immediately. She may be able to find some evidence of a botanical nature."

"I doubt that there will be anything for her to discover."

Caleb crossed the room to the cage. He looked at the motionless bodies of the six rats inside.

"I'm not so certain of that," he said.

"My *Ameliopteris amazonensis* was here," Lucinda said, fuming. "I can sense it. That nasty little thief Dr. Hulsey took it with him when he cleared out the laboratory. That makes twice that he has stolen it."

"The rats, Lucinda," Caleb said patiently.

With a sigh, she crossed the room to the cage and contemplated the dead rats. Her senses shivered. She pulled her cloak around herself.

"He fed them the same poisoned version of the drug that you found in the snuffboxes that Lord Thaxter and Allister Norcross carried," she said. "He must have tested it on the rats first to make sure it would kill."

"Hulsey wanted to be certain of his revenge," Caleb said.

Forty

"*I* brought the new version of the drug with me, sir." Hulsey produced a packet from the depths of his rumpled coat. He put it on the workbench. "Thought Mr. Norcross would drop around the laboratory this morning to collect it but when he didn't show up, I decided to deliver it myself. I know you are unable to leave your house these days."

Ellerbeck looked at the packet, trying to fight his rising sense of despair. Allister had left two nights ago saying that he intended to follow Caleb Jones. He had not returned.

Something had gone terribly wrong, Ellerbeck thought, but he had no means of making inquiries. Allister had been the one who brought him news of the outside world. There was little he could do now that he was alone. He dared not risk contacting Scotland Yard to inquire if the body of a certain gentleman had been discovered on the streets of London. He certainly could not contact the Jones agency for assistance.

Ellerbeck had racked his brain but he could not think of anything that his son had carried on his person that would lead anyone back to his home in Ransley Square. If Allister was, indeed, dead, it was likely that the first news of it would come in the form of a report in the press of the mysterious death of an unidentified man.

"You're certain this new version will work?" he said to Hulsey.

"Yes, indeed, sir." Hulsey bobbed his head. "The rats are thriving. There appear to be no ill effects whatsoever. I assure you that you'll be feeling much better in a day or two. Try it. You'll see what I mean. Very stimulating stuff and ever so much more stable."

Ellerbeck picked up the packet and opened it. He took a pinch and examined it closely, trying to assess it with what was left of his talent before he inhaled. He was aware of strong energies but that was all. The problem was that his senses were so badly warped now that he could no longer detect the nuances of botanical currents.

"It appears to be much more potent," he said. A tiny spark of hope leaped inside him. Maybe it was not too late.

"Yes, indeed," Hulsey said. "I can also assure you that in this new form it will keep much longer."

"How long?"

"Oh, a month or two, I should think." Hulsey surveyed the conservatory with great enthusiasm. "I say, very interesting collection you have here, sir. Mind if I stroll around and have a look?"

"Some other time," Ellerbeck said curtly. "I'm not feeling at all well today. I'm not disposed to give tours."

Hulsey flinched at the rebuff but recovered quickly. "Yes, of course, sir. Sorry, sir. Didn't mean to presume."

Ellerbeck inhaled a pinch of the powder. *Nothing left to lose.*

A diamond-sharp awareness blossomed inside him, driving out his anxiety. Power surged across his senses. For the first time in weeks he could feel the full force of the shifting currents that flooded the conservatory. Euphoria gripped him. *Not too late, after all.*

He would not only survive, he would become the most powerful member of the Order. According to Stilwell's notes, the drug had the potential to revive a man's potency and vigor. Stilwell had believed that it had the power to add a couple of decades to a normal life span. He would have time, he thought, to father more sons—healthy offspring—to take the place of Allister.

"You're right, Hulsey," he whispered, fighting to contain the sheer ecstasy that was flushing out his clogged senses. "It appears to be quite effective."

"Yes, sir. As promised, sir." Hulsey cleared his throat. "If you don't mind, Mr. Ellerbeck, I'm afraid I must request my wages. Expenses have been quite high in the laboratory lately, what with all the new ingredients needed to perfect the formula."

Disdain shafted through Ellerbeck, followed by amusement. "You may be a brilliant scientist, Hulsey, but Thaxter is right. You really are a shopkeeper at heart, aren't you? Just like the apothecary."

"Yes, sir." Behind the lenses of his eyeglasses, Hulsey's eyes glittered. "Just like the apothecary."

Forty-One

Caleb lounged against a workbench in Lucinda's conservatory and watched her examine the underside of a fern frond with a small instrument. It always gave him pleasure to see her at work here in her cheerful little jungle, he thought. The energy around her was so invigorating. Then again, he got similarly invigorated just watching her drink her morning coffee. Hell, all he had to do was think about her and he got invigorated.

"What the devil is that?" he asked.

"*Gymnogramma triangularis*," she said, not looking up. "Gold fern."

"Not the fern, the instrument you are using to examine it. Looks like a little spyglass."

"It's a folding brass linen prover. Those in the cloth trade use such devices to count the number of threads in a square of cloth. Very handy for looking at fern spores. One can carry it around in a pocket. Mr. Marcus E. Jones recommends it highly in his book *Ferns of the West*."

He smiled. "Is that so?"

She paused, a thoughtful expression on her face. "I wonder if he is a relation of yours?"

"Marcus E. Jones? I don't think so."

"Pity," she said. "He is a very well-respected pteridologist, you know."

"Jones is a common name."

"Yes," she said, "it is. So common, in fact, that a firm that specializes in a field as unusual as psychical investigations might want a more striking name than, say, Jones and Company."

"I disagree. The name, as it stands, provides a degree of anonymity that I think will prove very useful in the future."

"Hmm." She went back to peering through her glass again. "Any news on Hulsey?"

"Nothing, damn it. He and his son have disappeared. They'll no doubt be looking for new patrons soon."

"Not if word gets out that they poisoned their last financial backers."

"With luck, it won't. I told Gabe about the poison that was given to Thaxter and Norcross but he has decided not to inform the Council. He's convinced there are other highly placed members of the Society who are involved in the Cabal. Doesn't want to warn them that Hulsey might be a somewhat unreliable employee."

"So the case of the poisoned formula becomes yet another deep, dark agency secret?"

"At this rate it is going to be difficult to keep an account of all the secrets of the Jones agency."

Lucinda paused again, the little glass poised in midair. "Hmm."

"What?" he asked.

"I wonder if Dr. Hulsey and his son are using the formula."

"Good question. I've got one, myself."

"Yes?" she prompted.

"I keep thinking about the third snuffbox."

"What do you mean? Thaxter must have given it to Hulsey. He will have absconded with it even if he wasn't using it to keep a supply of the drug. After all, it was quite valuable, and Hulsey appears to be always in need of money."

"Maybe," Caleb said.

She beetled her brows. "You never say maybe, Caleb Jones. When it comes to assessing possibilities and probabilities, you always give numerical answers."

"Sometimes."

She cast her eyes up toward the roof of the conservatory in a silent plea for patience. "Well then, do you think Hulsey and his son have left London?"

"I'm almost ninety-nine percent certain that if they have left, it will be a temporary hiatus."

"Why temporary?"

"It would be difficult to find the kind of patrons they require in the wilds of Scotland or Wales. The problem is that the Jones agency isn't a police force, damn it. I don't have hundreds of agents to send out to scour the streets, let alone the countryside. And it is not as though I don't have other cases to see to. Got a new one this morning, in fact."

She looked up quickly, her eyes bright with interest. "Does it involve poison?"

Her enthusiasm was gratifying.

"I'm afraid not. Evidently someone endowed with a fair degree of talent is posing as a medium."

"What is so unusual about that? There must be several thousand people posing as mediums in London these days. They're all frauds."

"This one actually possesses some talent."

Lucinda gave a ladylike sniff. "Well, she certainly isn't using it to contact spirits in the Other World. That is quite impossible. Anyone who claims to speak with the dead is an out-and-out charlatan."

"Apparently this medium is supplying her own ghosts."

"What do you mean?"

"The client is convinced that the medium murdered one of the members of her séance group. The victim is certainly dead, so I agreed to look into the situation."

Lucinda pocketed the little glass and looked at him. "You don't have time to investigate every case personally, Caleb Jones. You are going to have to learn how to delegate. In addition, we really must build up a roster of agents who can be brought in to assist in various investigations."

He looked at her.

"We?" he repeated carefully.

"I've decided to accept your offer of a partnership." She smiled serenely. "Provided, of course, that my name will also go on the firm's cards."

"If you think for one minute I'm going to order a supply of calling cards with Bromley and Jones imprinted on each one—"

"Oh, very well." She held up a hand, palm out in surrender. "I'm willing to compromise. I'll accept Jones and Bromley but, really, Caleb, that just doesn't sound right. Admit it."

"No," he said. "It sure as hell doesn't."

"And neither does Jones and Company."

"Damn it, Lucinda—"

A movement in the doorway made him look around. Victoria stood in the opening. She had a very determined look about her.

"Victoria," he said. "A pleasure to see you today. But why have I suddenly been overcome with a sense of dark foreboding?"

"Very likely because you have psychical talents, sir." Victoria walked into the conservatory. She looked around, her expression lightening. "This is the first time

I've been in here. I must say, the atmosphere is quite refreshing."

"Thank you," Lucinda said. "I take it you are here to speak with Caleb. I will leave so that you may have some privacy."

"No need." Victoria paused to admire a large cluster of ferns. "As it happens, I would appreciate your assistance in this conversation."

Caleb watched her warily. "What is it you want me to do, Victoria?"

She turned away from the ferns. "I want you to find Mr. Fletcher a permanent position within the Society."

"He's already a member."

"You know very well that is not what I mean. He requires a steady, respectable income."

"Why?" Caleb asked.

"Because he is going to marry quite soon."

Forty-Two

Later that day Lucinda sat with Victoria in the library, drinking tea.

"I am making plans to introduce Mr. Fletcher to Patricia's parents in about a week's time," Victoria said. "I will have everything well in hand by then."

"How will you explain Mr. Fletcher's past to the McDaniels?" Lucinda asked with great interest.

"There is really very little to explain when one comes to the heart of the matter. Mr. Fletcher is a very talented gentleman, an orphan from a good family. He was born into the Arcane Society, of course, as was Patricia. For some time now he has been conducting clandestine investigations on behalf of the Council. Very hush-hush. The Master considers him invaluable."

"You make him sound like an agent of the Crown."

"Well, it is all true. I won't go into detail concerning his previous experience in the field." Victoria raised her cup. "I strongly advised Patricia and Mr. Fletcher not to mention such details, either."

"I'm sure they won't."

"I will also make it clear that Mr. Fletcher has been received in the homes of certain distinguished members of the Jones family."

"In other words, Mr. Fletcher has connections."

"At very high levels," Victoria added smoothly. "That should erase any lingering doubts the McDaniels might have concerning his respectability."

"Brilliant work, madam. Absolutely brilliant. I am very impressed."

Victoria allowed herself a small, satisfied smile. "I did tell you these things have a way of working out."

Lucinda picked up her cup. "Things did not work out by themselves. You are the one who is orchestrating the happy ending for my cousin and Mr. Fletcher."

"Well, one could hardly stand by and allow two young people to come to grief simply because the parents didn't approve of the marriage."

"You know as well as I do that a vast number of people would have had no problem doing precisely that. Most would consider other priorities such as social rank, inheritances and income to be far more important."

"Yes, well, I think I do have a certain talent for finessing those sorts of issues."

"Indeed," Lucinda said, filled with admiration. "It is always a pleasure to watch an expert at work."

"The final touch, of course, will come when I inform the McDaniels that the Master and the Council consider Mr. Fletcher's talent to be of such critical importance that he has been appointed to head the new Bureau of Museum Security, which will be under the auspices of the Jones agency."

"That should go far to reassure the McDaniels that Mr. Fletcher has an income of his own and is not marrying their daughter for her money."

"I must admit that I had Caleb's help on that last bit." Victoria arched a brow. "And yours, as well, I believe."

"I assure you it was not difficult to talk Caleb into creating the Bureau of Museum Security. He is starting

313

to realize that if it is to accomplish its mission, the Jones agency will require extensive resources and a number of consultants and agents. He cannot continue to oversee every investigation by himself."

"Indeed." Victoria took a delicate sip of tea and looked at Lucinda over the rim of the cup. "Now that I've finished with Patricia and Mr. Fletcher, what about you and Mr. Jones?"

"What of us?"

"Come now, Lucinda. You know as well as I do that you and Caleb belong together."

Lucinda blushed. "How odd that you should mention that. As it happens, I agree. Mr. Jones, however, is still coming to his senses."

"I see."

"Until he does, you will be interested to learn that I am to become a full partner in the Jones agency."

"Good Lord," Victoria said.

"The firm will henceforth be known as Bromley and Jones. Or, perhaps, Jones and Bromley. We have not come to an agreement on the matter of the name."

Victoria was dumbfounded.

"Good Lord," she said again. "Either way, I cannot imagine Caleb Jones agreeing to change the name of his firm."

Lucinda smiled. "Neither can I."

Forty-Three

"*I*t was very kind of you to call on me today, Miss Bromley," Ira Ellerbeck said.

"I came as soon as I got your message," Lucinda said. "I was so very sorry to learn of your grave illness, sir."

They were seated in the oppressive shadows of Ellerbeck's large library. All but one of the high Palladian windows was covered with heavy, blue velvet curtains, effectively shutting out most of the early afternoon sunlight. A pot of tea had been brought in shortly after Lucinda arrived.

"I appreciate your concern," Ellerbeck said. He sat behind his desk, as though he needed the large piece of furniture to support him. He sipped his tea and lowered the cup. "I confess I have not been up to receiving visitors in recent months but I fear the end is not far off now. I wanted to say farewell to some of my closest friends and associates."

"I am honored that you included me, sir."

"I could hardly overlook the daughter of a man who was one of my dearest acquaintances. In spite of what happened, I want you to know that I always respected your father."

"Thank you, sir."

"I confess that, in addition to wanting to say good-bye, I asked you here today in hopes of obtaining your advice. The doctors have told me that there is nothing more that can be done. Indeed, my own talent confirms that opinion. I do not expect a cure, of course."

"I understand," she said.

"Although you and I share similar talents, there are some distinct differences. It occurred to me that you might be able to suggest some therapeutic herb or plant that might alleviate the pain."

"I will do my best. Please describe your symptoms."

"They are both psychical and physical. My senses are failing quickly, Miss Bromley. They have become erratic and unreliable. I suffer from terrifying hallucinations and disturbing dreams. My nerves are shattered. In addition, I am experiencing severe headaches."

"I assume you have tried morphine or some other opium concoction?"

"Bah. You know how it is when it comes to the milk of the poppy. The quantity required to bring relief from the physical symptoms puts me into a deep sleep." He grimaced. "That is when the dreams come. I do not wish to end my life in a nightmare. I am seeking an alternative."

She glanced down at the satchel that she had placed on the carpet near her feet. Then she raised her eyes to meet his again. "I'm sorry. I don't think I have anything that will be effective in easing your particular symptoms."

"I was afraid of that. Well, it was worth a try."

"May I pour you another cup of tea?" she asked, getting to her feet.

"Thank you, my dear. Forgive me for not rising. I find myself quite exhausted today."

"Please don't concern yourself." She crossed to the

desk, picked up his cup and saucer and carried it back to the tea tray. "Do you have any notion of what brought on your unusual illness? Was it preceded by a severe fever or an infection of some kind?"

"No. The first symptoms appeared several months ago but I was able to keep them somewhat under control for a time. Gradually they have worsened, however. The doctors are at a loss and so am I. But enough of such depressing conversation, my dear. One hears that you have become a close friend of Mr. Caleb Jones."

She carried the cup and saucer back to the desk. "The fact that you have been housebound has obviously not kept you from hearing the latest news."

"Gossip has a way of filtering in everywhere, does it not?"

She returned to her chair, sat down and picked up her own cup. "Indeed it does."

"Dare I presume on my old friendship with your father to ask if Mr. Jones has honorable intentions?"

"Mr. Jones is a very honorable man," she said politely.

Ellerbeck's mouth tightened. He appeared to hesitate. Then he heaved a deep sigh. "Forgive me, my dear, but if you are entertaining a marriage offer from Jones, I feel I must bring up a very unpleasant subject."

"What is that, sir?"

"There have been rumors over the years that there is a streak of instability on the Jones's side of the family."

"Perhaps we should change the subject," she said coolly.

Ellerbeck flushed. "Yes, of course. I realize it is not my place to offer you paternal advice."

"Especially in light of the fact that you were involved

in my father's murder as well as the murders of Gordon Woodhall and my fiancé."

Ellerbeck started so violently that tea splashed on the desk. He stared at her. "I have no idea what you are talking about."

"I am quite certain that you are also connected to the attempt that was recently made on Mr. Jones's life. Perhaps you would care to discuss that, instead?"

"You astonish me, Miss Bromley."

"Why bother to lie. You are dying, after all."

"Yes. You are quite right, my dear. Quite right."

"I know that you are taking Hulsey's latest version of the formula. I sensed it in your aura the moment I walked into this room. It is deadly."

"You really do possess a most amazing talent."

She made a slight dismissing movement with her ungloved hand. "It is a poison. I am very good at detecting poisons."

Ellerbeck snorted derisively. He reached into his pocket and removed a small gold snuffbox. Green stones glittered on top. He set the box on the desk and studied it as though it were a strange artifact from another realm.

"Hulsey gave me what he claimed was the new, more stable version yesterday afternoon," he said. "I took three doses and was quite pleased. It seemed so much stronger than the earlier versions. It was not until the fourth dose last night that I realized what the bastard had done to me. To all of us, I suspect."

"He poisoned Thaxter and Norcross, as well, if that is what you mean. They are both dead."

"I thought as much. I estimate that I have a day or two left at most."

"The original version of the drug was a poison, too. You said your symptoms came on several months ago."

"The deterioration from the first version was much slower." He clenched his hand into a fist. "I had time. Now I have none."

"If you knew the founder's drug was dangerous, why did you take it?"

He fixed her with a bleak look. "All great scientific advances involve some risk. You cannot begin to imagine the power of the drug. One is infused with the most thrilling sensations. My talent rose far beyond its previous limits. I could see colors in the botanical world that I had never before been able to observe. I could comprehend aspects of plant life that had always been just beyond my reach. I could have accomplished great things, Miss Bromley."

"If it had not been for the unfortunate fact that the drug was killing you," she concluded.

"It transpired that I am allergic to it."

"In other words, it was killing you faster than it will kill the others in the Order."

"Much faster. Most will have years. Time enough to produce a more stable version of the drug. But I soon realized that I had only months."

"If you are severely allergic to the formula, how did you survive this long?"

"I used my talent to buy myself some time while Hulsey worked to improve the drug. Yesterday he gave me the results of his latest research." Ellerbeck's mouth twisted. "The bastard assured me that it would soon alleviate all of the allergic symptoms. Instead, it will put me into a coffin within forty-eight hours. He has murdered me as surely as I sit here."

"Why did you ask me to come here today?"

"I refuse to die until I have had my revenge on you, Miss Bromley."

"You blame me for what has happened?"

"Oh, yes, Miss Bromley, I blame you."

He pushed himself to his feet with great effort. She saw the gun in his hand.

"Do you intend to shoot me here in your library?" she asked, rising slowly. "That will be somewhat messy and rather difficult to explain to the police, will it not?"

"I no longer give a damn about the police, Miss Bromley. It is too late. You have destroyed everything. But I will have my vengeance on you if it is the last thing I do on this earth. I am feeling quite weak, however. I need some of my special tonic. Come with me. You are very likely the only other person in London who can truly appreciate what I have created."

She did not move.

He jerked the gun toward the conservatory and then pointed it at her again. "Open the door, Miss Bromley. Do it now or I will shoot you where you stand and to hell with the mess on the carpet."

She crossed the room and opened the door to the conservatory. She was braced for the impact but the currents of twisted, malevolent energies struck her senses with such force that she swayed. She grabbed the doorframe, instinctively trying to close down her senses.

Ellerbeck came up behind her and shoved her into the glass-walled chamber of botanical horrors.

"Welcome to my private hell, Miss Bromley."

Still off balance, she stumbled forward and nearly went down. She reeled, barely managing to catch hold of the edge of a workbench. Her skirts twisted treacherously around her ankles.

The sound of a key in a lock sent another shiver through her. Ellerbeck had sealed them inside the conservatory. She looked around, amazed and horrified.

Malformed plants and darkly luminous greenery filled the glass-and-iron chamber. She recognized an array of bizarre hybrids, cultivars and varieties of dozens of dangerous and poisonous species. Other specimens were so distorted that it was impossible to identify them. When she opened her senses very cautiously, she could detect traces of the original plants but the disturbing energies the strange new creations produced iced her blood.

"What have you done here, Mr. Ellerbeck?" she whispered, stunned. "Nothing is right in this conservatory."

"Nature does not recognize right or wrong, Miss Bromley. Only that which survives."

"You have distorted everything in here."

"After I developed the allergy to the founder's drug, I discovered that the atmosphere in this chamber could alleviate the worst of the side effects. Indeed, it has been all that has sustained me for the past few months. I have been unable to leave it for more than an hour or two at most. I was forced to *sleep* in here. In effect, this conservatory became my prison."

"Why did you do this to these plants?"

"This conservatory contains my life's work. Years ago I devoted myself to psychical plant research in an effort to find a cure for my son's insanity. What you see here is the result."

"Did you ever find the cure?" she asked, the botanist in her unable to resist.

"No, Miss Bromley, I failed in that, as well. And now Allister is dead."

Understanding slammed through her. "Allister Norcross was your son?"

He nodded bleakly. "Yes, Miss Bromley."

"Tell me why you murdered my father and his partner."

Ellerbeck took out a handkerchief and mopped his sweating brow. "Because they found out that I was the person who had taken one of the plants that you brought back from the Amazon."

"Mr. Jones was right," she said. "It all goes back to the last expedition."

Forty-Four

"Thaxter was insane at the end but oddly lucid," Caleb said. "He was the leader of the Seventh Circle of Power. As was the case with the Third, there is no obvious link to the other Circles or to those at the top of the Cabal."

He and Gabe were in his library-laboratory. He was attempting to provide his cousin with a full report of what had transpired, but a growing sense of unease was gnawing at him. It was not just the restless sensation that always came over him when he knew he was overlooking some vital piece of a puzzle. This was something else, something connected to Lucinda.

"We must assume that we did not find all of Stilwell's notes and papers," Gabe said. "There are obviously other copies of that formula floating around. That is very likely how the members of the Cabal obtained the recipe."

"The genie is out of the bottle, Gabe."

"Yes." Gabe folded his arms. "Hulsey deliberately altered the drug in such a way as to kill both Norcross and Thaxter in order to avenge the death of Mrs. Daykin?"

"She was his longtime lover, business partner and the mother of his son. He discovered that the Seventh Circle had arranged for Norcross to murder her. One can understand his desire for revenge."

"You're still uncertain about how many members there were in Thaxter's Circle?"

"According to the jeweler's records, three snuffboxes were ordered. The first two were commissioned about six months ago. The third was purchased a month later. Evidently Thaxter gave them out to the members of his Circle."

"Three snuffboxes means that there were three members in the Seventh Circle," Gabe said patiently.

"Thus far, only two snuffboxes are accounted for. Norcross's and Thaxter's."

"Hulsey must have the third one. When we track him down we will find it."

The need to go to Lucinda was growing ever stronger. "I'm ninety-seven percent sure that Hulsey doesn't have the third snuffbox," he said. *Calm yourself. She is safe at home.*

"What makes you believe that?"

"Thaxter did not consider Hulsey a social equal. As far as he was concerned, Basil Hulsey was merely skilled labor. He claimed that the Order of the Emerald Tablet only accepted members from what he considered a proper social background."

"In other words, Thaxter would have been willing to employ a man like Hulsey for his talents but he wouldn't have invited him into the Circle?"

"To him it would have been like inviting his gardener or his coachman to join his club. I certainly can't see him giving Hulsey an expensive gold snuffbox that, to his way of thinking, had been designed for a gentleman."

"Perhaps Hulsey insisted on being treated as an equal in the Circle and demanded a snuffbox of his own as part of his fee," Gabe offered.

"From what I have learned of his nature, I don't think

Hulsey gives a damn about social status. All he cares about is his research. There is something else that bothers me, as well. The third snuffbox was ordered five months ago. Hulsey was not involved in the Seventh Circle at that time."

"If you're right, then there is a third member of the Circle still unaccounted for."

"And another unsolved theft of a plant." Caleb looked at the paper he had put on the workbench. "There has to be a connection to Bromley's last expedition to the Amazon."

"What have you got there?"

"Lucinda's list of names of the botanists who viewed the specimens from the last expedition immediately after the Bromleys and Woodhall returned from the Amazon."

"What are you looking for?"

"The person who stole the first plant eighteen months ago. Do you have any notion how much effort is required just to discover whether or not a certain individual happened to be in London on a certain date a year and a half ago?"

"Sounds difficult," Gabe allowed.

"It's more than difficult. It's damn near impossible. I'm going to need more assistance, Gabe. And more money."

"Just to find the other plant thief?"

"Not just for that, for the agency. The regular clients pay for their investigations, but trying to chase down the rest of the Circles in the Order and identify the Cabal leaders will require a number of consultants. Consultants, it turns out, are expensive."

"I thought we agreed on a budget for the Jones agency."

"It will have to be increased."

A knock on the door interrupted him.

"Yes, Mrs. Perkins, what is it?" he called.

The housekeeper opened the door. "Inspector Spellar is here, sir."

"Send him up immediately."

"He's already here, sir." Mrs. Perkins drew herself up. "You will recall that I have given notice, Mr. Jones. I will be leaving your employ at the end of the week."

"Yes, yes, Mrs. Perkins," Caleb muttered. "You did mention it."

"I'll be expecting my wages then, sir."

"Never fear, Mrs. Perkins, you'll get your money."

"Mr. Jones." Spellar strolled into the room. He was munching on a pastry. He looked first at Gabe and then at Caleb. "And Mr. Jones. Good day to you both. As you can see, Mrs. Perkins very kindly gave me a bite to eat."

"What news, Spellar?" Caleb asked.

Spellar swallowed the last of the pastry and brushed the crumbs from his hands. "Thought you might be interested to know that I finally discovered Allister Norcross's address. Tracked him down through his tailor."

"The tailor remembered him?" Gabe asked.

"Tailors always remember their expensive customers," Spellar said. "This one informed me that he sent Norcross's bill to Number Fourteen Ransley Square."

Caleb frowned. "That is a neighborhood of large houses, not a street where a single man would rent lodgings."

"Norcross was staying at the home of his uncle, who evidently is quite ill. I stopped by on my way here to make inquiries but I was told that the owner of the house was too ill to receive callers." Spellar smiled. "It occurred to me that perhaps it might be easier for a Jones to get past the front door."

Caleb looked at the list of names and addresses. The last passages of the maze were suddenly illuminated.

"Ransley Square," he said. "The bastard is supposed to be dying. If he took Hulsey's last version of the formula, that is probably exactly what he is doing."

He had told Lucinda that he could not always understand why people acted the way they did but some motives he comprehended very well, indeed. Vengeance was one of them. And that was all that was left for a man in Ellerbeck's situation.

He was on his feet and heading for the door without thinking about it, relying entirely on his intuition.

"Out of my way, Spellar," he said.

"Where are you going?" Gabe called after him.

"Ransley Square. Lucinda is there."

Forty-Five

"**Y**ou are the one who stole the first plant from my conservatory," Lucinda said. "Why did you take it?"

"You will recall that immediately after you and the others returned from that last expedition, your father and Woodhall showed me the specimens that had been collected. With my talent, I comprehended the true potential of one of them. But I also knew that Bromley and Woodhall would never allow me to grow it for the purpose I intended."

"You made some poison from it?"

"I made a most interesting drug from it, Miss Bromley. It puts an individual into an extremely suggestible hypnotic state. While in that state he will do whatever he is told to do without question. When the effects of the drug wear off, the victim does not recall what happened while under the influence. As you can well imagine, there are those who would pay dearly to have such power over others."

"You sold this drug?"

"It wasn't that simple," Ellerbeck whispered. He was starting to slur his words. "I realized I had an astonishingly valuable product but I did not know how to go about finding buyers for it. I'm a gentleman, after all, not a shopkeeper. I discovered Mrs. Daykin one afternoon

328

when I went to her establishment. I sensed the poisons she kept behind the counter and knew she might be open to a business arrangement."

"She found your customers for you?"

"She found one customer in particular," Ellerbeck corrected. "An underworld lord who was willing to pay the very high price I charged for the drug. In exchange, he agreed to acquire all that I could supply. It was a very profitable association for all concerned while it lasted."

"When did it end?"

"Six months ago, when I joined the Seventh Circle."

"I would have thought this criminal lord would have objected quite strongly when he discovered that you no longer intended to supply him with the drug."

"Allister took care of Jasper Vine for me." Ellerbeck's mouth twisted. "Caused quite a sensation in the press. The villain's associates and Scotland Yard were all convinced that he succumbed to a heart attack. I did society a favor, I assure you."

"How did you get involved with the Order of the Emerald Tablet?"

"Lord Thaxter came to see me. He was a member of the Order and he had been authorized to recruit botanical talents for a new Circle of Power."

"The Order wanted you to work on the founder's formula, I assume."

"It had become clear that the version created from John Stilwell's notes was deeply flawed," Ellerbeck said. "The members of the First Circle are quite anxious to make it more stable."

"So the Order is conducting research to improve the drug?"

"Yes. I was eager to take on the project. I was certain that with my heightened talents I would soon find the answers. But when my son and I began experiencing side effects, the work took on a new urgency."

"You gave the formula to your own son? How could you do that? It is one thing to experiment on yourself. Why would you put him at risk, too?"

"You know nothing about my son," Ellerbeck whispered. "The formula was his only hope."

"What do you mean?"

"As I said, he was quite insane, Miss Bromley. I was forced to put him into a private asylum when he was only twelve years of age. I did that the day after he murdered his own mother and sister with a carving knife."

"Dear heaven."

"I told the police that Allister died at the hands of the unknown intruder who had killed my wife and my daughter. I changed his last name when I put him into the asylum. As far as the world is concerned, Allister Ellerbeck has been dead for years. Now, thanks to you and Caleb Jones, he truly has been taken from me."

"What made you think that the formula would cure his insanity?"

"I was certain that his mental illness was linked to his unstable psychical senses. I thought that if they could be strengthened, he might become sane. For a short time it appeared to work. I was able to take him out of the asylum and bring him here to live with me. I introduced him to my friends and associates as my nephew since I could hardly claim that he had come back from the dead."

"But soon the toxic side effects of the drug began to show, didn't they?" Lucinda said.

"He was plunging back into insanity before my very eyes but this time he was so much more dangerous because the formula had heightened his senses to a level that allowed him to kill with his talent. I knew we were both doomed unless the drug could be stabilized and made less toxic."

"You weren't making any progress improving the drug, though, were you? Was that when you discovered that the penalty for failure within the Order is death?"

"Yes, Miss Bromley."

"That was when you and Thaxter went looking for a modern-day alchemist to assist you, wasn't it?"

"Believe it or not, I considered inviting you to join the Order, Miss Bromley. But Thaxter wouldn't hear of taking a woman into the Circle. In any event, I feared that if you ever learned the truth about the death of your father and Woodhall, you might go to the police or to the Council."

"I would never have agreed to help you work on the formula," she said tightly.

"You are so like your father," Ellerbeck said wearily. "All that bloody self-righteousness is very tiresome. In desperation I turned to Mrs. Daykin for advice. I knew she was aware of other botanical talents in London who might abide by a somewhat different set of ethical standards. She suggested I discuss the matter with a certain Dr. Basil Hulsey, who, as it happened, was looking for a new patron."

"Why did you send Hulsey to my conservatory to steal my *Ameliopteris*?"

"*I did not send him to steal that damned fern,*" Ellerbeck hissed. "He wanted it for his own, private experiments. Daykin had told him about it. Nothing would do but that he had to have it."

"But he was supposed to be working on the founder's formula."

"In order to get him to help us, we had to strike a bargain with him." Ellerbeck slumped against a workbench and blotted his brow again. "We agreed to finance

331

his private research as long as he made progress on stabilizing the formula."

"But he wasn't successful, was he?"

"I have no notion, Miss Bromley, and I never will now because I will soon be dead. Everything has gone wrong because you brought Caleb Jones into this affair."

The hand holding the gun was shaking.

"One more question," she said softly. "Why did you kill my fiancé?"

"I had no choice." Ellerbeck snorted. "Glasson was nothing if not a consummate opportunist. He suspected that I was the one who killed your father and Woodhall. He followed me to Daykin's shop and realized that I was dealing in poison. He tried to blackmail me. I had to get rid of him. That little scuffle between the two of you in the Carstairs Botanical Society gardens set the stage very nicely."

"You are responsible for the deaths of a number of people, Mr. Ellerbeck, but it ends now. You will not kill me."

"You are wrong, Miss Bromley." The gun wavered precariously in Ellerbeck's hand. "I will have my vengeance if it is the last thing I do."

"You are no longer capable of aiming that gun at me, let alone of pulling the trigger. You are quite exhausted and you will soon collapse into a deep sleep."

"Wh . . . what are you talking about?"

"I put a drug into your tea," she said gently. "It works very rapidly."

Ellerbeck trembled, as though in the grip of a raging fever. He blinked, trying to clear his vision. The gun slipped from his hand. He stared at her, uncomprehending.

"You poisoned me?" he whispered.

"The moment I walked into your house today I sensed the terrible energy emanating from this conservatory. I knew something was very wrong. When your housekeeper went to inform you that I had arrived, I took a sleeping powder from my satchel. It is odorless and tasteless. I had no difficulty slipping it into your tea. You have drunk two full cups of it."

"Impossible," he gasped. "I watched you pour the tea. I saw no bottles or packets that could have contained poison."

Glass splintered and shattered. Caleb walked into the conservatory. The gun in his hand was leveled at Ellerbeck.

"Are you all right?" he said to Lucinda without taking his eyes off Ellerbeck.

"Yes," she said.

Ellerbeck crumpled to his knees. "How did you do it?" he demanded. "How did you poison my tea?"

She held up her ungloved hand so that he could see her lapis-and-amber ring. Very deliberately she opened the tiny, hinged lid to reveal the hidden chamber.

"Some of the stories about me are true, Mr. Ellerbeck."

Forty-Six

"The good news is that Hulsey did not have an opportunity to return to Ellerbeck's residence to remove any files and records," Caleb said. "There may be something useful among the papers and notebooks that Fletcher and I confiscated."

They were in her library. Caleb was stalking up and down in front of the hearth. He had been doing a great deal of stalking about since arriving a short time ago. She was seated at her desk, hands clasped on top, doing her best to hang on to her patience.

"Hulsey was probably waiting for the full effects of the poison to take hold," Lucinda said. "He no doubt meant to go back last night when he could have been certain that Ellerbeck was dying. Fortunately, I got there yesterday afternoon, instead."

"There was nothing fortunate about your presence in Ellerbeck's household." Caleb shot her a dangerous look. "Damn it, Lucinda, you could have been killed. What the devil did you think you were doing, dashing off alone to see him?"

"That is approximately the fiftieth time you have asked me that question," Lucinda said. "And I have given you the same answer at least as many times. I went there because he sent me a note saying that he was dying and wanted to say farewell."

"You should have waited until I could accompany you," he said.

"You forget, sir," she said, resigning herself to the endless lecture. "This is Ira Ellerbeck we are discussing. I believed him to be my father's friend. And it was not as though I went alone. I took Shute with me."

"For all the good it did," Caleb muttered. "Shute was in the street outside the house. He had no way of knowing you were in danger. You should have left the instant you sensed the dangerous energy in that household."

She pursed her lips. "I suppose that would have been the appropriate course of action."

"You *suppose* so?" He stopped in front of the desk, flattened his hands on the surface and leaned forward in what could only be described as a menacing fashion. "What sort of shabby reasoning is that?"

"I never said logic was involved. The moment I entered that house, I knew that the solution to my father's murder was there. I could not leave without the answers."

"Let us be clear on this, Lucinda. I will not tolerate such reckless behavior in the future. Do you comprehend me?"

Her strained temper finally snapped. She shot to her feet. "I am not the only one whose behavior could be considered reckless. What of the manner in which you went to interview that kidnapper? You insisted on going alone and you were nearly murdered by Allister Norcross as a result."

"That was different."

"I fail to see how."

"Damnation, Lucinda, if you are going to be a partner in this firm, you will learn to follow orders."

"I will be a *partner*, not an employee. By definition, partners do not take orders."

"Then you will damn well learn to confer with the *other* partner in this agency before you take such rash actions."

"Come now, Caleb. You are overreacting here."

"I have not begun to react. You will never again attempt any such ventures without consulting with me." He circled the desk, seized her by the shoulders and hauled her hard against his chest. "Do we have an understanding, Lucinda?"

She thought about the harrowing energy that she had sensed emanating from him when he crashed through the door to Ellerbeck's conservatory yesterday afternoon. In that moment she knew that he had been driven half mad with fear for her safety. A half-mad Caleb Jones was a very dangerous man, indeed. She did not want to put him through that kind of ordeal ever again.

"Yes," she said softly. "We have an understanding."

A discreet cough from the doorway made them both turn toward the entrance. Edmund and Patricia stood there, expressions carefully composed.

"This had better be important," Caleb said. He did not release Lucinda.

"Inspector Spellar just sent word that Ellerbeck died during the night," Edmund said. "He never regained consciousness."

"Hell," Caleb said. "That means I won't get any answers out of him."

"I killed him," Lucinda whispered, stunned. "It was only a heavy dose of a sleeping drug but combined with the damage the formula had already done, it was more than enough to kill. Heaven help me, I knew it at the time."

"Hush," Caleb said, tightening his grip on her. "He would have been dead within a day or two in any event."

"Yes, but not by my hand."

He cast a quick, meaningful glance at Edmund and Patricia. They both vanished without another word, closing the door very softly.

Gently Caleb drew Lucinda to the pair of chairs in front of the hearth. He pushed her lightly into one and sat down next to her. Reaching out, he took her hand in his and threaded her fingers through his own.

For a long time they sat there, gazing into the fire, hands tightly clasped.

After a while, Caleb spoke. "You were right the other night when you told me that there would be times like this in the years ahead," he said. "Times when the results of our actions will be difficult to live with."

"Yes," she said.

"The only way I will be able to do this work is if I know that I will always have you by my side. Marry me, Lucinda."

"Oh, Caleb," she said gently. "You would go so far as to marry me just to ensure that the agency carries only the Jones name?"

"I would walk into the fires of hell to marry you, Lucinda."

A great sense of certainty rushed through her. He would do exactly that, she thought. Without a moment's hesitation.

"Caleb," she whispered.

He rose and pulled her up out of the chair and back into his arms.

"Early on I told you that I was not convinced there was such a thing as love because I could not define it," he said quietly. "But I comprehend it now. It is the overwhelming sensation that struck me the first time I saw you. Even before that. The moment I saw your name on the message you sent requesting my services, I knew, somehow, that I would need you in ways I could never explain. I love you, Lucinda. Now and for whatever lies beyond."

She put her arms around his neck. "I fell in love with you the first time you entered this room. I will love you always. Of course I will marry you."

She went up onto her toes and brushed her lips lightly across his. He wrapped her close and kissed her, sealing the solemn vows between them. They stood there, holding each other very tightly for a long time.

Forty-Seven

One month later . . .

The noise of the construction going on below in the gardens was annoying but the day was too fine to close the windows.

Caleb stood with Gabe at the long laboratory workbench. Together they contemplated the array of notes, papers, journals and records that had been removed from Ellerbeck's house.

"The vast majority of the materials here relate to Ellerbeck's botanical experiments," Caleb said. "He attempted some work on the formula but it is clear he was out of his depth. So was Thaxter. That was why they hired Hulsey and son."

"I suppose it was too much to expect that we would find a neat diagram that described the various Circles of the Order and identified the leaders," Gabe said, studying the heap of papers.

"The Cabal behind this affair is very good when it comes to strategy. So good, in fact, that I suspect the leader and perhaps his closest associates have a talent for such elaborate planning and secrecy."

"Strategy talents?" Gabe looked intrigued. "Makes sense."

"Damn it, we need a more complete record of the talents of the various members of the Society."

"That won't be easy. In fact, I'm sure it would be impossible to identify the talents of even a fraction of the members. This organization has existed in the shadows for two hundred years. We are, all of us, including you and me, Cousin, very obsessed with keeping secrets. The habit is in our blood."

Caleb rubbed the back of his neck and exhaled deeply. "I must get back to work on that psychical taxonomy chart."

"Lucinda is right. You don't have time to do everything. You must learn to concentrate on the most important objectives."

Light footsteps sounded in the hall outside the chamber. A pleasant sense of anticipation whispered through Caleb. He would know those dainty, high-heeled boots anywhere.

The door opened. Lucinda swept into the room, bringing fresh energy and the warmth of the sun with her. She carried a small box in one hand. He noticed she looked very pleased with herself.

"Good afternoon, gentlemen," she said cheerfully. "A lovely day, is it not?"

Gabe smiled. "Indeed it is. You appear to be in excellent spirits this afternoon, Mrs. Jones."

The wedding had taken place a week earlier. The guest list had comprised the entire Jones family and the residents of Guppy Lane. The crowd had filled the conservatory. Caleb suspected that Lucinda's former neighbors in Landreth Square would be talking about it for months.

"About time you got here, my love." Caleb rose and crossed the room to where she stood. He kissed her, savoring the little rush of satisfaction that accompanied the act. "The workmen have been pestering me for instructions. I have explained to them on several occasions that it is your conservatory that they are building and that they must get their directions from you."

"I do hope they have made some progress." Lucinda whisked up her skirts and hurried to the window to look down. "Oh, good, the herb wing is coming along quite nicely."

Gabe smiled at Caleb. "A conservatory is a most unusual wedding gift to give your bride."

"It is nothing compared to the amazing gift that she gave me," Caleb said with great feeling.

"Herself?" Gabe was amused. "What a very romantic notion, Cousin. Didn't think you had it in you to be carried away by such poetical flights of fancy."

Lucinda turned away from the window and walked back toward the men. "Caleb was not referring to my person. My wedding gift to him consisted of the Shutes. They very kindly agreed to take charge of this household. Luckily they have had some experience with an eccentric employer. Henceforth Caleb will not need to worry about finding new staff on the first of every month."

Gabe nodded. "That explains the expression of rapture on his face."

Caleb looked at the box in Lucinda's hand. "What have you got there?"

"New cards for our firm." Lucinda removed the lid of the box. "They have both of our names imprinted on them."

Gabe chuckled. "You won that battle, did you?"

"Certainly," she said. She extracted a crisp white pasteboard and held it so that he could read.

"Jones and Jones." Gabe laughed. "Has a ring to it."

Caleb smiled at Lucinda, basking in the bright, warm, effervescent energy that shimmered in the air around her.

"Yes it does," he said. "It sounds right."